DEEP NORTH

A BRENDA CONTAY NOVEL OF SUSPENSE

BARRY KNISTER

OPEN WINDOW

Livonia, Michigan

DEEP NORTH

The poem, *Peonies*, by Mary Oliver
used by permission of the author.

Published by Open Window
an imprint of BHC Press

Library of Congress Control Number:
2017932135

ISBN-13: 978-1-946006-49-3
ISBN-10: 1-946006-49-1

Visit the author at:
www.bwknister.com &
www.bhcpress.com

Also available in eBook

Book design by
Blue Harvest Creative
www.blueharvestcreative.com

ALSO BY BARRY KNISTER

BRENDA CONTAY NOVELS
The Anything Goes Girl
Godsend

OTHER NOVELS
Just Bill
Dating Service

Deep North is dedicated to
Bob Nelson and Jim Sheahan

CHAPTER

1

The housekeeper glanced in the rearview at the teenager in the back seat. "You got everything now? Pillow? CDs? You take a sweater?"

"God, for the zillionth time—"

"I'm just checkin' like your mamma told me to." She looked back to the road. "So you got no reason to go back in that house."

"Tanya—"

"Yeah, you 'Tanya' all you want. Your mamma seen that *Risky Business* picture. She know what goes on when parents leave home."

The girl looked away, and Tanya again faced the road. Carrie Ross was a good girl, though. A nice girl. Nevertheless, the housekeeper kept her face hard for the rearview. She slowed on Maple and turned onto Mallard Lane. Ahead, Brittany Remnick stepped out of her parents' big Dutch colonial.

Hugging herself in the gray and chilly afternoon, she started down the brick walkway.

"Maybe I should go in and talk to this girl's mamma."

"Oh, please don't." Carrie undid her seatbelt and leaned forward. "Please don't embarrass me. Mom talked to her; she told you everything's cool."

"Yeah, you cool all right."

But that was probably true, the two mothers arranging for Carrie to stay with her friend while Mrs. Ross went fishing in Minnesota. Tanya slowed at the curb and stopped. Carrie was out instantly, the two girls jumping and jabbering the way they always did. Tanya popped the trunk and looked again in the rearview. Almost instantly it was slammed shut. Wants you *gone*, she thought and smiled. Wants you history.

She watched Brittany start back up the walk, carrying the duffle bag. Carrie fell in behind with her box of CDs and the pillow she always took on sleepovers. The housekeeper put the car in gear and pulled away. Deposit her check, and she was home free for a week. Then she remembered: the check was still on the countertop in the Ross kitchen. *Damn*. Carrie had forgotten her pillow and run back upstairs. Waiting for her had thrown Tanya off a second.

Resigned, she swung into the next driveway, backed down and around. She passed the Remnick house and thought again about where Mrs. Ross and her friends were going. Some big old houseboat floating around in Minnesota in some string of lakes called the Boundary Waters. Bunch of ladies don't know nothing about it, Tanya had said. That's the point, Mrs. Ross told her. To see if we can manage.

Minutes later, she pulled in at the Ross house, got out, and crossed the back drive. A flagstone path led to the patio. At the French doors she pressed the security button. The light blinked off, she inserted her house key, and turned the handle. Still locked. She turned the key again, and this time the handle levered down.

Tanya studied the key. The door had already been unlocked. It made no sense; she had checked all the doors before leaving with Carrie.

That little monkey. Carrie had come after and unlocked it for some risky business later. But that made no sense, either. She had her own key, plus a spare was kept under the firewood box on the patio.

Tanya let herself in, and eased the door shut. She stood in the big dining room. Familiar silver and china glinted in the two breakfronts. The porcelain pheasant centerpiece stood where it belonged on the table. Through the arch lay the sprawling living room; groups of furniture rested on Oriental carpets in the milky light coming through sheer curtains. She listened a moment before stepping through the open door into the kitchen. Silence. The room was spotless as she had left it, her check still on the counter.

She crossed the glossy slate floor. A dish towel draped over the sink reminded her of towels loaded earlier in the clothes dryer. As with her check, the delay for the pillow had made her lose track of time, and the towels might mildew. Still troubled by the unlocked door, Tanya crossed to the basement stairs.

Something was wrong. "Who's there?"

She started down, reached the landing and looked below. A light was on. "Let me hear whoever you is, 'cause I know you down there." Nothing. You crazy, she thought. It was just the big house being empty, and a rusty door lock.

She continued down the stairs, turning right into the laundry room. It was clean but gloomy, with naked floorboards overhead, ductwork, and wires. At the dryer she knelt and began pulling the still-warm towels out onto the open door. When she had them all, Tanya gathered them in her arms, kneed shut the dryer, and turned.

Now, though, she saw another light.

Holding the warm towels, she retraced her steps, moved around stored patio furniture, and stepped into the dim furnace room. Beneath the naked bulb, on the gray-painted floor, rested what looked like two clocks. Not clocks, though. Timers. Like what Mr. Ross used on lamps when the house was empty. *Why down here?* You put timers on lights or a radio to make people think you was home. Wires trailed from the boxes, back behind the furnace.

She turned away, walked back to the stairs, and started up. She would phone the police to be on the safe side.

"Hello."

"Jesus God!" Clutching the towels, she looked up. He was standing on the landing, looking down.

"Hey, sorry."

"What the *hell* you doin'?"

He was white, wearing a uniform of some kind, blue. He pointed to a badge on his chest. "MichCon."

"The gas company? Bullshit." She felt her heart pounding, but glared up at him.

"No, lady, really. You got a leak that showed up on our computer." He fished in his pants pocket and brought out a piece of paper. "I got a work order here says to get the patio key and let myself in." He unfolded the sheet and looked at it. "Name's Ross? We called her office and got her cell phone. She explained about the alarm and the key under the firewood."

Tanya wasn't buying it. "Where's your truck? I didn't see no truck."

"My partner has another call, same problem. It's probably just faulty sensors. He dropped me off, he's coming back in a half hour. You must be the cleaning lady. This Mrs. Ross—"

"She didn't say nothing about it."

"Well, she couldn't, could she? We just got the readout and called. On her way to Milwaukee, she said. 'No one's home, do what you have to and let yourself out,' is what she said."

Tanya stared at him. He did seem to have his facts straight.

He smoothed the sheet of paper and held it out. "It's no break-in, lady. Here's the work order."

She started up the stairs again. It was his white-blond hair, she now realized, that made him look strange—not the color, but the way it lay on his head. Understanding this made Tanya feel less fearful.

She stopped two steps below him, took the paper, and studied it. It looked like a work order, the name and address right. "Backhoe break" was scrawled across the page. Except...

He couldn't call Mrs. Ross. She'd turned off her cell phone. That was part of a promise to Carrie—except for emergencies, no calls. And those timers in the furnace room...

Let him think she believed. "Okay, that looks 'fficial to me. I come back from running some errands is all. You go on finish up on the leak, but give me the key so we don't got to change the locks. The missus got a lot of nice things someone like to get their hands on."

"Sure."

He reached in his pocket and handed her a key. It was shiny and new, not weathered like the one kept on the patio. And now she saw he wore latex gloves. Paper boots covered his shoes.

"I'll leave the way I came in. You can lock up after you're done with the laundry."

"Good, you leave."

She hoped her fear didn't show in her voice. The fake work order meant he had known exactly when the house would be empty. She needed to get out and drive. Straight to the police. He was still blocking her way. "You don't believe me."

"'Course I do, you got a work order—" She took a step up and moved to push past with the laundry.

He held out his arm. "It's Tanya, right?"

He knew she knew. Heard it in her voice.

"You let me pass," she said, not looking up. "Lot of people know I'm here, start wondering pretty quick—" She butted at him with her shoulder. "Don't want no trouble. You got a wrong house or something, all right, that happens, you just let me pass—"

"Lady, don't fuck around—"

She butted again. Suddenly he shoved her shoulders with both hands.

As her feet left the steps, she felt sick and weightless. Falling away, she glimpsed his white-blond hair, the low ceiling's gray paint, and remembered her check before she hit the stairway's bottom step.

Her shoulder struck first, whipping her neck. The back of her head struck the concrete floor. She saw and felt stars. Groaning, she felt her heavy body like a thing thrown after her. It shoved her down, until it lay like a thing apart, on top of her.

Pain and white light. Skull and shoulder both fractured, Tanya closed her eyes and groaned. It was bad, but she was alive. She would make it.

She looked up at the bright bulb overhead. Again Tanya closed her eyes and lay still. Moving made it worse.

Shoes were scuffing, going. He was gone, and she was going to make it. Eyes shut, she felt pain thudding with her heart in waves. In whatever time had passed, a profound sleepiness came to her. It was still there with the creak of floorboards above, then nothing.

CHAPTER

2

WESTBOUND INTERSTATE 94

Gently rocked in the passenger seat, half smiling, Brenda Contay stared out the Chevy Suburban's windshield. Slowly the anonymous fields faded. She saw herself standing under the shower in her bathroom—and the door banged open. The curtain was scraped away and there stood David Santerro, thick-muscled from college football. He reached in and lifted her out as you would lift a child from a bath, flattened her against him, and kissed her.

"Brenda?"

She felt herself being walked from the bathroom, feet off the ground—

"Brenda? You okay?"

The windshield materialized. "I always want to smoke in cars. I drift off thinking about it."

Hands on the steering wheel, Marion Ross shook her head. "As Carrie would say, you are *so* lying." She glanced over and back to the road. "I bet it was sex. You should see your cheeks."

"All right, you got me." Brenda lifted her coffee from the cup holder.

"David?"

"Yes, David."

"Do you miss him?"

She pretended to think about it. "Yes and no. I was always glad to see him. I was just never really sorry to see him go. Which he did all the time."

Was that true, or said for effect? This time, Brenda actually thought about it, in the focused way that sometimes happened at odd moments. A kaleidoscope skipped through her memory—bits and pieces of concerts, football and basketball games, restaurants, bedrooms. It now seemed that her memories of David registered only as data, as information without meaning. What she missed was missing him.

"Does he email you?" Marion asked.

"Oh sure, I'm his default girl. His numero uno cybersqueeze."

She looked back to the road. It had been nice enough with David Santerro, in a haphazard, generous sort of way. They had both known it would not "become something." But after being with someone for five months, there had to be something wrong with not really knowing him beyond his basic stats and style, his body type and commando approach to sex.

No. Not being bothered, *that's* what was wrong. Five months of beepers and apologies as he walked away, hand cupped over his left ear, cell phone clamped to his right. In lines at movie theatres and restaurants, waiting for the ski lift at Boyne Mountain—and she hadn't cared.

"You told me his mother named him for David Brinkley," Marion said.

"Correct."

"So now he's a journalist. Destiny at work."

She had lied about it just now, but for the last hour Brenda Contay had wanted a cigarette. Clean for a year, she decided it must have to do with the motion of driving. That also might explain thinking about sex. Certainly nothing in the Chevy Suburban provided any temptation to smoke. The ashtray would be as untouched as the day it was made.

She looked over her shoulder at the gear mounded behind the back seat. Fishing rods, tackle boxes, canvas duffles.

"Everything still there?"

"Still there." She turned back and folded her arms. "Aren't you tired? I could take the wheel."

Marion shook her head. She was dressed for the outdoors in a red chamois shirt and jeans. In profile, with her chestnut hair swept behind her ear, she looked gentle. Maternal. Face to face, though, Marion Ross could be sharp-eyed and intimidating. Even a little scary. It was a quality she put to good use in court, but it made for problems at home. With Carrie.

"I'll get us to Wisconsin," she said. "You can take over there. If you aren't having one of your sex spells."

"You must love to drive." Brenda pointed to the clock. "It's been almost five hours."

"In this thing I do. Sitting up high, cruising the interstate. My best closing arguments get worked out this way."

Having passed the derelict steel factories of Gary, Indiana, they were now south of Chicago. Franchise hotels and corporate office buildings slipped by on both sides of the expressway.

"Hear it?" Marion smiled. "No radio or TV. Pager on the dresser, computer on the desk. I can't tell you how much I need this."

Yes, the big SUV was quiet. And it was quiet back home. These days, Brenda made only occasional trips to WDIG. She had returned last year to television but on her own terms. Her book about a drug company scandal in Micronesia was the reason: *Blue Sky Six* had won a Pulitzer, and the book's success had freed her from regular reporting. Now, she did think pieces once a month, in a sound studio.

"About the others," she said. "You mentioned someone had to cancel."

Marion finished passing a trailer truck and eased back into the right lane. "Right, Marcie Long. From my office. She was supposed to be our brain trust; she does a lot of camping. When she backed out, I called Heather Reese."

"Your college classmate." Marion nodded. "You said she's a throwback."

"I suppose that was snarky of me. But Heather does sort of take you back to the fifties. Home and hearth, committees. Her husband fishes, he's letting us take his boat. After college I went to Europe, Heather and Brian got married. You'll see what I mean tonight."

"Did you tell her about me?"

"Of course."

"And were you snarky?"

"I told her about *Zapped!*"

"Oh, great, *Zapped!* Thanks a lot."

"Hey, you wrote it, I didn't."

Two years before, Brenda had done a profile on Marion for *Elle.* It was how they'd met and become friends. A well-known local lawyer had secretly sold off his assets in preparation for divorce. When a friend called his wife and told her what was going on, the husband was just then soaking in the hot tub on the deck. Hold on a minute, the wife said. She had stepped outside and tipped the bug whacker into the tub. All right, I'm back, she told the friend. A bug needed whacking. Thanks to Marion Ross, the new widow had spent just eleven months in a psychiatric clinic.

"And someone named Tina," Brenda said. "She taught in Milwaukee?"

Marion nodded. "At a community college. She has MS and just retired. Heather asked if she could come along. I've never met her, but she sounds interesting."

It was just like Marion Ross to turn a fishing trip won in a raffle into a week of fresh-air camp for shut-ins and housewives. And a stray like her journalist friend.

◆◆◆◆◆

They stopped at six for gas, bought candy, and more coffee.

As they walked back through the service plaza, Marion glanced at the bank of pay phones. Outside, she reached in her jeans pocket and pulled out her cell phone.

"Don't do it." Brenda stepped up to her. "Come on, you promised Carrie. Calls only in emergencies, plus one after we get to Milwaukee."

"I know, I know..." Marion looked down at the phone. "Worry is an addiction, okay?"

"And this is an intervention. Why don't I keep it for you?"

Marion sighed and handed over the phone. "You should've been a cop. I suppose you want to conduct a cavity search to check for a backup."

"Not before we eat dinner."

They returned to the Suburban, and Brenda took the wheel. The day was ending as it had begun, overcast and chilly. Soon, she was driving through the rolling hills of Wisconsin dairy country. Slopes marked by penned herds and unplowed acreage stretched away under dark skies. In the waning light, the farmhouses and barns looked cared for and prosperous.

"Does the idea appeal to you?" Marion asked. "Farm life?"

"Yes, but only as an idea. From the safe distance of your car. People working the soil, doing meaningful labor. I see them eating huge meals and never gaining a pound. Everyone's spinning yarns about calving season, and yes, I'll have another biscuit, please. Then they read a few pages in the latest Burpees seed catalog and go to bed without drugs."

"I like the part about meals."

"So do I. But I'd go nuts in a week."

"Ever do a story on farmers?"

She thought about it. Her two-part series on urban gardens in Detroit didn't really count. Neither did the one on genetically modified plants.

"I did a piece on a man who killed horses," she said. "A rancher in Wyoming. He was gaming the government's 'Adopt a Horse' program. You could adopt wild horses for a dollar, it was meant to save the remaining free-range mustangs. After a year they were yours. He was letting dozens of wild horses graze on his land. A year and a day later, he could slaughter them and sell them for dog food. All legal. He hauled them up by the heels, then slit their throats. He preferred bleeding them out that way."

"How disgusting. Did your story shut him down?"

"Yes."

"The power of the pen. I bet that made you feel great."

Brenda shook her head. "No, it didn't. It wasn't enough. He was just going to keep on being what he was. Hurting people, hurting animals. I interviewed him, you must know the type from your practice. In his own mind he didn't see anything wrong. And he had a way with words. You could almost imagine how he might be good company. If he hadn't been a monster."

After a moment, she glanced over. Her friend was staring out, thinking. Brenda faced forward and tightened her grip on the wheel. Like an acid flash, she saw herself and the rancher in his barn. They were standing beside two skinned horses. He was smiling, dressed in camouflage, explaining how much he was paid per pound. Hearing him, and remembering the beauty of grazing horses she'd passed on the way to his ranch had made her close to crazy.

"It wasn't just killing horses," she said. "It was how he treated his wife. His sons. It was always their fault when he hit one of them, 'for their own good.' They accepted it, too. For them, it was the natural way of families."

Marion bumped out some M&Ms. "You need these. Give me your hand."

Eyes on the road, Brenda held out her right hand. Chocolates dropped into her palm, and she popped them in her mouth. Both women crunched in silence.

"Yeah, they're out there," Marion said. "Just before I cut back my practice, I had a client mixed up with someone *born* with a chip on his shoulder. Every negative in his life he blamed on others. And my client, my God—" Marion sighed. "All this talk about independence and making your own decisions? Not Doreen. When her significant other moved in and laid his 'plan' on her, she was completely grateful."

"What was his plan?"

"Skimming funds. They both worked for this plumbing company. He snaked out sewer lines, she was a bookkeeper. He talked her into falsifying invoices. I still have a suspicion she never fully understood what she did was wrong. Of course, he insisted everything was her responsibility, he had nothing to do with it."

After a moment, Brenda glanced over. Marion now looked thoughtful.

"What?"

"It's hard to explain," Marion said. "They were actually pretty happy. We called them Mickey and Minnie in the office. You know, symbiosis, co-dependency, whatever. But she had what she wanted. Someone telling her what to do. Yes, it was embezzlement, it was fraud. But she was happy. They belonged together."

Brenda again thought of the skinned horses. "But you said he was cruel."

Marion sighed again. "Sure he was. Oh, he didn't hit her, he was just manipulative. A control freak. The kind of man who needs someone to give orders to. To manage."

She laughed. "He was such a hopeless klutz. He'd failed at everything. Dishonorable discharge from the Navy, fired from MichCon. And *literally* a klutz. Tripping in court, spilling soft drinks out in the corridor. When I asked her about it, Doreen just said he was this capable guy who could fix anything. I'm sure he was like that, but only around her. They connected. He's up for sentencing in a few days."

A beep sounded from the dashboard. Then a light began flashing. Brenda glanced at Marion. "Am I doing something to make your car unhappy?"

"It's a fax."

"In your car?"

"I'm a lawyer, Bren. Discovery documents, deposition transcripts, blah blah. Not to mention my phone being seized, remember?" Marion secured her coffee and tapped buttons. Now paper began issuing from a slot below the radio. It went on, stopping and starting, then gave a smooth run and stopped. She tore off the sheet and brought it close.

"It's from Drew," she said. "Dear Mark Trail, are we having fun yet? Jay and I just got back from *The Mouse Trap*. I think Jay was bored. Tomorrow, it's Savile Row for a fashion makeover. Then I see our future business partner for lunch, and Jay does Parliament. Don't forget your promise to Carrie. She needs her space, or whatever it's called now. Take a whizz in the woods for me, and give my best to Bambi. I mean Brenda. Jay says love yuh."

Marion folded the paper and tapped the dashboard clock. "Jet lag, he's still up." She put the paper in her breast pocket, buttoned the flap, and turned to look out her side window.

It was dark now, lights on in the farmhouses. Brenda saw herself in the windshield and felt isolated. It had to do with yellow windows in darkness, and the story of two misfits who were happy together. And with Marion Ross folding a fax and putting it in her pocket.

CHAPTER

3

9:20 P.M.

"**Shit, it's** cold."

Hands behind his head, Jerry Lomak lay stretched out on the girl's bed. Carrie, her name was. The bedspread had blue and gold unicorns and was crowded with stuffed animals.

He glanced again at the clock on the nightstand. He got up, stepped to the side window, and separated the curtain. The lights were now off next door. The Heanys lived there, retirees. They had come outside to work in the yard, making it impossible for him to leave before dark.

"The missus made him his favorite heart-smart special. They watched *America's Favorite Home Videos*, and packed it in."

He dropped the curtain, needing to pee. The bathroom was next door, but Rohmer would say no, to hold it. Don't touch anything, he'd say, there's DNA in your urine, yadda yadda yadda. That's how Rohmer's mind worked. But when you gotta go, you gotta go. It was because of the cold. The thermostat had been turned down for the ten days no one would be home.

He remembered the maid. Better check her again.

He turned away and crossed to the open door. What if she had only skipped a few beats? Just in shock? Lomak now scuffed along the dark second-floor hall, but slowed to glance in the master bedroom. The bedside lamps were now on, from a timer. He'd checked it out earlier, picking up framed photos, smelling the perfume he remembered from court. Smelling it again when he opened her closet. Ross's husband was a tie freak, at least a hundred in his own closet. They had a fireplace in the bedroom with a mantel. Clay pots she had made rested there. Smelling her scent had made him want to smash everything.

He turned away and started down the stairs. Below, the hardwood entrance hall was arranged with Oriental rugs. Two big planters with little trees stood before windows on either side of the front door. In the room on the left, light came from another timer lamp.

Hell with it. Squeeze out a quick pee, then leave.

He stepped off the staircase and crossed, zipped open his fly, and began peeing into the left planter. Lomak sighed with relief and looked in the lighted room.

Floor lamps bathed the study in a soft yellow glow. One wall was nothing but floor-to-ceiling books. A little mahogany ladder ran along a rail for reaching the upper shelves. A whole room, he thought. Just for sitting on your ass and reading. Two big, green leather chairs flanked a computer desk. It all made Lomak think of the conference room in the law office where Marion Ross was a partner. Sitting across from him, next to Doreen, Ross had said he could confess to fraud and cop a plea, or take his chances in court. The memory and the softly lit room filled him with a mix of rage and loss.

Lomak finished and zipped up. He moved back along the hall to the kitchen with its slate floor. How much would a floor like that cost? He reached the basement stairs and headed down, careful in the dark. But in dim light from the basement's glass-brick windows, he could make out the maid's body below. The towels were heaped at her feet on the last couple steps. He stopped now, squinting to see. The blood pool next to her head had developed a skin. He saw she was stiffer.

Coming back for towels. He shook his head. The luck of the draw, bad karma.

He turned, went back up to the landing, then stopped and glanced back down. His own timers were connected to small charges on the gas line. All at once Lomak wasn't sure he'd set them correctly. That was Rohmer. It was like Louis Rohmer was watching him through the little professor glasses he wore, with his bald head and white beard. Someone like that made you doubt yourself.

Nah, you set them right, he decided. Out the back and across the yard.

He passed through the kitchen and stepped into the dark dining room. Bottles glinted on a butler's cart parked against the outside wall. It was like the cart they used for cooking next to your table at Mario's on Second Street. Steak Diane, Cherries Jubilee. That's where he and Doreen liked to go. Valet parking, waiters in tuxes. He saw himself there, Doreen sitting opposite in the purple dress that showed some cleavage. Duke and Pilar—that's what they called each other for fun. Duke for John "Duke" Wayne, Pilar for his wife.

Not purple, Jerry, aubergine.

Auber-whatever was French for eggplant. He now moved to the patio door.

CHAPTER

4

"**Remnick residence.**"

"Carrie?"

"No, Mom, it's the house. The Remnick residence."

"Very funny. Are you two all right? Is Mrs. Remnick there?"

"She's in the shower. She burned her hand on the grill, making tuna kabobs."

"I'm sorry. Was it bad?"

"She has a plastic bag on it, in the shower. Like Jay did on his cast."

"Where's Mr. Remnick?"

"He and Brittany went to Cosi Fan Tutti to pick up a pizza. We gave up on the kabobs."

"All right, kiddo, I'll let you go. Give my best to Mrs. Remnick. Tell her—"

"She has the number, Mom. For Milwaukee, the boat place, the FBI."

"Okay, I did promise, didn't I? What can I say? Once a mom always a mom."

"And when I have kids, I'll be a pain in the butt just like you. You told me enough times."

"All true. Maybe you'll be even worse. Well, I guess that's it, then. Wish us luck."

"Just don't bring anything home we have to put on the wall."

"Not a nice big northern pike for your room?"

"Gross. Look, Mom, I'm online with this really cute serial killer, I have to go."

"Very funny, all right. Carrie?"

"Yes, Mom, I love you too."

♦♦♦♦♦

Smiling and nodding as Heather Reese continued talking about her son's hockey team, Brenda was trying to overhear Marion. She was making her call next door in the kitchen. Now she hung up.

"Of course, to anyone else it's just kids' stuff, but for us it's incredibly—"

Heather turned as Marion stepped into the dining room. "Is everything all right?"

"Everything's fine." Marion sat again at the table. "Carrie's getting ready to stuff herself on pizza. Go on with your story."

"I'm just boring poor Brenda here about Brian Junior's hockey," Heather said. "All us moms and dads go crazy watching. Those little guys really skate their hearts out. You'd think 'lock those people up' if you saw us, but we wouldn't miss a game."

"Jay played football," Marion said. "Flanker or end, something like that. It always scared me, watching him being chased around. You think, well, they're padded all over, stop worrying. Then you read some spinal-injury story."

Heather nodded, then downed what was left of her wine. She reached for the newly opened third bottle of chardonnay.

"The cross-checking in hockey *is* a problem for me," she said, pouring. "They discourage rough stuff, and the coaches change players a lot. So everyone gets a chance. But there *are* the skates. With the girls it was different. Jamie threw up sometimes in swim practice, but I guess that just goes with it. And Robbie—well, Robbie always did her own thing. *Does* her own thing, I should say."

Heather smiled too quickly, put down the bottle and raised her glass. "Oh, *I'm* sorry—" She set down the glass and got the bottle. "Who's ready? Mar?"

"No thanks, I—"

Heather poured into Marion's glass. "Oh, come on. We're celebrating, no one's driving. This is girl talk, catching up."

When she turned with the bottle, Brenda put her hand over her glass.

"Sure?" Heather said.

"Very sure."

"Oh, come on. We all know famous writers are big drinkers."

"I'm not famous, so I'm not allowed."

"Well, you're famous around here. Wait, *I* know."

Heather got up quickly and went into the kitchen. Her napkin had fallen, and Brenda retrieved it. She placed it next to Heather's plate, and looked across at her friend. Marion shook her head and mouthed *don't ask me.*

Behind her, the wallpaper presented colonial American troops in blue uniforms, marching in formation. A rack of antique plates circled the room, maintaining perfect alignment like the troops. More plates were displayed inside a large hutch that covered the dining room's back wall. Brian Senior had made the hutch in his garage workshop. He had eaten early and was out there now, running a saw.

"Here we go." Heather stepped from the kitchen, holding a half-full brandy snifter. "I figure a Pulitzer winner for a cognac girl." She set it down next to Brenda's coffee cup and took her chair.

"Thanks. I'm going to take this with me and get some air. You two can duke it out over Little League or whatever's next."

"You must be going bonkers," Heather said. "Listening to us rattle on about children."

"Not at all." Brenda pushed back her chair, feeling like someone in a book club who hadn't done the reading.

"Once Mar and I get through the catching up, I want to hear all the gossip about the book you wrote." Heather sipped her wine and winked. "Marion's told me a lot about you."

"You mean *Zapped!* You shouldn't judge—"

"Not just that. She says you kick serious butt in your work." Heather winked again. "'Get 'em by the balls, their hearts and minds will follow'—who was it said that? Oh God—" Her face dropped, and she covered her mouth. "Forgive me, I can't believe I said that."

Brenda smiled. "I think Nixon's guy Chuck Colson gets the credit."

"I'm sorry, really. It's all this talk about hockey. When we go to Chicago, the Blackhawks games are *so* violent. We try to watch the language around Brian Junior."

Marion raised a hand. "Point of order. I just said you don't pull any punches to keep your sources happy. You sure didn't with me."

"Yes, exactly." Heather nodded. "That's what I meant."

Brenda reached down for the brandy snifter. "Eight hours on the road. I feel like someone kicked my butt for real. Back in ten minutes."

She walked into the hall and moved toward the front entrance. Yes, they were now actually talking about Little League baseball. But clearly Marion had been caught off guard by whatever was going on in the Reese household. Ahead, hooked rugs lay on pegged flooring. There were appliqued milk cans, and clay pickle crocks stuck full of bats and hockey sticks.

She reached her room and opened the door. Everything here fit with the rest of the house: antique washstand, distressed chest of drawers, a bedspread themed with ears of maize and Pilgrims. The bedside table was draped with a quilt. Centered there, a hurricane lamp glowed red, fitted with a pink bulb. Because of the lamp, Brenda had dubbed the décor Molly Pitcher Bordello. *If you stay in my room, you have to put out when a Minuteman needs a comfort woman*—that's what she whispered to Marion when Heather went to fetch Brian Junior. Fourteen and suited up for hockey practice, he had looked like a kid's version of the Detroit Red Wings' Darren McCarty.

She set the snifter on the table and knelt to look in her duffle bag. Jokes aside, something was definitely going on in the Reese household. It felt like Ibsen's *A Doll's House*, with Early American props. Here, though, the husband took the orders. And the doll—very fit, with streaked-blond hair and preppy clothes—seemed almost conscious of playing a part.

Brenda got her beige crewneck from the bag and pulled it on. She took the drink from the table and stepped into the hall. At the garage entrance, she stopped and listened. A woodworking machine was screeching again inside. She had intended to throw away the drink but on impulse opened the door.

Wearing coveralls and goggles, Brian Senior was cutting plywood with a table saw. Seconds passed. Now he sensed her, looked up and shut off the saw.

"Hi." He dusted off his hands and raised the goggles.

"Hello, Brian. I brought you something." She stepped down, smelling pine. "What are you making?" There was a pack of Marlboros on his worktable. Instantly the craving was on her. She hoped he would follow her gaze.

"Thanks." He took the snifter and pointed. "It's a sleigh."

She looked at it. Half finished, it made her think of a buckboard on runners. "I see, just like Santa's. Will you use a snowmobile or an actual horse?"

"For what?"

"To pull it. You said it's a sleigh."

"Oh, no. It's for flowers. It's a planter."

"Of course, silly me." Again she glanced at the box of Marlboros.

"Heather sees us using it at Christmas, too," Brian said. "Maybe on the roof. You aim floodlights, fill it with gift-wrapped boxes. She saw it in a magazine."

"I see."

"Then, in summer, you line it with polyethylene, fill it with dirt. Plant geraniums or whatever. We had a little Amish gig, but she decided to go with the sleigh this year."

"What happened to the gig?"

"Pardon?"

"The Amish gig."

"The annual community rummage sale. Heather is more or less the permanent chairperson on that. She put it up for auction. I think someone bid three hundred for it."

For no reason, Brenda felt sorry for him. She could tell his sleigh was going to be beautiful and authentic, but never serve its real purpose. "I think Heather must keep you pretty busy out here," she said and smiled.

"She does, that's true. Lays on the lash, keeps me out of trouble."

"Well, okay, I'm on my way out to get some air. I'll let you get back to it." She turned, but swung back and stared at the Marlboros. "I sure would like one of those."

"What? Oh, sure, sorry." He got the box open and held it out. "It never occurred to me to ask. No one smokes anymore."

She took one, hesitated, and took another. "For later. Thanks a lot."

"Here, take the box." He handed it to her, then a book of matches. "And if you would, please, be sure to light up outside. Smoking's a no-no in the house."

"Will do."

"I smoke out here when Brian Junior's not home. I use a smokeless ashtray." He pointed to it.

Brenda waved again and let herself back into the house. The saw started up as she opened the front door. She stepped out and moved away from the front windows. On the walk she readied a cigarette and struck a match. A whole year, she thought. Why start again now? She saw herself behind the wheel of the Suburban. Folding the fax from Drew, Marion now put it in her pocket.

Brenda lit up and inhaled. She felt momentarily dizzy, always the same when she fell off the tobacco wagon. The night was chilly and clear. Stars were out.

Smoking, she studied them.

If you were thirty-three and had no partner or husband, no child, you faced doubts often enough. But Heather and Brian Reese made going solo look better. Still, looking up and hearing distant traffic, Brenda knew this was too easy. No, if she were honest, what was here—the kids and committees, the make-work projects and country-cute decorating—it was full of connections. Meaning. She thought of her condo on the eighth floor of her high rise. No pickle crocks or hockey sticks there. Just gray walls and unfinished furniture, a frayed couch left over from college days. No Molly Pitcher Bordello or power tools.

She looked from the sky to the driveway. At some point, Brian Reese had hitched his trailer and fishing boat to the Suburban. Fixed above the garage door was a large eagle, held captive in static flight. Maybe Brian would take it down for the next auction.

CHAPTER

5

The bungalow next to Doreen Taylor's was in foreclosure. The aluminum siding had been stripped off, and someone had bolted sheets of plywood over the windows. The house on the other side was lit up, the blinds down. Heavy Metal thudded through the dark.

If it was the same hippie renters as before, they would be stoned by now. Lomak listened to the music, standing in the side entrance to Doreen's garage. Minutes before, a patrol car had crept past but kept going.

The music stopped, and a dog began barking. There were lots of dogs in Hazel Park, just north of Eight Mile Road. That was the dividing line between Detroit and the suburbs, whites to the north, blacks to the south. On the Detroit side was all the crack and black hookers you could dream of. And on the north side...Hazeltucky. That's what people called Hazel Park, from the Kentucky and Tennessee rednecks who lived here. They were so proud of the name Hazeltucky, they used it themselves. Most of the rednecks took care of their property, but none of them had any class. They used fake sandstone on the front of their houses. Covered the porches with shit-green indoor/outdoor carpeting. If you had any class you moved out of Hazeltucky as soon as you could. That had been the plan before Doreen got herself caught.

"Before you screwed me," Lomak said softly.

Light came from her own covered windows. It fell on the fallow section of the backyard, where he'd put in the garden. At the Ross house, Lomak had seen huge, neatly-edged flower beds waiting to be planted. When he slipped out the patio door and crossed the dark yard, he wondered what she usually planted. With beds that big, you were talking hundreds of dollars in annuals.

As he drove, Lomak's sense of betrayal had given way to the image of the cleaning woman on the basement floor. Why had she come back? She done it to herself, he decided. When she pushed you. Pushing back was just a reflex, completely natural. But once the Ross house blew up, they would find the maid and say it was all his fault.

"Just like they claim I brainwashed you," Lomak said.

Facing Doreen's small house, he reached down and hefted the five-gallon can of gas. It had been waiting for him on a shelf in her garage. Except for her Ford Focus, nothing was left now. They had taken the outboard motors he stored there. The boat. Even the cottage had been seized.

He was just taking care of business, tying up loose ends. Because there were *two* sides on the scales of justice. Not the fake scales on *Court TV*, real ones. Scales of inner truth that was still true, even after some woman lawyer in a pinstripe pantsuit and a moron like Doreen Taylor screwed you over. To re-balance the scales of justice, both of them had to pay.

The music started up again next door. Lomak tightened his grip on the can and glanced at his watch. 10:50, Friday night. If he wasn't showing Doreen how to act in a decent restaurant, he'd be inside with a tall one, in the Barcalounger, watching *Law and Order.*

But what made Jerry Lomak most angry and now led him forward with the heavy can was the outline of the addition. Almost finished, it arched out from the back of Doreen's bungalow. It had floor-to-ceiling plate-glass windows, and because it was a clear night, he could see inside. Twin sets of wires were still hanging down. They had belonged to top-of-the-line ceiling fans, with blades just like real palm leaves. Those had been the last thing he'd installed. Like everything else, the fans were gone, seized and sold at auction.

As he neared the back of the house, Lomak tripped and dropped the can. Hearing gas slop inside, he straightened and listened. No noise came from the house. The music next door was still going. He looked down and now saw the garden hose. It was just like Doreen to leave the hose out all winter. He righted the gas can, then walked down the driveway. At the front, he stopped and looked in the side window. A single floor lamp was on; otherwise, the living room was empty. No projection TV, no Barcalounger.

He turned away, moved back along the house, and stopped at Doreen's bedroom window. She had the Venetian blind closed, but bluish light flickered in the slats. A woman's shrill TV voice. The Home Shopping Network. Totally broke, Doreen was still watching that crap.

But like with the lawyer, the point of justice with her wasn't death. In fact, it would be better if they both lived. The point was, they should be humiliated. Humbled. Neither woman should be allowed to keep the life they had before. Not after what they had done to him.

Lomak went back to the gas can, bent, and began unscrewing the top. Fridays, her kid Ben went to his aunt's house for the weekend. Ben wasn't part of it. You made it nice for him, Lomak thought. Put a dropped ceiling in the basement, laid down a quality piece of carpet. Took him to Tigers games.

He hefted the can and walked back along the house, pouring as he moved. When the smoke reached her bedroom, Doreen would wake and run out the front door. As she watched the fire, she would know who had done it. And after, every time she took the bus. Every time she had to wait up on Eight Mile with pond scum for the bus, she could think on what she did. Lomak kept pouring. Dumb as she was, maybe she would realize the size and weight of her betrayal. Her crime against the only person to ever give her the time of day.

Sloshing gas around the unfinished addition, smelling the sharp odor, he couldn't look inside. All that work. Cherry wood for both the built-in cabinets and the floor. Skylights with louvers you could open.

The house and garage were both made of wood and would burn fast. He moved with the can, slopping as he worked his way around the far side. Checking the hippie house, he recrossed the yard to the garage. He reentered and slopped the remaining gas around her car. Saving just enough, he trailed the last of it across the yard to the house.

Music was still pounding next door. He got matches from his pocket, lit one, then the whole book. When it was going, he dropped it and moved quickly to the drive. As he passed along the house, Lomak slowed to glance once more in the front room.

His shadow leaped before him. He turned away and loped now, down the incline to the sidewalk.

CHAPTER

6

"Knock knock. Still awake?"

"Come in."

Brenda was propped in bed with Elmore Leonard's latest novel. The book's pages were tinted pink from the bedside lamp. Marion stepped in, closed the door, and moved to the Boston rocker in the corner. She sat and leaned forward.

"Listen, you can back out," she said softly. "We'll make up something. You can pretend to call WDIG. You can say they need you back in the studio right away."

"Relax, Mar. Everything will work out. Heather's not that bad."

"Isn't she?" Marion looked around the room. "Okay, she's always been over the top about home and hearth. That's fine. But in the two years since I was last here, something's happened. The way she went on about hockey. Then all these loony collections, it's…" She shook her head. "I'm serious. You don't have to go."

"She'll be all right," Brenda said. "Plastic knives and forks. Peeing without a hardwood toilet seat. Maybe it'll do her some good. She'll be fine."

Marion looked to the door and back. "Plus, there's an actual problem. Her friend Tina has MS."

"You told me."

"Yes, but Heather never said anything about a wheelchair. I just assumed Tina could still walk."

True, that could be tricky. But paraplegics bungee-jumped, even went waterskiing. Except Marion Ross was a lawyer. "You're thinking litigation?"

"Four women who know nothing about it," Marion said. "On a houseboat. In the Boundary Waters. One of them in a wheelchair. It's a lawsuit waiting to happen."

"Okay, then. Just tell Heather her friend needs to sign a waiver."

"I feel guilty, but I'm thinking about it. Drew has this big deal on. That's why he and Jay went to England. All our assets are positioned for it, he's been setting it up for months. This is my party, which makes me liable. But I hate meeting someone for the first time and handing her a waiver. That's exactly why people hate lawyers, isn't it? How would you like it?"

"If I wanted to see the great out-of-doors, it wouldn't bother me a bit."

"You mean that?"

"Anyone who wants to go fishing in a wheelchair will sign on the dotted line."

Marion nodded. "One of your great gifts is not being another goddamn lawyer." She stood and again looked around the room. "Mine has a Victorian pram full of Beanie Babies. My lamp has a blue bulb."

"Very chaste." Brenda picked up her book. "In here, it's rape and plunder. See you in the morning."

The door closed. She changed her mind, put her book on the table, turned out the light and lay back. In the dark, something about moonlight on the room's ceiling related to the scene with the rancher. They were in his barn. He was a survivalist, and stacked high along the inner wall were sacks of rice and flour. *For the coming apocalypse*—that's what he'd said. The barn door was open, the air busy with flies drawn by the two skinned mustangs.

They were hanging from their hind hooves. Roped, then drawn up alive, they had been killed that way the day before. Tendons and muscles were exposed, the skinless heads grinning with big teeth. *Saved a couple rounds doing it that way. It's a hard world, missy, and sure to get harder. That's why I had my boys do the cutting, one each. So they can learn and be strong.*

She could still smell the blood. It had been sluiced away, but not the awful smell. Feeling her nails cutting into both palms, she closed her eyes and relaxed.

CHAPTER

7

Lomak woke facing the room's other bed. It was unmade, the covers mussed. "Rohmer?"

He threw back the blankets and listened. Hearing no click of computer keys, he got up and crossed to the open entry. The front room stood empty.

Rohmer was gone. He had learned about the fire at Doreen's and split in his float plane. In his mind's eye, Lomak saw it taxiing away from the marina dock, out into Lake St. Clair. He felt hot and clammy, watching as the plane rose off the water.

Time out. No way. He needs you, Lomak thought. Besides, there were dozens of fires every night not worth putting on the morning news. Plus, Louis Rohmer wasn't dumb. He wasn't someone you would want to drink or hunt with, but he was not dumb. He was just out buying supplies. Dicking around with his laptop in the lobby. If you broke in and robbed his house, a computer freak like Rohmer wouldn't know until he went to the kitchen and found the microwave was gone.

Lomak liked this. Getting his pants from the chair beside the bed, he saw Rohmer using the laptop. Behind him, people were lugging shit out the door as he typed away, in a room with no furniture. Lomak smiled and zipped up.

"Mother*fucker*—"

He hopped from foot to foot, holding himself, eyes watering. At last he stopped. With great care, he unzipped his twill pants. He waddled to the bed and sat heavily before pulling down his briefs.

No blood this time.

"Jerry?"

The suite's outer door closed. Still seated, Lomak pulled up his pants and stretched to look casual as Rohmer came through the bedroom entry. He crossed and held out a paper sack.

Lomak took the bag. "Where'd you go?"

"I fueled the plane. I have some email to send, then we're off."

"What's this?"

"Egg McMuffin."

"We got time to eat in the snack bar. McDonald's sucks."

"We don't have time, Jerry, and we don't need another scene in a restaurant."

Rohmer went back into the front room. Lomak reached in the sack and brought out the sandwich. He unwrapped it, took a bite, and chewed. It was somehow both soggy and dry, but he quickly wolfed down the rest, then stood to button his pants. Clicking started in the front room as zipped up with care, and moved into the bathroom. His blue MichCon shirt hung from the door.

"Last night?" he called. "The waitress in Brownie's?" He shook out the shirt. "That wasn't my fault. She was coming on to me."

He put it on and did the buttons, feeling for stickiness where the waitress had spilled the daiquiri. Brownie's was on the lake, where the plane was tied up It was where he and Rohmer had arranged to meet. Hold it now, Lomak said to the waitress as he wiped his shirt with cocktail napkins. This was a banana daiquiri. You sending me a message? When she left, Rohmer told him the waitress had spilled the drink on purpose. Stop bothering her, he said. Don't draw attention. In Costa Rica, do what you want, not here.

He ran the cold water, drank some, then straightened and ran both hands through his hair. He checked his teeth in the mirror, turned off the tap, and walked into the front room.

"Take that dolly to Mario's; it's a done deal," he said of the waitress. "Feed 'em, fuck 'em, forget 'em. If I followed that advice with Doreen, everything would still be cool. Move in with 'em, they screw you every time. This is a known fact."

Rohmer went on typing at the dinette table.

"Treat 'em right, they turn on you."

"You told me cooking the books at Damon Plumbing was your idea." Rohmer didn't look up.

"It was my *suggestion.* Doreen never had an idea more advanced than taking a pee. I gave her confidence. If she left it alone with just the boat and remodeling, they'd of never caught her."

"I thought buying the cottage was also your idea."

"Well, shit, Rohmer, if you do something, don't fart around. Make an investment. Something that builds equity. Without me, she would've pissed it all away on the Home Shopping Network."

He waited for a reaction.

"They don't think is the whole deal," he said. "Amazing. I tell her, tangible assets, Doreen. Something for later. You think there's going to be any Social Security when you hit the big six-five? Advanced thinking like that, it wouldn't enter her head until she was using a walker."

"You told me." Keys clicking, Rohmer still didn't look up.

"Yeah, and I'm telling you again. Not until she was asking what day is it every ten minutes. This is what I get for teaching her money. I give a totally ignorant woman knowledge on how to make a better life. This same woman gives me up the first opportunity."

"Marion Ross had that idea." Still Rohmer didn't look up. It was one of several things about him that irritated Lomak.

"There you go," he said. "Exactly. We're together five years—five fucking *years*—and some cunt lawyer turns her against me in one hour. 'It's not your fault, Doreen. We'll get a therapist expert witness, Doreen. He was dishonorably discharged for black market scams in the Philippines, and did you know he was charged with destroying a car at Macomb College?' Like the Philippines wasn't entrapment, any way you cut it. At Macomb I was working maintenance. Trying to better my education. Their goddamn backhoe had faulty brakes. From this kind of unrelated crap I'm looking at five to seven, while Doreen Taylor sees a self-esteem facilitator twice a week."

Rohmer finally logged off. He pulled out the power cable.

"Just like the stranger," Lomak said.

Now Rohmer looked at him. Winding the power cable around his hand, he frowned. "Are you talking about Albert Camus's novel? *The Stranger*? You read it?"

"Yes, Louis. I read it at Macomb College. This guy offs an Arab. On a beach in North Africa. He doesn't plan it, it just happens. Shit happens, bad karma. The sun's in his eyes, he sees a knife, he defends himself. This guy—"

"—Gets the death penalty for not crying at his mother's funeral," Rohmer said. "Yes, I read it too."

"There you go, same deal. With me, there was men on that jury. Men that had to see what Ross was working."

Still looking at him, Rohmer closed the laptop. He slipped it into the canvas case and zipped it closed. He was bald with a white beard, and his rimless glasses were glinting. He had on a green plaid shirt that made his hands look more pink. They were not hands that had ever done real work.

He carried the computer to the front entry, leaned it next to the door, and straightened. "So, you think Marion Ross was working something?"

"Right on. She played…whatever you call with women would be the same as the race card."

"The gender card."

"There you go, queen of fucking hearts." Lomak liked this, too, and thought Rohmer should at least smile. "With a bull dyke judge, eight brain-dead women and…what is it when they cut off your balls, your voice changes?"

"Eunuchs."

"There you go. Four eunuchs along for the ride."

Rohmer checked his watch and looked up. "Anyway, Jerry, we agree she should pay. And she might as well pay us. If you need to pack anything, do it now. We leave in an hour."

CHAPTER

8

MINNESOTA,
EAST OF INTERNATIONAL FALLS
7:20 P.M.

Renewed with coffee in the town of Virginia, Brenda had again taken the wheel. She had driven through what the map called the Mesabi Iron Range, and then, just after passing through a hole-in-the-wall called Orr, she felt the steering go funny.

She glanced in the rearview. Tina's dog had felt it, too. Sonny was now sitting up on the mound of sleeping bags. Behind him, the boat trailer was swaying. She slowed and eased onto the shoulder.

"What is it?" Heather asked. "A flat tire?"

"Feels like it." She came to a stop.

"Oh, God."

"I'm sorry, but I like it," Tina Bostwick said. "It's an adventure. We may have to sleep in the car. I've never done that."

"Let me have my phone," Marion said.

Looking at her in the rearview, Brenda undid her seatbelt. "There's no need. We're just outside Orr. I saw a service station."

"I'll go with you."

"No, Mar, it makes more sense if you and Heather unload. So we can get at the spare. It'll save time. Please hand me my jacket."

Marion reached in back. "Good boy, lie down—" She patted the golden retriever, got Brenda's windbreaker, and handed it over the seat. "This is a bad omen. We can't be more than an hour from the turnoff."

"Listen to Tina," Brenda said. "Have more coffee and a donut. Pretend you're on stakeout, watching for poachers."

She opened her door and stepped down. Stiff from sitting, she slipped on her jacket and walked to the back of the Suburban. The left rear tire was flat but looked undamaged. She zipped up the jacket, flipped her hair outside the collar, and started along the shoulder.

It would be dark soon, but Orr was not more than a fifteen-minute walk. The air felt brisk, not cold. A long day sitting, she picked up the pace. It felt good to move and to be alone.

They had left Milwaukee just after nine. Traveling north, they reached the state line at two and crossed into Minnesota by way of Route 53. About five they had reached Duluth. The big Suburban passed huge rust-colored conveyor lines that stretched out into the bay. Everyone agreed Duluth's hard-blue water made you cold just looking at it. To Brenda, the town's tidy, old-frame houses spoke of tough lives that had not broken the owners' sense of self-respect.

She smiled as she walked, thinking about the trip. On stops to walk the dog, for gas and rest rooms in diners, Heather had pushed Tina's wheelchair. Truckers in caps and quilted vests watched over their coffee mugs. At the second stop, one of the men had come over. "How you doing, Professor Bostwick. Remember me? I still remember the three to's, affect, effect, the different no's. Like you said, a spell checker does nothing for you there."

"And don't forget the three there's," Tina said. He had grinned at her, a middle-aged kid with his old teacher.

A pickup truck whipped past, towing a covered boat.

You could see why students would come up years later to say hello to Tina Bostwick. Rolling to a stop that morning before her small house, Brenda had watched the front door open. A dog bounded out, and seconds later Tina followed in her wheelchair. From the passenger seat, Marion had watched with a pained expression as a stranger in a parka and stocking cap rolled down the ramp. Shaking hands a moment later, Tina had handed Marion a sheet of paper.

"It's a waiver," she said. "I'm grateful to be going, and I don't want you to worry about me." Tina had then asked if Sonny could go. "Otherwise, we'll drop him at the kennel. But to be honest, he needs this more than I do." Relieved about the waiver, Marion said she was a dog person, and that Sonny was more than welcome.

Yes, Tina Bostwick was simpatico. She made no mention of her illness and told great stories. The Arab student who claimed to love Shakespeare and skydiving equally; the Desert Storm veteran whose unifying point of reference in all his papers had been the tank. Or the identical twin girls who ran an "escort service."

Brenda smiled as she walked. When detectives from the Milwaukee vice squad arrested the two in the middle of a diesel mechanics class, the girls had made their one allowed phone call to Tina. "It was all in their essays," she said. "S and M freaks, someone stimulated only by Sousa marches. They were taking the diesel course to have more in common with the truckers they serviced. In some loopy way, I thought that demonstrated an admirable commitment to customer service."

A horn blared. And blared without stopping. Brenda looked back. She had walked about two hundred yards and could see Heather and Marion on the shoulder, next to the truck. Up the road, she saw no taillights from the pickup that had passed her. That meant the driver had pulled off in front of the Suburban.

She started jogging back, and now saw someone coming from the front. A man. She heard his voice and Marion's as they looked down at the flat tire. Gear from the Suburban had already been stacked on the shoulder. Sonny was sitting in the empty cargo space.

As she approached, Marion looked up. "This nice man is going to help us. If the spare tire has air in it. I never thought to check."

"Let's see what you have."

He looked convincingly outdoorsy. About six feet and solid, he was dressed in jeans, a red buffalo plaid shirt, a Milwaukee Brewers cap. He stepped from the side of the truck and straddled the trailer hitch. The dog barked and came to the opening.

"Hi, there, buddy…"

He held out his hand to be sniffed, and now scratched Sonny's head. Petting the dog. It was a scene they used in movies to establish the good guy. Tina was turned in her seat, holding the leash.

"That's it," he said, stepping clear. "Hold him while I check the spare."

It was upright, on the left. He unzipped the cover and pushed the tire with his thumb. "Feels solid, but we won't know until we get it down."

"I have no idea where the jack is," Marion said.

"On Suburbans, I think they store it over the wheel well."

Brenda watched him crawl inside. "Good," he said, hidden behind the tire. "It's all here." He backed out, holding the jack and a kit of tools. "First, we have to unhitch your trailer. Got a wrench?"

"My husband gave me one," Heather said.

Hunched in her parka, she moved to the mound of gear and began searching her bag. Marion was watching the man work off the plug socket for the trailer's taillights. She folded her arms. "We're extremely grateful, but I don't know," she said. "You could hurt yourself."

"The shoulder's pretty level here," he said. "We should be all right."

Heather came back with a wrench and handed it to him. "Tina's still in the car. Should she get out?"

"Not necessary."

"You don't have back problems?" Marion asked. "Heart trouble?"

He looked up a moment, and back to the trailer hitch. "You must be a lawyer."

Looking small in her heavy fisherman's knit sweater, Marion gave Brenda her resigned look. The one reserved for lawyer jokes.

◆◆◆◆◆

Quickly he got the hitch unlocked. Then he had Brenda inch the truck forward and back until he could raise the cup and lower the trailer. This done, he asked her to pull up six feet. He got the heavy spare tire down, then fitted the jack in a receptacle in front of the rear wheel. Soon, he had the tire off. Ignoring the hard gusts of passing trucks, he raised the heavy spare, aligned the wheel posts, and worked the holes into position. He shoved on the new tire and began screwing on the lug nuts. His name was Charlie Schmidt.

"Michigan plates," he said. "All you ladies from there?"

Marion pointed to Brenda. "She and I are from outside Detroit. Heather and Tina are from Milwaukee. We're headed for the Ash River."

He nodded.

"It's something called Northern Lights Houseboats."

"I know Northern Lights," he said. "It's a reliable outfit. They'll take good care of you."

"We're all tenderfeet," she said.

"You'll be fine. Pete Gustofson's son owns it now. The same family's had the concession maybe thirty years."

"You're from the area?"

"Milwaukee. I have a place up here on Lake Kabetogama." Seeing he was ready for the lug wrench, Brenda handed it to him. "Thanks. There's a can of WD-40 under the passenger side in my truck. We should put some on your hitch."

"I'll get it."

Marion hurried forward. Heather was now talking to Tina through the open side window. Brenda turned back, watching Schmidt wield the tire iron.

It was always unexpected, how attraction happened with her. It had nothing to do with his stopping to help. Or with petting-the-dog acceptance by Sonny. It was his deft movements. His hands. The familiarity with which he was doing an ordinary task, a job easy to describe, but impossible for any of them to manage. Not with a tire that heavy.

And his smile. Seeing his hands were dirty, she remembered a rag in the console. She stepped to the driver's side, got the door open, and reached over.

"What a nice guy," Tina said softly, stroking Sonny. The dog lay sprawled on the back seat, head in her lap.

"Damsels in distress." Brenda got the rag and closed the console.

"Coming through Norse country on his trusty charger." Tina grinned. "Heading back to the castle but stopping to do his chivalrous duty. It's mythic."

"Sorry, Tina, he's almost done. You aren't going to get to sleep out here."

"I was lying. All I want now is a stiff drink and some grub."

Brenda smiled, already liking this person. She ducked from the cab and stepped back to Schmidt. When he looked up, she handed him the rag.

"Question." With her back to the truck, she waited as he wiped his hands. "We have an MS patient with us. Are we in over our heads with this, or not?"

"I wouldn't take her out in a fishing boat without help."

"She just wants to see the sights. But you see how it is. We're really out of it."

"The houseboats are good-sized. You shouldn't have a problem. Most people doing houseboats are families. Or city guys with girlfriends. The lake's got buoy markers to keep you clear of rocks and sandbars. Gus will take you through the river, show you how to operate everything. The boats all have ship-to-shore. You won't ever be far from land."

"Ours is something called *The President*."

"*That* thing." He finished with the rag. "Sixty-five feet, I think. I don't know how they got it through the access road. Potscrubber dishwasher, VCR, full bathrooms on both decks. Hot tub. Your friend will have a ball."

Marion came back with the WD-40. He used it, then lowered the jack before hefting the flat tire inside. As he attached it to the side mount, Brenda and Heather began passing gear to Marion. Charlie Schmidt finished, stepped away, and watched. She liked that about him, too. He was letting them do their part, a real mensch. As she passed sleeping bags to Marion, he again used the rag. Fifty or so—no, a little more—he was someone you wanted to like. Someone you hoped would prove that first impressions could be dead-on right.

After they were done, she backed up the Suburban. He dropped the trailer on the hitch, tightened it, refastened the safety chain, and refitted the light plug. He asked her to pump the brakes, then stepped alongside the truck.

"You're good to go." He handed her the rag. "You have jigs and Rapalas?"

"I wouldn't know if I did. What are they?"

"Lures. Artificial bait. The fishing's not so hot this early. Rapalas are your best bet. Gus has them, you might pick some up."

"Will you be up here this week?" Brenda asked.

He looked at her, and she felt herself blush.

"A guy I know is flying in to do some fishing," he said. "I'll be here."

"You say this boat of ours is some kind of monster. It must be hard to miss."

"True."

"Come to dinner," she said. "Bring your friend. We don't do tires, but we grill a mean steak."

"*Yes,*" Marion called from the back. "Please say yes. With or without your buddy, I want the chance to do something. You've been very kind."

Charlie Schmidt smiled. "Maybe so. Have fun."

He walked forward. In the glare of their headlights, he turned and waved before moving again toward his truck. All at once he staggered and held his back, but kept walking.

They all laughed, and she glanced in the rearview. Marion was shaking her head.

CHAPTER

9

Louis Rohmer had told Schmidt he didn't care if the fishing was poor this time of year. He just needed to get away.

He called at the beginning of April, upset about some drug-company stock he'd bought on margin. A sure bet, he said. Convinced the Food and Drug Administration would approve the company's new drug, Louis had taken out second mortgages to buy the stock. When the drug was rejected, the stock tanked. This didn't exactly raise Louis's own stock in Schmidt's estimation, but he sounded strung out, so Charlie said yes, to come in the first week of May. After the call, he went online and looked up Rohmer's properties. They were pricey row houses in upscale Brooklyn Heights, now in foreclosure.

Even so, Rohmer was still leasing a plane. He would fly in for a long weekend.

He'd flown it to Cabo San Lucas the previous spring, when Schmidt and his nephew Kenny were there for Kenny's spring break from the University of Wisconsin. Schmidt knew his good-looking nephew would hook up there, and sure enough, a girl from Penn State snagged Kenny's full attention their first night in Cabo, in a bar called Carlos 'n

Charlie's. The next day, Kenny had taken their Jeep rental and headed for the beach.

Schmidt went then to the harbor, in search of a crew that spoke English. Rohmer was there, and they agreed to share a charter. They'd done pretty well—three yellow fin tuna, and a black marlin Rohmer almost landed. He invited Schmidt up to his condo overlooking the bay. The Mexican housekeeper did up one of the tuna as sashimi, and steaks, this followed by key lime pie and brandy.

Rohmer talked about his Brooklyn Heights properties. He'd grown up in Michigan, gone to school there, then gone to New York to make his fortune. After Cabo, Louis had flown up to Minnesota in July, to fish for walleye. That October, Charlie was in New York for a builders' show, and called. Louis took him to his club, a great old place off Gramercy Park full of guys in huge leather chairs, sleeping with the *Wall Street Journal* on their stomachs. That had seemed the last of it, until Louis's call.

◆◆◆◆◆

Just after nine, he swung off the county road, onto the trail leading to his property. With the boat trailer bouncing hard in back, Schmidt tunneled through the arc of light formed by his headlights. Pine boughs swept the cab. The headlights glanced off a pair of eyes before a deer vanished in the dark.

He had told Louis where to find the keys, and now saw lights through the trees.

The house was barn-like and made of cedar. His father had built it. Reaching the gravel turnaround, he snapped on the high beams to see the cabin's roof. Just like every spring, lichen was growing there and would have to be scraped off. He swung the truck to the right, stopped in front of the new pole barn and turned off the ignition. In the quiet, Schmidt heard music.

He got out and crossed the spongy mat of pine needles. The music grew louder, blaring when he opened the door.

Greeted by smells of chili and mildew, he saw a fire was
going in the big stone fireplace. He looked to the open bedroom doors, two each on either side of the big, all-purpose
room. The wood of the walls and pitched ceiling had grown
dark over the years. Depending on your mood, the place was
gloomy or cozy. An old wagon wheel with electric candles
hung from the rafters.

He closed the door and walked to the front. A boom box
rested on the plank coffee table, and a man lay face down on
the leather couch. It wasn't Louis Rohmer. Schmidt stepped
around and turned off the radio. The man didn't move. A half-
empty bottle of Jack Daniels rested on the rag rug.

He moved to the kitchen, around the table to the glass
door wall leading to the patio. Cupping the glass, he looked to
the lake. The Nielsons had made good on their promise to get
the dock in early, and Rohmer's Cessna was tied to it. A light
glowed in the plane's cabin. Schmidt's utility skiff was tied up
in front of the plane. Someone had put a motor on it.

He glanced back at sleeping beauty, then to the kitchen
table. Stacked there were cans of smoked oysters and goose-
liver pate he remembered Louis bringing last summer. He
stepped to the refrigerator and looked in. Lots of Beck's and
butcher-wrapped packages.

Schmidt got out two beers and opened them. He pulled
open the heavy door wall, stepped out and eased it shut. The
night was country-silent. Moonlight lay splayed out on the
lake, the Canadian shore opposite completely dark. He took
the shallow steps and started down the grassy slope.

"Hey Louis—"

He reached the aluminum dock, and as he walked toward
the plane, the light went out. The cockpit door swung open.

"Hi there." Rohmer swung down. Schmidt reached him,
knelt, and pulled the tie-up line until the plane's pontoon
nudged the dock. Louis jumped across.

"Sorry I'm late." Holding both beers in his left hand, Schmidt stood and held out his right. "Good to see you, Louis."

"Right, yes—" Rohmer shook his hand. "How have you been?"

"Okay. I see you brought someone."

"Listen, Charlie, I'm sorry about that. It was a mistake. He works for me and got into some trouble. It was a last-minute thing, I should have called you."

"No problem, plenty of room."

Hands on his hips, Rohmer looked toward the house. "His name's Jerry Rizzo. A sewer cleanout guy. He was doing some plumbing in a building I bought. Try to do someone like that a good turn, it never works."

"Here." Schmidt held out a beer.

"Thank you." Louis took it, drank and shook his head. "I knew he was strung out…" He drank again. "I thought it was just trouble with his wife. Said she left him, emptied the savings and checking. Took the car. An ordinary Joe Sixpack, you know? Hell, okay, I said, if you can leave town for a few days, come with me. Take your mind off it. In the plane he starts drinking, telling me how she got mixed up in some accounting scam where she works. She was cooking the books. He claims it was her idea, but I know he put her up to it. They nailed him at the trial, not her. Something over two hundred thou they stole. He's up for sentencing soon, looking at jail time."

"Has he done time before?"

Rohmer looked back at the house. "No idea."

"I've hired people who did time," Schmidt said. "The ones that get it straight and climb back on the bike do fine."

"I think you told me. That's maybe why I thought you wouldn't mind. But I don't know." Louis drank and looked out over the lake. "You talk to him?"

"He's asleep."

"Ideally, he'll drink and sleep. He's not a bright guy. Very sorry for himself, a whiner. I told him, this is not the woman's fault. Get yourself together and do your time. Keep your nose clean, I'll help you later. All he can talk about is how some lawyer blind-sided him."

Schmidt drank his beer and studied the dark Canadian shore. It almost made sense. But Louis Rohmer was a fussy guy. Smoked oysters, liver pate. He took himself seriously and didn't come off as likely to invite someone who worked for him to join him for a long weekend. Maybe post bail, or put in a good word, but not bring him fishing. Louis was a bit of a dandy, even up here. Everything new—expensive Orvis clothes, top-of-line fishing tackle. He had shown up last year with the "right" stem- ware for the wine he brought. In a fancy picnic hamper from Harrods, the London department store.

"I see you got the ten-horse from Nielson," Schmidt said.

"I walked down, he drove me back with it. I wanted to refresh my memory. See if I remembered anything."

"How'd you do?

"Pretty well. Lost Bay, Mica Bay. I went up the Ash River to Gustofson's. They had charts for sale."

"Good idea. If you aren't familiar, everything starts to look the same."

Rohmer nodded, drank from his beer. "They were prep- ping boats. He said the season hasn't started yet."

"Not for another couple weeks. He has an early party up this weekend."

Rohmer nodded again, looking out. A loon called. The sound echoed out over the quiet night. "Yes. Gustofson told me someone won a trip in a charity raffle."

Schmidt listened to the loon. The haunting sound was one his wife Lillie had said made her feel at home here. "I met them outside Orr," he said. "Four women. They had a flat."

Louis lowered his beer and looked at him.

"I knew you'd be waiting, but I saw a wheelchair in their truck. Two from Detroit, two from Milwaukee."

"Huh."

"One was a lawyer. She was worried I'd pop a disc and sue."

"This is the same party going on Gustofson's boat?"

"Same ones. They had enough stuff for a month in the Yukon. Anyway, we're invited to dinner."

"A lawyer," Louis said. "Better not tell Jerry. The one who jerked his chain was a woman."

CHAPTER

10

The cutoff from the county road was clearly marked with a large Northern Lights sign. Next to it were family names on picket-fence boards nailed to a post, as if every family here were a town.

Brenda slowed the Suburban, turned, and crept forward. In the dark, the two-track dirt road ran between narrow ditches. Cedars and pines had been bulldozed on both sides in a wide swath, leaving only plowed earth and tree stumps. For the next three miles, the women were jolted along in weary silence.

At last, the headlights revealed shuttered cottages and log houses. Then came boats stored under blue shrink-wraps, large steel sheds, Old Style and Miller beer signs. Behind the sheds shone the Ash River, black and narrow. The opposite shoreline rose sharply in the glare of the truck's high beams.

"There—"

Marion pointed. A broad gravel parking area appeared on the right. At the far end rose a bulky log barn or lodge. Brenda pulled in and stopped. The headlights were now trained on houseboats moored in the river. Brightly lighted inside, the largest boat loomed massively at the dock.

"That must be ours," Marion said. "They rent it mostly for corporate retreats."

"Looks good to me," Tina said. "Home sweet home."

"God, at last." Heather zipped up her parka.

Other houseboats, ranged in descending order of size, floated between pilings. They were oblong with flat roofs, like mobile homes. When someone stepped from the big house-boat onto the dock, Sonny started barking.

Marion got out and crossed in front of the headlights. Once she disappeared behind the lodge, Brenda turned off the ignition. "Thank you, Mr. Schmidt." She stretched her arms and neck.

"You must be exhausted." Tina sat forward and kneaded her shoulders.

"Yes, I'm sorry," Heather said in what Brenda now thought of as her little-girl-lost voice. "It was the boat. It just made me so nervous."

Heather was apologizing for not having helped with the driving. She had taken the wheel once, in Wisconsin, but kept letting the truck veer onto the shoulder. She had said it fright-ened her, seeing the trailer sway in the rearview.

"Thanks, that feels great."

As Tina kneaded, Brenda studied the coarse gravel park-ing lot. It would be tough going in the wheelchair, but the sloped path leading down to the dock looked to be asphalt. From here, the massive houseboat was level with the shore. Getting Tina on board would be simple.

Floodlights came on. The river and opposite shore leaped into garish brightness. Rounding the corner of the lodge, a man lumbered toward the Suburban. He was huge, in jeans cinched under an enormous belly. His flopping hands looked like fielders' gloves. The sleeves of his flannel shirt were unbut-toned, his wrists too big. He seemed to move like a force of nature, a land mass.

"See you made it!" he called in a high-pitched voice. More first impressions. Man Mountain sounded like Don Knotts.

Brenda got out. "Right, sorry we're late. We had some car trouble."

"No problem, we got 'er all ready for you. Get you unloaded in the A.M., take you out first thing. I'm Gus Gustofson. You eat on the way?"

"We were hoping to eat here."

"That'll work. You got your microwave, your ovens, two 'frigerators. Two gas grills—" He pointed to the dock. "Anyone in your party knows boats?"

"Not really."

"No matter. Get you out to the channel in the morning. After that it's pretty simple. Looks like you timed it good. A front went through this afternoon, sunshine due in starting tomorrow. Should work out. We'll finish unloading you in the morning."

The dog barked again and the back seat's window buzzed down. "Hello," Tina called. "Sonny here is demanding a walk. Heather wants to know if it's safe to take him along the road."

"Sure is," Gustofson said. "No one's around except us regulars. But city dogs go kinda nuts up here, critters and stuff like they never smelled before. I'd keep him on a leash. Otherwise, you could be looking for him half the night."

Heather got out the other side. The dog was straining at the leash, nose to the ground. "Sonny... Heel, Sonny..."

"So much for obedience school," Tina said. "He must think he died and went to heaven."

Brenda explained about the wheelchair. When she opened the Suburban's rear gate, Gustofson swung the chair out with one hand, shook it open and brought it to the open door. He lifted Tina out and down into the wheelchair, as though she were a weightless doll.

He straightened and studied the gravel. "Tell you what, let's do this simple. Can you stand?"

"If you can deliver."

Tina pushed up on the armrests. Gustofson reached down and again gently cradled her in one motion. He turned and carried her casually toward the floodlit path. Brenda bumped along behind him with the chair. When they reached the lighted patio in front of the lodge, she saw Marion inside, doing paperwork at a counter. Canned goods and sundries rested on shelves, there were racks of sweatshirts, caps, and novelties. She guided the chair behind Gustofson, remembering what Charlie Schmidt had said about... Raphaels? Rapellers? No, Rapalas.

He reached the dock, and smoothly carried Tina aboard. The two disappeared inside. Seconds later they reappeared forward, in the bright windows of what looked to be a lounge. The huge man set Tina on her feet, then pulled a captain's chair out from under a table. Tina sat and began clapping.

Seconds later, Gustofson came out the stern entrance. He crossed the loading ramp, folded the wheelchair and took it aboard.

"Great idea." Brenda followed. Maybe up here, people thought less about lawsuits.

"My wife's sister was in one of these last summer," he said. "Got both legs busted between cars in an outlet mall. Comes up here in August, lands a thirty-pound northern. Did it sitting right on the dock, using a spinner and twelve-pound test."

Gripping the wheelchair, he opened the door and led the way. As she followed, Brenda glanced into tidy, lighted cabins. There were four, with freshly made-up double births. Each cabin had a tin sink, open mahogany storage bays, shelves. She passed a bathroom bigger than her own back in Michigan.

This would work. This was *not* roughing it.

CHAPTER

11

But three hours later, she was still awake.

Staring up at the cabin's low ceiling, she looked again at her watch. 2:10. She turned to the window next to her bunk and parted the curtain. The Northern Lights lodge was now a massive, dark presence, not even a nightlight on.

After Heather came back with the dog, Gus Gustofson had taken them through the boat. Storage lockers stuffed with life jackets, fire extinguishers. Be sure to seal your trash in plastic bags and store it topside, he said. You don't want a bear coming on board for a snack. They all wanted a nightcap, and Gus had taken the keys, returning with their box of wine and liquor. Water in the tanks for bathing, he explained. Spring water in jugs for drinking.

Ten minutes after he left, a young girl Brenda took to be his daughter had come down with a tureen of potato soup. But not the daughter. No more than five feet tall, with her small face wreathed in cherry-scented blond hair, Mrs. Janey Gustofson told them the soup was a favorite with her three children. "I'm chief cook and bottle washer around here," she said. "Bookkeeper, purchasing and booking agent, shop manager. It's sixteen-hour days for five months, but then we get to veg out all winter in the Florida Keys."

Brenda reached out from under her sleeping bag, released the window latch and slid it open. The scent of pine floated in on cool air. A slight movement rocked her, followed by the sound of the big boat easing against rubber bumpers. Forces at work. Hidden currents.

It was the first time she'd been on a boat since the *Nauro Maru*. Her book *Blue Sky Six* dealt mostly with corporate crime, but its big selling point had been the story of her ordeal at sea—two weeks adrift in the Pacific, on a rudder-less tuna trawler.

For no reason, the idea made her again crave a cigarette.

That's why she was awake. Not strange low ceilings. Not even the friendly, well-worn features of Charlie Schmidt, though off and on his face had come to her as she drove. No, it was tobacco.

She unzipped her sleeping bag, swung off the bunk and shoved into her boat shoes. Thinking of Brian Reese's smoke-less ashtray, she got her jeans from the wall hook and pulled them on. She groped in her bag for the pack of Marlboros. Secretly she had purchased two more packs at the last rest stop and squirreled them away, like a drunk hiding bottles for later. She found the cigarettes, then her heavy rag-wool sweater. She pulled it on and stepped out into the passage.

Marion's cabin door hung open, her friend curled in sleep. Good for you, she thought. Turning over your phone, giv-ing Carrie some elbow room. Brenda now padded along the spongy shag carpet and stepped out onto the open upper deck. The wet bar was moon-blue, also the cover on the hot tub. Chaises and deck chairs stood waiting. She crossed to the lad-der and stepped down to the stern. Carefully she opened the door and moved in darkness, through the narrow passage to the big front lounge.

A light had been left on under the cupboards. She got a plastic tumbler and poured from the water jug on the counter. Ready now to commune with the night, ready to *smoke*, she found an ashtray, and crossed to the glass door wall separating the lounge from the forward deck. She pulled it open, stepped out, carefully shoved it closed. Brenda lit up, suppressed a cough, then stretched out on a chaise facing the river.

The water lay at peace under moonlight. Up the river, docks jutted from either bank. Wooden stairs led to cottages and decks; motionless trees hung above the water. It was placid. Peaceful. She smoked and tapped the ash, glad now that sleep had not come. What were they all dreaming? Three women asleep on a boat. Families and houses, so many connections.

The idea led to the image of her mother, in her big house in Larchmont, New York.

Brenda saw Reva Contay in the den, smoking. She was just sixty-four, but already starting to forget things. That was because of early widowhood, and no second marriage. During their last phone call, she had said the garden would be too much to manage this year. Brenda had seen it coming, the next retreat from better days. Reva Contay now spent her time on cruise ships with other widows, or shopping in New York. Otherwise, it was television, smoking, and popping mints in front of the set.

Still Brenda saw her mother in the house's gloomy, stuccoed den. Unchanged for twenty years, the room glowed sub-aquatic blue from a huge TV. Around Reva Contay's red leather club chair, the fireproof beige carpet was spotted with scorch marks from the cigarettes she often dropped.

Brenda put out her cigarette and lit another. Mother and daughter and nicotine. There were worse family connections. Dozing in the big leather chair, Reva Contay would wake soon. Confused by a movie or talk show different from what had been on earlier, she would use the remote. After a moment, she'd push up and slowly make her way through the cave-like living room to the hall. In a few years, she would be living in a one- or two-bedroom apartment, in an upscale retirement center. A place with perpetual mahjong and bingo, where staff members called everyone dear or honey—the turnover would be too fast to keep track of residents' names.

Seeing her mother slowly mounting the stairs, Brenda knew the retirement home would give Reva Contay a better life. But thinking this was also self-serving, to ease the guilt of not being there. Still, once the move came, there would be others with her mother. And some sense of community. Connection.

She heard a small click, and turned.

Inside, Heather Reese, in a powder-blue nightgown, was closing a cabinet, holding a glass. She stepped from behind the sink, reached to the liquor bottles next to the galley's side window, and got the vodka. She began working off the plastic seal. A nightcap, Brenda thought, until Heather began pouring. And pouring. At last she set down the bottle and reached for the jug of drinking water. Popping off the cap, she raised the jug with both hands. With practiced skill, she topped up the vodka bottle, checking twice to get it right. She set down the jug, got her glass and drank.

Watering the liquor. It would figure back home, too, in suburban la la land. Brenda watched as Heather now took a magazine from the counter. In slippers that matched her robe, she crossed to the couch under the port-side windows and flopped down. She snapped on a lamp, opened her magazine, and began leafing through. Glass in hand, she stopped to study pictures. Turned pages. She crossed her legs, and a slippered foot began wagging.

Watching the slipper, Brenda felt trapped. It was impossible to turn away and enjoy the silent river. If she said nothing, it could go on a long time. Or Heather would hear something, make her own discovery, and feel spied on.

She looked at the woman's youthful face, her girlish hair, the engagement ring and wedding band. Brenda decided it would be better to make herself known. Besides, it might help to improve things. During the trip, Heather had sniped several times from the back seat about single women and their careers. What's it like? she asked. All that praise and fame as a Pulitzer prize-winning journalist? All that freedom? It's a job, Brenda said, driving. I talk in front of a camera once or twice a month. I write articles for magazines. Heather had not looked convinced in the rearview. Whatever you call it, those of us holding the fort at parent-teacher meetings don't see much of it.

She reached out and tapped the glass door wall. Heather looked up quickly, staring at what would be her own reflection. She dropped the magazine and stood. Brenda swung off the chaise and pulled opened the door wall.

"Oh my God—" Drink in hand, Heather closed her eyes. She began patting her chest. "You scared me, I thought... I don't know what."

"It's just your local insomniac journalist."

Heather looked up, still patting, shaking her head. "You have no idea how jumpy I get in strange places," she whispered. "Whooh. My heart's going a mile a minute."

"I couldn't sleep. I came down for a smoke."

Heather stopped patting. "How long have you been there?"

"Not long. Ten or fifteen minutes."

"Why didn't you *say* something? God—" She took a drink, eyeing Brenda over the glass. "You were spying on me."

"I was spying on the river."

"Uh huh." She set down the glass and held herself. "What you saw, it's not what you think."

"Get your coat," Brenda said. "It's nice out here, we'll talk."

"I hate bugs."

"It's too early for bugs, come on."

"That man, Gus. He said bears sometimes come right on these boats."

Little Girl Lost. "He was talking about garbage. If you don't want to talk, that's fine. But I'm pretty sure this is a low-risk area for bears. We're in camp, only a bear out of Marlboros is going to attack under these conditions." She held up the cigarettes. "Come on, get your coat. Keep me company."

Looking trapped, Heather turned away. Brenda lit another smoke before stepping back to her chaise. She stretched out again, determined to admire the river in the seconds left to her alone. Then would come disclaimers about booze, about how leaving home always gave Heather Reese the jitters. But there was more to her than collectibles and Shaker hutches. First, though, would come layers of boilerplate armor. Some people had so much of it that weeks could pass, months or even years with nothing more. It was one way of understanding others: how quickly they could let go of safe talk about children or jobs, and be intimate with someone outside their known world.

Heather stepped out, gray parka over her nightgown. Holding herself, she looked at the water. "I shouldn't have come."

"No, Heather. We're going to have a great time. Your friend needs it, we all do."

"Tina's really the reason I'm here," she said. "In that house with Sonny all day.

Alone, dependent. Imagine being married to someone for thirty-one years. You're diagnosed with MS. When you get to be a 'problem,' he leaves you. Then he dies, leaving you wondering if it's your fault. It's sickening."

"Tina thinks her husband died because of her?"

"As far as I'm concerned it was his own fault, and he had it coming."

Tina didn't seem like the self-blaming type. "Is that what she says?"

Heather glanced down at her glass and back to the river. "Of course not, she's too classy. Too proud. Tina doesn't talk about it at all. I've never known anyone so strong, so—" She shook her head. "Besides, it doesn't matter what she says. He was a bastard any way you slice it."

Here was passion. Anger and outrage at a friend having been betrayed.

Heather drank, and now sat gingerly on the second chaise. Knees pressed together, she cupped the glass. "What you saw in there, with the water, I want to explain."

"There's no need."

"Yes, there is. People see things, they come to conclusions. I didn't want anyone finding the vodka and wondering."

Brenda got her own glass of water, and took a drink to be communal. Here we go, she thought.

"Do you see what I mean?" Heather said. "A little toddy when you can't sleep. A little something, and before you know it you're getting sidelong glances. Raised eyebrows."

The hubby. Brenda saw Brian Senior's eyebrows, lightly powdered with sawdust.

"You don't believe me." Heather swung her legs up and sat back, facing the river. "I could tell what you were thinking at dinner last night. All the wine I drank. The simple truth is, you made me nervous."

"I'm sorry."

"You really did. The way you looked at the house. The collections. I knew you were making mental notes for a story. The daffy wifey in la la land." Heather drank and lowered the glass to her lap. Looking out at the river, she barked a soft laugh. "The ultimate product of patriarchy, I think they call it. That's what people like this Susan Faludi would say."

The Faludi reference came as a surprise. Heather Reese didn't seem likely to read high-profile feminists. "You're right. I think your house is nutty and compulsive."

"I knew it." Heather smiled grimly. "Hummel figurines aren't great art, but they're charming and valuable. So are Hallmark Christmas ornaments."

"It was the Beanie Babies. I was managing pretty well until we got to those. But it doesn't matter, Heather, because people really are nuts. I know this with great certainty. If you saw the space I occupy in Michigan, you'd know for sure I include myself."

She waited for Heather to look at her.

"My condo has almost no furniture. Nothing on the walls. No plants, no pet. No collections. And it isn't because I'm too famous to have time for decorating. Too busy with my Pulitzer winner's life. It's because I have no sense of...I don't know, call it environment. No sense of spatial occasion. I've thought about this a lot, and I still can't explain it. I just have this paralysis about...things. Sometimes when I come through the door, I can't believe someone thirty-three years old lives like this. I think it's because I'm not really responsible to anyone but myself. I should be, but I'm not. And don't bother bringing up your backyard. I'm sure you saw me out there this morning before we left, gathering material."

During this monologue, Heather had stopped twitching her foot. She gave a laugh and drank. "Yes, I did. I could see the wheels turning out there."

"Are you talking about the Dutch windmill or me? The windmill was going at gale speed."

Heather laughed again, then covered her mouth.

"Listen, I'm serious," Brenda said. "I want you to tell me how it works, what it's about. The cement squirrels and frogs. The geese with bow ties."

Mouth still covered, Heather was shaking her head.

"No, I *am* being serious, Heather. Because you're not alone. I see it everywhere. Disney characters, Bugs and Mickey, the

Seven Dwarfs. When I see that sort of thing, at first I think it's for the kids. But kids aren't the ones buying it."

Composed again, Heather took a drink. "Oh, it's not so hard to figure out. People are lonely. They need company, something besides themselves. Something to love. It's pathetic, actually. Grownups buying little elves and bunnies to peek out from the shrubbery. Maybe your place is empty because you have enough love, being by yourself."

Heather took another drink. She lowered the glass and nodded. "Or maybe something or someone was taken from you. So you can't risk losing anything else."

As it still did, even after twenty years, and never when Brenda saw it coming, the image of her dead father snapped into place. He lay on his back, on a beach. She was next to him, rocking on her haunches. Nervously she was patting the back of his hand with the tips of her fingers, too afraid of him to hold his hand. It was summer and night in South Truro, on Cape Cod.

The river restored itself, black and shiny like the coiling Atlantic waves in her memory. Insight from a woman in powder-blue slippers. Who would have guessed? It made Brenda feel gratified. And exposed. Intimate in the moment with another.

Heather Reese, she thought. Welcome aboard.

CHAPTER

12

SUNDAY, MAY 6
8:10 A.M.

Lomak woke hung over. Stiff and funky-smelling, he rolled over and stared at the ceiling. A wagon wheel hung from the rafters. You could do that kind of thing with cathedral ceilings, and he pictured the wheel hanging at Doreen's, between the addition's two skylights.

Then he remembered the fire.

A truck engine revved outside, followed by the squeak of brakes. Stop-and-go, stop-and-go. They must be launching Schmidt's boat. He sat up. Jesus, just put the fucker in.

Schmidt's place was old and big, like a barn. Snowshoes hung on the wall, family pictures. There was an old photo blowup of an Indian over the fireplace. Big Chief Slopehead. Got his headdress on. Got his peace pipe, his wampum mojo pole. In the plane, Louis had said Indians fished the lake, that they were allowed by treaty to use gill nets. He said Schmidt's family history included an Indian somewhere. Maybe that was him, the dude in the blanket.

Lomak stood and crossed the kitchen to the glass door wall. A hundred feet to the right, Schmidt stood at the water's edge. He was watching the ass end of a trailer hitched to a pickup, motioning *come on, come on.* The cover was off the boat, a nice one. The big outboard was tipped up for launching. Schmidt didn't look Indian. Fifty-plus, big in the shoulders, with a cap. He held up a hand, another squeak of brakes. Now the boat lifted free in the water and floated off the trailer.

Lomak turned from the window. He went into the bathroom, snapped on the light and leaned over the sink to study himself. He parted his hair. The weave had been re-knotted last week, the ties still new and tight. They would be good for a month or better. Plenty of time to find someone in Costa Rica to take the place of his regular technician. The hair feathered down perfectly to blend with his own. Older women said it made him look like Jerry Vale, the singer. Vale was old but in good shape. A Golden Oldies favorite on TV specials. He still did Vegas, the women said. Vale's hair was white, not blond like his own, but the matching first name gave them the idea.

He smoothed it back with both hands. Righteous. Hair you could swim in, fuck in, stick your head in a wind tunnel. First thing after Doreen started skimming, she'd had her ears done at the Straith Clinic. She thought they stuck out, which they did, but not that much. Not like Will Smith, the darky actor. Still, she had them done.

It had been good then, early on. Doreen had gone back later for permanent eye liner they tattooed on. Then her tits. The titties were solid after, serious tits she said were for him. But mostly she had them done because Doreen didn't think much of herself. Lomak had gone to Hair's the Point, first reading up on options. You had your traditional transplants, or this deal where they took out skin, pulled both sides on top and sewed them together. They showed him pictures, said the new micrografts were individual hairs you couldn't see any difference from, compared to the original part in your own hair. Nothing like the old hair plugs that gave every guy the pegboard look. Like it fooled anybody, seeing you that way. In the end he'd gone with the hair weave, something you could change if you got tired of it. You should get one, he told Rohmer in the plane. Take ten years off. Who's your cue-ball role model, Michael Jordan? Bruce Willis?

He smelled himself and decided to shower. Outside, the big outboard came to life, revving hard. He undressed as the sound moved away from shore. Being hung over always did something weird to his mind—anything loud gave him a hard-on. He stepped out of his pants and saw one in progress. He pulled back the shower curtain, inspecting the stall. Clean, anyway. Soap in the dish, a bottle of Head & Shoulders.

He turned on the water and adjusted it, seeing the waitress from Brownie's. She had nice ones that bounced when she walked. Definitely her own, you could tell from the way they moved. Not the Twin Peaks on Doreen. The waitress— Connie? Gail?—she had commented on his hair. And Louis was all wrong about the spilled drink. Just a mistake from her being flustered. Jerry Vale's younger brother coming on to you. Getting you nervous.

When the water was right, he stepped in and got the soap. Eyes closed, he got himself soapy and worked the hard-on, seeing the waitress doing a little number as she undressed for him. In a thong bikini, looking over her shoulder, wagging her ass. Some day after Costa Rica he would come back. Just like now, the waitress would be slipping down, falling forward on a desk or table. They would be in her place, whatever, falling over and holding on, spreading her legs—

"Jerry."

"Yeah?" Still holding himself, he stuck his head around the curtain. Louis stood in the open door.

"He's out testing the boat. We have a few minutes."

"For what?"

"He met them on the road. Marion's party. He stopped and changed a flat tire for them. There are four, and he knows where they're going."

"Close the door, it's cold."

"We have to get this straight before he comes back." Louis stepped in and closed the door. "Tell him you're sick. Make an excuse why you don't want to go out. He says they invited him to dinner, and he wants me to go with him. This is perfect. I'll meet them, make contact with Marion. But she mustn't know you're here. If she sees you before Monday, we'll have to abort."

"Oh she's going to see me," Lomak said. "You can take it to the bank, absofuckinglutely, she's—"

"Yes, yes, but not before Monday. And remember, please. We don't know what they have out there. Phones, computers. The houseboat will have ship-to-shore. Until we have a read on their setup, you have to stay out of sight. Follow me?"

Remember, please— That kind of bogus being polite, it pissed you off. "What's there to follow, Louis? We worked it out, *remember?*"

"Don't forget your name."

Jerry stared at him, shiny-headed, the beard some kind of compensation for being bald. "You're pissing me off," he said. "We're going to Costa Rica, who gives a fuck?"

"We aren't there yet, and your own name leaves a paper trail."

"I'm Jerry Rizzo, from Flint. I worked for MichCon, now I snake your buildings. Okay?"

"Once we know what we're facing, this will go down as planned." Steam now filled the bathroom. "I can't do it alone, you're crucial."

"Yeah, I'm crucial. That's good to know. Now leave."

"I just want you to understand," Rohmer said. "Nothing on this end can go wrong. We have a window on Monday, and it won't be open long. The Rosses' brokerage opens at nine, the market opens at nine-thirty. We will have one or two hours, no more. After that, the Northern Lights people will know the ship-to-shore is out. That means we need to be finished and gone by noon."

"Tell me this again, you can do it yourself," Lomak said. "Which you can't."

"I know I can't. That's why you're here. Just follow the script." Rohmer backed out and closed the door.

The hard-on was gone, along with the waitress from Brownie's. Lomak slapped the curtain back in place. He began soaping his armpits. It was Rohmer, always fucking with other people's minds. In Costa Rica, he would definitely get some of that shit himself.

CHAPTER
13

By seven Sunday morning, Gus Gustofson had launched Brian Reese's boat. He tied it to the stern of the houseboat, then moved the Surburban to the incline leading to the dock.

Marion and Brenda dressed quickly and went below. They began toting tackle boxes, rods and coolers down the ramp as Gus handled the Styrofoam lockers full of dry ice, frozen steaks, shrimp and chicken.

By eight, everything was on board, and Gus left the boat. Moments later, he appeared on the river, guiding the skiff he would use to return. He reached the transom, jumped on and tied the bowline. "Want a canoe?"

The idea made Brenda think of Micronesia. "Yes, please."

He went ashore, came back with one over his head, and set it gently in Brian's boat. Minutes later, they were underway.

Standing next to him as he steered, she listened carefully as he described the boat's operation. Marion actually took notes. Compass, sonar, controls for the two outboards. "On-Off switch here for your ship-to-shore," Gus said. "Just set it on channel 1 or 2." Marion wrote everything down as he worked the wheel. "They had the dam open at Kettle Falls. To regulate the lake. Water's low now."

"What's that mean?" Marion kept writing.

"Not much. It won't matter once we get through the river. Not a problem with the other boats, just this one."

From time to time Brenda felt a gentle nudge under her feet. The huge boat was kissing the bottom, even in the middle of the passage marked by rubber floats.

Gus pointed to one. "They work the same in open water. In the channel, it's green on your left, red on your right." Marion wrote furiously. "Do that, and you're staying in deep water."

The shoreline was muddy, fatigued-looking with winter debris. An occasional runabout hung suspended before a cottage. The river snaked slowly in wide loops. Birds darted before the bow; trees seemed to grow straight out of ledge rock on the eastern shore.

But it was sunny and clear, the air smelling of earth and wood. It wafted through the bow's half-open door wall and mingled with cooking odors. In the galley, Heather was frying eggs and bacon, making toast. Presently she brought them plates. Tina rolled her chair to the oval dining table and ate looking out.

"How are the loons these days?" she asked.

Gus nodded, huge hands on the chromed wheel. "Plenty of loons. You got your mallards and mergansers. The moose herd they say is big now. Bear, I told you about."

"You told us," Brenda said. "We won't forget."

"I have a place in mind you'll like, about six miles from here. A beaver dam you may want to see. When you go ashore—" He reached out and tapped a roll of duct tape next to the compass. "—wrap this around your pants. At the ankles. This has been a wet spring, we got a lot of deer ticks. There's another roll in the silver drawer."

"And eagles," Tina said. "I read they're back."

"Plenty. I don't know how many nests. You could go a year and not see one when I was growing up. Now, they're all over. You'll see some for sure."

"Good. Everyone should see an eagle at least once."

Brenda looked at her, and Tina winked. She pivoted her chair from the table, and wheeled herself down the passage.

♦♦♦♦♦

Negotiating the channel took almost an hour. Marion went topside and showered in the upper-deck bath. Fifteen minutes later, she came down in fresh clothes, toweling her hair. "I now know something of life among the high rollers," she said. "Traveling off the beaten path, on your own private yacht."

"Maybe that's your future," Brenda said. "After Drew's deal, you can buy a Greek island. You can fly your low-roller friends in for the weekend."

"An island's too much worry. This is better. All the fun without the responsibility."

Brenda went up then. She undressed, feeling liberated before the open window with nothing outside but rock and tree branches. Under the shower it was cozy and bright, the skylight open. Steam funneled up. An odd pleasure came from the big boat gently rocking. Birds calling. Like the canoe, it made her remember Micronesia. She had showered this way on Pirim atoll, under the soft, tepid spray that fell from a rain barrel in Calvin Moser's little grass shack. She could tell from the open hatch above her that the air temperature was rising.

She came down, and minutes later the water widened. "Sullivan Bay," Gus said. The channel narrowed again, then finally gave way to big water. To the right, fishermen in a runabout sat raising and lowering their rods. Both men waved and Gus sounded the horn. The houseboat passed up between two big, forested islands. Once they were through, he shoved the twin throttles forward. As the motors grew loud, the air freshened, paper plates blew off the table. Brenda closed the door wall.

"Yeah, we're going to move good here," Gus said. "There's a little chop. You might want to check your friend in the chair. Tell her to hold on." He slipped off the high stool and motioned for Marion to take the wheel. "Go ahead, it's easy."

She took his place, looking intent.

A captain's peaked hat rested on rolled charts in front of the controls. He got it and set it on her head. "Steady as she goes, captain."

Brenda stepped away, feeling for her sea legs. She used the dining table for balance, then lurched down the passage and stopped at the bathroom. She knocked on the door. "Heather? Everything all right?"

"God, what's happening?"

"Hold on to something, we're making time."

"Is it safe?"

"Just hold on, everything's fine." She braced herself in the passage and worked back to the rear door.

Outside, Tina sat facing the stern. She was gripping the ladder, her chair locked. Sonny sat next to her, head raised, nose working. Brenda stepped out, feeling the loud motors' vibration underfoot. Water foamed below the transom. It formed a wedge that fell away in twin wakes. The churning water was a rich brown.

"You all right?" she shouted.

"Never better! It takes me back!" Tina had put on sunglasses. Her salt-and-pepper gray hair was blowing.

"You've been here?" Brenda held on to the ladder.

"Near here, with Bert. Years ago."

Good times before nature pulled a fast one. Before the mister said goodbye. Brenda couldn't help the thought. But she was glad to see Tina happy.

"I want to thank you!" Tina shouted.

"For what?"

"Bringing me. You're never going to know what it means."
Tina smiled again and looked away, out over the water.

No, I won't, Brenda thought. She wondered what it would
be like, the MS. To be going forward just like everyone else.
The days full or not, but passing like a train on a track, the
rails ticking off the months and years, the simplest acts taken
for granted. Until one day you lost your balance in a new way.
Then again.

At first you would take it in stride, maybe for years, thinking to yourself, this is just how it goes. This is just middle age,
saying, Hello, there, Tina, guess what? You're not young anymore. Until one day you blacked out and woke lying on a sidewalk, looking up at strange faces. And pretty soon questions
with no answers would be part of your new, radically altered
take on things.

Brenda steadied herself, straddle-legged. "Ever catch a fish?"
Tina nodded. "You?"

"Bluefish, Cape Cod. Growing up. My dad taught me."

"We went to the Cape in '75. I'm a natural-born scaven-
ger, low tide was my thing. Shells, driftwood. Lakes are great,
but nothing beats the ocean. Heather told me you had quite an
experience in the Pacific."

"Micronesia."

"She said you almost died. You were on a drifting boat for
two weeks."

"Until a cruise ship picked us up, yeah."

"Is this taking you back?"

"A little bit. But it was very hot."

Tina took off her sunglasses and looked up, holding to the
ladder with her free hand. "I think you must be a tough cookie.
I mean that as a compliment."

"And that's how I'll take it. I think you must be one yourself."

"I have a question."

Brenda waited.

"Out in the Pacific, when you were drifting. Did you ever give up?"

"How do you mean?"

"Quit. Say to hell with it. Believe you wouldn't make it."

Brenda was looking into intelligent, gray-green eyes. She felt held by them as she rose and fell with the big boat's heavy progress. *In whose wake, no waters breed or break.* The line came to her, a poem of Philip Larkin's. And with it came a weighted sensation, the gravitational fact of mortality. In a moment, the sunny lake seemed too bright. A reproach.

"The person I was with did the quitting," she said finally. "On the fishing boat. He gave up, and I think that's why I didn't. He became my project. I had to work on him hard. He set the perfect bad example to keep me going."

Tina nodded. "You mean he was a distraction. Your pupil in survival. Did you write about it in your book?"

"Some. I think he decided what was happening would get him fired or passed over for promotion. We're starving, but he's worried about a bad performance review. Why live if you aren't going to make vice president? Something like that."

Tina shook her head. She put her sunglasses back on and looked away to the water. The trailing islands were small now, lumps of green. Buoys danced in the boat's wake. To their left, the shoreline was perhaps two hundred yards off. Sand beach lay exposed, and now gave way to rock, sheer and fortress-like. Traced on the rock, white sediment marked the drop produced by the dam Gus Gustofson had described. Kettle Falls.

"Without your student," Tina called. "Your pupil. What then?"

"No idea. Glad I never had to find out."

Tina nodded, holding on, jostled in the chair.

CHAPTER

14

Eyes narrowed against the wind, Schmidt reached up and turned his Milwaukee Brewers baseball cap backward.

Doing it made him think of his son. Andy didn't wear caps that way anymore. He said it looked stupid, plus the sizer band left a mark on your forehead. Out on job sites now, Andy wore his cap the regular way, A & M DESIGN printed on the front. It was more important these days to advertise his landscaping business than to make a fashion statement.

Fitting the cap more firmly, Schmidt gripped the throttle and shoved it forward. The big Honda responded, the bow rose. A&M stood for Andy Schmidt and Mike Vreeland, friends through childhood, now business partners. After high school, it had been pickup trucks and ponytails, lots of beer and no doubt everything else. Lillie had been sure Andy would kill himself some night after closing. Let him run, Schmidt told her, knowing any preaching would go unheard. Trust me on this, he said. You're seeing me thirty years ago.

He squinted against the wind at the familiar shoreline. Remembering himself young here, his son now a man, he thought of Jerry Rizzo. The guy hadn't moved on. In his thirties but stuck somewhere around eighteen. It had been evident

last night when Rohmer woke him. Surly, not drunk but acting it, Rizzo had not bothered to get up and shake hands.

You saw it in bars, and at Miller Park. Or the way some guys
manhandled snowmobiles and boats. *Attitude*, everyone called it
now. The fake hair and fuck-you stare, the bad mouth and gravel
voice lifted from the movies. If you didn't give it back to them,
most guys with a chip like that on their shoulders would let it
go. Not this one. Beyond some point, if guys like Jerry Rizzo
didn't get lucky for real instead of just laid after closing—if they
didn't find work they could go after, and someone who mattered—the kid thing just kept going on.

So why had Rohmer brought him along?

A boat on his right sat at anchor off a starboard island. He
throttled back and aimed for it. Two men were jigging for walleye. He and Louis had fished the same spot last summer.

Louis Rohmer's problem wasn't a chip on his shoulder.
It was emptiness behind the eyes. Even in Cabo San Lucas,
Schmidt had sensed it. A laugh that didn't quite work, a certain inability to take pleasure from what he was doing. Always
Rohmer was somewhere else. Divided. Last August, from the
time he climbed down from his plane and handed Schmidt
a two-hundred-dollar bottle of Pauillac, it had been there.
When he had called last month, only loneliness explained saying okay to Louis Rohmer.

He neared the runabout and slowed. The two men were
looking his way, rods suspended.

"Any luck?"

"Two keepers in four hours," one said. "We're packing it in."

"It's the falls, the water's down."

The man shook his head. "Always messes it up."

"Any houseboats come out this morning?"

"The big one, an hour back. They went east."

Schmidt waved, put the engine in gear and moved slowly
away. Gradually he shoved the control forward, the bow rose.

He cut left to pick up the channel. Gus would take them east four or five miles, into Lake Namakan. He would find a nice place to tie up and leave them for a day or two, to get used to the boat. Schmidt doubted they would move themselves, and that was a shame. Every tie-up point offered something different. Beaver dams, the waterfall at Lost Bay. Mica Bay was always good for northerns, in front of the little runoff that kept fish interested.

He veered right, leveled the Stratos and began the passage between two more islands. But whether they moved or not, he would make sure they got to Johnson Bay. If the warm weather held, they would get its full effect at sunset. The water would be orange and brown, all weedy shadows and perfect calm. A real picture. Whenever he thought of selling his place, Johnson Bay changed his mind.

He glanced left and right, twin islands rising on both sides. Where the shale rock ended, red and white pine and spruce trees rose steeply. Alone now, as he had been last night in his truck, he could think about it better. Think about *her* better. Moving fast this way, once more he saw her coming toward him.

Even in the semi-darkness, her hair had looked red. No gas can and no wave, walking along the shoulder to Orr. On her own, not waving to him for help. Then Schmidt had seen two others at the back of the Suburban. If loneliness explained agreeing to fish with Louis Rohmer, it also explained thinking about the redhead. Just small talk during the twenty minutes he spent changing the tire, but there she still was.

Leaving the two islands behind, he aimed straight. The boat trimmed nicely as he shoved the throttle. Lonely. That's what he was. He felt foolish, but very clearly saw himself and the redhead. They were fishing in Johnson Bay. The look was still there, the one she'd given him, arms folded and talking to him as he worked.

What look?

It had to just be her face, her eyes looking friendly that way for Bozo the clown or anyone. Nothing special in that look for him. But if you were hard up enough, that's not what you made of it. Knowing you were being foolish, you dropped back thirty years, not Jerry Rizzo's ten or fifteen. And it wasn't like there was any chance. Even screwed-up lonely, you knew that. Someone that young turning on the charm, that was just a bonus. A tip for the old boy for changing your tire. A sexual courtesy. Something to cheer him up for the rest of his drive.

No, he wasn't thinking of her because he actually thought Brenda Redhead was sending him something at the side of the road. It was just better than thinking anything else. Better and more fun, to make it up as he drove down a dark road. Or after he went to bed.

Or guided his boat over Lake Kabetogama, seeing the two of them on Johnson Bay, at dusk.

CHAPTER

15

"That's about it."

Gus stepped down onto the transom. "Fuel tanks are full. The one in your Lund is topped up. If it looks like rain, be sure to close the windows. You don't want to come back to soggy beds. Got rain gear?"

"We do," Marion said. "I wish you'd stay for lunch."

"Thanks, but we got a lot of work. If I'm not there, the boys goof off. Now, it's channel one or two on the radio. You call any time. Right around this inlet—" he pointed "—you have a nice place for bass. A little farther up is good for northern and walleye. If you decide to move, remember, green left, red right. You got to pay attention when the water's low like this. Lot of big rocks and sandbars, and they aren't all marked."

"Don't worry, we won't be moving," Marion said. "This is perfect."

He looked relieved. "Okay, then. Catch you later."

As he stepped down into the skiff, a motor was growing louder. Gus looked out to the lake. Brenda shaded her eyes, and now a sleek boat passed in the channel and disappeared behind the cove's far side. Then the motor changed pitch. Seconds later, the boat reappeared. The driver swung sharply and came at them. Planing smoothly, the hull rode the waves, hardly touching the water—until the motor's pitch dropped.

Charlie Schmidt. Seconds later he stood and waved, cap on backward. It made her smile. She waved back, Marion, too, and Tina. Sonny was at the railing, barking, tail banging the wheelchair as Heather stepped from the passage. "What's—" She looked out. "Why, that's him, the man on the road."

"Sonny, quiet." Tina stroked the dog. He whined and paced next to her, looking out.

"Good." Marion still wore the captain's hat. In white jeans and the fishermen's knit sweater she looked the part. "We owe that guy."

Gus looked to them. "You know Charlie?"

"He fixed a flat for us outside Orr," Brenda said. "We asked him to dinner."

"You're all set, then." Gus reached to the cleat and untied the rope. "Get him to take you in that Stratos of his to Kettle Falls. Take you only ten minutes in that thing. Don't know if the hotel's open, but it's worth going for the falls alone."

Slowing to a stop now, Charlie waited for Gus to push off and start his motor. The huge man pulled the rope, sat, and worked the tiller. As he neared the other boat he said something. Charlie nodded and laughed. Guy stuff about us girls, Brenda thought. Charlie said something more, nodded again and took off his cap to smooth his head. Before he put it back on, peak in front this time, she saw his hair. It was receding some, cut short. Brown with plenty of gray. He looked his age.

Gus's boat now nosed up and headed away. Rocking in the wake, Charlie floated toward them. He shut down his engine, moved forward, and grabbed a yellow bowline.

"Hello there," Brenda said. "As you see, we made it."

He looked at her and threw the line. She caught it and pulled, amused at the corny symbolism—*throw me a rope.* She held on as he jumped to the transom. The dog barked again. As he had on the road, Charlie crouched to eye level before holding out his hand. He scratched the dog's head, stood and stepped up onto the stern.

"The Viking knight returns," Tina said. "On a new charger."

"How'd you know where to find us?" Marion asked.

"Some guys fishing saw you. Your upper deck's visible from the channel. I thought Gus would bring you about this far."

"How about a beer?" Brenda handed him the rope.

"Sounds good." He knelt and tied it to a cleat, his hands purposeful and practiced as she remembered them. He finished and stood, the dog wanting more, nuzzling his hand. Slightly awkward, he scratched Sonny's ears. "So, you're ready for bear." He looked at the overhang above the stern, then to the gas grills. "Roughing it this is not."

"Please don't talk about bears," Heather said. "We've had enough warnings."

He held up both hands.

"We have Old Style and Heineken, or gin and scotch. And there's wine, too, chardonnay, cabernet—"

Brenda smiled at the missing vodka.

"Don't insult him," Tina said. "Norsemen don't drink white wine or mixed drinks."

"An Old Style would be good," he said.

"Would you like to see our private yacht?"

Marion doffed her captain's hat and motioned with it to the door. She opened it and Charlie stepped aside, waiting for Tina. She rolled past, into the passage. The others followed. Brenda waited until last and held the door for him, seeing he was slightly nervous. She followed. Charlie moved straight ahead, not looking into rooms. Maybe he wasn't a Norse god, but he had manners.

In the lounge they made him sit, brought the beer, asked about his friend.

"He was there when I got in," Charlie said. "Flew in yesterday afternoon. I have to get back soon, but thought I'd look you up."

"Can you stay for lunch?" Tina asked.

"Thanks, but they're waiting on me. I launched my boat and was just testing it. I should head back." He pointed to the houseboat's instruments. "Are those charts?"

Brenda stepped to the control panel and brought them back. The others sat as he unrolled one. Marion held down one end, Tina the other.

"Here's the Ash River." He pointed. "Then you came up through the channel. We're here now. This is all park, the least used in the national park system. This in-and-out pattern here is Canadian water. You don't want to fish there without a Canadian license. The fines are steep."

"We bought Minnesota licenses from Gus," Brenda told him.

"You all have the Canadian visitor's card and the Remote Crossing pass?"

"We got them by mail."

"Good," Charlie said. "You can't fish, but you can visit the Canadian waters."

"It looks very confusing—" Marion moved a finger from their site to the islands. "On our way, it all started to look the same."

"It's a problem," he said. "People get lost out here, and not just tourists. But your Lund is a good boat, and I see you have a trolling motor. That's a big advantage."

Marion looked to Heather. "Do you know how it works?"

"I've been along, that's all. Brian sits up front and uses a foot pedal."

"That's really all there is to it," Charlie said. "You'll need to charge the battery every so often. There's a hookup in back, to the generator. With a trolling motor, you can compensate for drift and maintain your position along the walls."

"Gus mentioned something about Kettle Falls," Brenda said.

He tapped the chart. "There. It's pretty, you should see that. I'll take you. All in this area here is pretty tricky—" Again he tapped. "And Johnson Bay, you don't want to go home without seeing that. In some places, you might see white bobbers. Chlorox bottles. This would be at the entrance to bays. They mark gill nets. Give those a wide birth, they belong to the Indians."

A minute later, he let the chart roll up. "Before I go, why don't you show me the tackle you brought."

Heather and Marion went to their cabins and came back with tackle boxes borrowed from their husbands. They opened them on the table.

"Okay, you have some weedless spoons here," he said. "Some jigs and spinners."

"You told us to get Rapalas," Brenda said. "We bought some at Northern Lights."

"That's good. Some run deep, others close to the surface. If you aren't having luck with one, try a different color until you get a strike."

"I strongly doubt that will happen," Marion said.

"No, you're going to catch fish." Charlie smiled at her. "Around here, you can hardly help it. Even this early."

"I appreciate your optimism." He looked up at Brenda. "You have way too much confidence in this bunch."

"We'll see." He stood. "Thanks for the beer."

"Dinner." Marion got her cap from the table and put it on. "This is the captain speaking. Charlie Schmidt will report to the officers' mess this evening."

He smiled and looked at them. "I'd like to. Let me see how things are at my place."

"Bring your friend," Tina said.

"Promise us." Brenda folded her arms. "Night falls on the forest. Moose mass on the shore. All we have to defend ourselves are cooking spatulas and trail mix."

"Forgive her, she's a journalist," Marion said. "But we also have some nice Delmonicos and a decent cabernet. I think some kind of frozen pie, too. Which you will be doing us all a favor to eat most of."

Before leaving, he explained how to use the trolling motor, and what to look for when fishing. Then he stepped out on the transom with one of the rods. Brian Reese had seen to it they had plenty of line and swivels. Charlie attached one of the new Rapalas and made a cast.

"Don't get discouraged," he said, reeling in. "Just practice. Let your lure hang off the rod about five inches. Release the bailer and use your forefinger."

He flipped his wrist and the filament sailed out again, the lure plopping seventy feet into the inlet. He repeated this, and made Brenda try. He stood close, guided her arm. Then again. On the fourth attempt, feeling his hand on her wrist, she managed a crude version of what he'd shown her.

"See?" he said. "It's simple. Now you're in charge."

He untied the bowline, shoved and jumped. Soon, he was headed toward the channel.

CHAPTER

16

It was eleven when he got back. Near shore, Louis was in the aluminum utility, casting toward the point. He waved. Schmidt slowed, looking down into the amber water. Granite boulders glinted below the surface. He used the lift to tilt the engine several inches. Schmidt's son Andy said the Stratos worked like a Corvette with girls, making them nervous, screaming. He neared the utility and put the motor in neutral.

"Any luck?"

"One strike," Rohmer said. "A nice northern, eight or nine pounds. He took my lure."

"Where's Jerry?"

"Inside. Listen, Charlie, again, I'm sorry about that. I don't know what I was thinking."

"I found the ladies."

Louis put down his rod and stood. He waited for the Stratos, grabbed the gunwale and held on. "How many did you say?"

"Four. Listen, Louis, I want your help on this. They asked us to dinner and I don't want Rizzo along. I'm sorry he has trouble. He's here and that's fine, but he's not handling it. I don't think he'd be good company."

Louis nodded. "It won't be a problem. He's not interested in fishing. We'll just tell him we're going out and take our tackle boxes. He doesn't have to know."

"No, Louis, he may meet them later. He'd know we lied. I'm going to tell him straight. If he doesn't like it, he doesn't like it."

Schmidt put the half-raised motor in reverse and backed away. He felt angry. The more he knew about Rohmer, the less he wanted to know. He swung the boat in a slow arc and motored slowly toward the dock. It was probably how Rohmer always operated. You wouldn't know it right away, in Cabo or New York. You would get a taste of it when he handed you a bottle of wine and told you what it cost, coming out of his plane with it, no handshake first. Okay, maybe that was just how they did things where he came from. But with something like this—suggesting they lie to Rizzo, ashamed of him and ready to dump him—that's when you would know.

He neared shore, shut down the engine and raised it fully. When the hull touched the sand beach, he stepped forward and jumped, then pulled the boat up more firmly. All right, he was here, time to deal with it. He moved up the grassy incline. The door wall was closed and he again heard music. Rohmer would come with him to dinner with the ladies. He would do a couple more days, and that would be it. Goodbye, Louis, he would tell him. Take care of yourself, but don't call again. It's just the way it is.

He reached the porch slab, pulled open the door wall and stepped in. Rizzo was seated on the couch, playing solitaire.

"Morning."

"That's what it is," Rizzo called.

"You guys find some breakfast?"

Rizzo looked up from the cards. He turned down the radio.

"I asked if you had some breakfast."

"None of that fucking chili, I can tell you. I was in the crapper twice this morning."

Schmidt opened the refrigerator. He got out a Beck's and used the opener. "Some women I met on the road," he said. "I think Louis told you. They asked us to dinner."

"That's cool, you and Louis go." Rizzo slapped down cards. "Women are on my shit list right now."

Good, easy enough. Schmidt sipped his beer. "I have some work on the roof," he said. "Screens to put up. You and Louis take the Stratos. He knows the channel from last time, you won't have a problem. Fish or just look around. Maybe go up the Ash River. You might find a tavern open."

"A bar would be good." For the first time, Rizzo looked up and smiled. "Some neon. After too much woodsy shit, I get spooked. Your boat looks like a righteous pussy magnet."

"According to my son."

Schmidt finished his beer and crossed the big room to the front entrance. He stepped out, then moved toward the pole barn. Bigger than needed, he and John Nielson had put it up the summer before Lillie died. The corrugated steel was still shiny. Reaching it, he got out his keys, worked off the big Yale lock, and shoved open the sliding door. Inside were the snowmobiles and jet skis, gas and kerosene tanks, the big rotary field mower.

It was windowless, with a dirt floor. On the back wall hung an aluminum ladder. He got it down, swung it clear of his son's dirt bike, and lugged it out into the sun-dappled front clearing. At the house he settled the ladder against the roof. He went back to the barn, got out a metal brush and a broom, went back and started up.

It was something he did every spring, and enjoyed. Broom and brush in one hand, he now stepped onto the gently sloping roof. Carefully he began working his way up the cedar shingles. The opposite shore slowly appeared, then the lake. At the top of the roof he straddled the peak and enjoyed the view. Jack pines rose on all sides, blue sky above, puffy clouds.

On the lake in direct sun it was warm. Up here, a little cooler. Schmidt looked down on the greensward that would soon need mowing. At the shallow beach, the dock. Rohmer's plane.

And felt what was missing. Always when he did the roof, Lillie painted the Adirondack chairs on the greensward. It was one of many paired tasks formed over the years. Looking up to check on him, making sure he didn't break his neck, she'd have on old sweats, be wearing work gloves, holding the paint can. The chairs would be turned over, so she could paint them on the underside. That was Lillie all the way, painting where no one could see. It had not been necessary for them to talk. When they did, it was mostly in code. In the last years, as often as not they would be thinking the same thing, life grooved and smooth without words.

He edged down the lakeside slope, seeing the luminous blue-green of the lichen at the base of the chimney. It was stone, capped with chicken wire to keep out squirrels. He braced against it, and began working on the fungus. It came off easily, and now he used the broom. Roughing up the shingles gave him better footing. He stood in the cleaned area and worked left to right. The shingles changed color to a honey brown.

Working, he saw himself changing the tire on the Suburban. There she was next to him, smelling of coffee, and something feminine. Powder or cologne.

CHAPTER

17

"What's wrong with staying close to the houseboat?"

"Nothing."

Brenda cranked the lure close to the end of her rod. She set the bail on her spinning reel. "But this is just our practice pond. I want to see what's around the point."

"We just got here. What about currents? It's nothing but rocks down there. It's dangerous."

As Charlie Schmidt had showed her, she tautened the line on the tip of her forefinger. Not at the first joint. Do that and you'll miscast, he said. She had tried it that way and now knew what he meant.

"I wish Brian were here," Heather said again.

"Come on, it's a great day."

"I'm freezing."

"It's sixty-one degrees, Heather. This could be a cool day in June."

True enough. The sun felt warm on her shoulders. There was little or no breeze. She raised the rod, whipped and released, watching the lure sail out into the sunny cove. The Rapala landed with a satisfying plop, and she began reeling slowly. Here in the inlet, it was shallow, the clear water topaz-colored. Ribbed sand and smooth boulders blinked on the bottom.

She glanced again at Heather. She was still bundled in her parka, looking bleak. Following lunch, after much coaxing and many false starts, she had finally stepped down awkwardly into the Lund. Once she was seated, Brenda had pushed off and used the paddle to move them into the center of the inlet. An hour later, Heather was still seated behind the boat's controls, hands under her arms.

As she worked the reel, Brenda looked back to the houseboat. Tina hadn't moved in twenty minutes. She was on the stern, hatless, with her head back, taking the sun. A book lay face down on the white bait tank. Topside, Marion mimicked the pose, head back, arms draped along the sides of the hot tub. She was still wearing the captain's hat, arms shiny with sunscreen.

Oh yes, Brenda thought. This will *do*.

She looked again to the water, still cranking. Her lure was visible now, silver, with three treble hooks. It wiggled as she brought it in, looking alive. Twice a fish had followed, darting away as the Rapala neared the boat. It got you excited knowing they were interested, making up their minds.

"Are we having fun yet?" she called.

Tina and Marion raised up and waved, then settled back in their separate reveries. Brenda looked back to her lure. When it reached the stern she lifted it out, lowered the rod. Careful of the hooks, she inserted one in the top guide as Charlie had shown her. She rested the rod on the gunwale.

"Let's crack a brewskie."

She had taken off her windbreaker and now felt hot in the flannel shirt. She stepped to the back of the boat and popped open the small cooler, got out two Old Style and straightened.

Hands still clamped under her arms, Heather shook her head. "Not if we're going away from the boat."

"What's this? You can't fish and not drink beer. I think it's on your license."

"It'll make me go. Anything cold makes me go."

"Heather, we have a whole national park to pee in. Look around." Brenda faced the lake, the shore, turning in an arc. "No one's here. No spies or neighbors. No hall monitors. In an hour we've seen one boat." She turned back, holding the cold beers. She had to get those hands loose. So she tossed a can.

Heather snatched a hand free and caught the beer. She held it away from her. "Why do they always have to be frozen?" She brushed off the water. "They can't be cool, they have to be like this."

"It's part of the sportsman's code." Brenda popped open her can. "Cold as possible."

"Brian says that. It's ridiculous."

"When you're with him and have to go, what do you do?"

"He takes me to shore. I use the marina, or go to one of the restaurants."

"Truly? You never peed in the great out-of-doors?" She drank, feeling the beer slip down her throat like an icy minnow.

"Only swimming, but I'm certainly not doing that here. I'm sure Brian does it when I'm not along. You know, over the side."

Brenda drank again and studied Heather. Little Miss Muffet, sat on a tuffet. In the middle of nowhere, Heather Reese wanted her oak toilet seat, her bluebird-patterned bath mat. Already she was forgetting last night's honesty.

"I've decided something," Brenda said. "I've decided you're my project out here. My mission. Remember last night?"

"What about it?" Perhaps the memory plugged into the need for a drink. Heather popped the can, holding it out.

"You were candid. Honest. You said serious things, smart things. You weren't just killing time."

Heather drank and lowered the can. "I shouldn't have come. If Tina didn't need this, I wouldn't have."

"There's no wind. They can probably hear us."

Heather looked quickly to the houseboat.

"If we go around the point, they won't hear."

Heather went on looking, making up her mind. Nothing was simple for her. Like everything else, leaving sight of the houseboat was loaded with risk. Like a pike following a lure.

"Come on, start the motor. We'll go slow."

"I have agoraphobia."

"No, you don't."

"I mean it," Heather said. "I hate being outside. When I go with Brian, I do what I did last night. I make a thermos of Bloody Marys. If we're going anywhere, you have to drive."

Progress. Heather moved and Brenda sat at the controls. She used the cupholder for her beer, put the throttle in neutral, and turned the key. The motor whinnied and caught. She edged the control to Forward and throttled gently. They began to move.

Happy, feeling in charge, she stood to see. She kept to deeper water, eyeing the bottom.

"See? Nothing to it. I promise, Heather. We won't take chances."

She left the throttle where it was and watched the sandy bottom. Very gradually the rocks and boulders darkened as the yellow water turned to brown. They neared the point where inlet merged with lake. Once there, Brenda spun the wheel and began a slow, gentle turn. The motor chugged, she looked at Heather. She was gripping the boat's gunwale with her left hand, the beer in her right.

"Look, if this—"

"Go on, get it over with."

More progress. As they edged forward, the shoreline behind the point came into view. It was like throwing a switch, from feminine to masculine. A hundred feet ahead, sheer rock rose in dark shade. It formed a perfect wall of shale, or maybe granite, twelve to fifteen feet above the waterline. This extended for perhaps two hundred feet, and ended at another point. At the base, fallen slabs jutted from the surface. Charlie Schmidt called it structure. Protected, rocky pools or weedy hiding places where fish felt safe. It was along such walls he said the trolling motor would be needed, to keep the boat steady.

She straightened the wheel and guided the Lund into shade before turning off the engine. In silence, they began to drift very slowly with the current.

"What now?" Heather was still gripping the boat.

"Now we're going to use that nifty trolling motor." He had shown them that, too, how to lower it and work the foot pedal. "And you're going to fish."

"It's gloomy here. Like a dungeon."

"Moody, not gloomy. It's primordial. Peaceful. Come on, Heather, get with the program. Take off the parka, you can't cast in that. If you're cold, put on my windbreaker."

Brenda moved between the seats and boosted herself up onto the cowling over the bow. Like Charlie's boat, a raised seat was fitted there, the trolling motor bolted in place. It had a hinge, and she worked it to lower the small plastic prop. In front of the seat was a foot pedal. She sat, placed her boat shoe on the pedal and pressed. A soft hum issued from the motor.

She looked back at Heather. "See? I work this thing, you fish. Once I get it down, we can both cast."

Doubtful, Heather stood slowly, hands half-reaching for the gunwales. She unzipped her parka and laid it carefully on the driver's seat. After several seconds, she crept to the back and picked up Brenda's rod. "What now?"

"Do just like Charlie showed us. Unhook the lure and cast for the base of the wall. Bounce it off the rock, you won't hurt it."

CHAPTER
18

Lomak leaned back in his seat and sighted along his arm as if holding Schmidt's thirty-ought-six. Schmidt kept his guns in a cedar chest, not a gun safe. Lomak had found them while Schmidt was on the roof. There was the Remington, a twenty-two probably for target practice, and a Browning over-and-under for duck season.

Bingo. Lomak lowered his arm and watched the doe. Even in a moving boat, he was sure his shot would drop it. The deer stood motionless on the beach, looking at them. Simple as shooting in an arcade, a video game.

He watched until it bent to drink before facing forward in the boat. He ran a hand over the glossy Stratos's gunwale. The boat was black, with glitter in the plastic. Like what Doreen put on her face at New Years. It would run at least twenty thousand without the motor. The motor would set you back at least another six. He could see himself in such a boat on the Detroit River, hauling ass under the Belle Isle Bridge. Fuck the Canadian tunnel toll with a boat like this. If Louis had balls, Schmidt said the Stratos would do sixty. They were moving only half that.

He looked at Rohmer behind the wheel. His back was arched, hand on the throttle, playing big-time hydroplane cowboy. He had on another fancy wool shirt and a vest made of pockets. Ernest fucking Hemingway. He sort of looked like Hemingway, with a hat to go with the pants. Like an ad for Eddie Bauer.

"I want to drive."

"On the way back." Rohmer didn't look at him. "Are you keeping track? I'm checking the distance. Here in the channel there's no problem. Even with the lake down."

"I can see the buoys, Louis."

"Good. We'll locate their boat, then I'll show you the way to Kettle Falls. I researched it, but we should check the wireless hot spot there. Just to be sure, for the Internet connection. Now, tonight, you follow us in the utility. Charlie called them, we're leaving at five. He wants to eat early and show them Johnson Bay."

"Stop the boat."

Now, finally, Rohmer looked at him.

"Go on, stop it."

Rohmer throttled back. The bow dropped, and the hull rose in the backwash.

"I want to run through what we got here." Lomak smoothed back his hair and closed his eyes. Once stopped, the sun felt good on his face. Get a little color, why not? "You tell me we're talking four mil in the money market."

"Maybe more," Rohmer said. "They added to it in the last week. They sold the last of their equities and municipal bonds. It's there, I showed you."

"Yeah, you showed me."

"Ross needs at least four million for his share of Saxon Services. That's why he's in London. He has three partners. The house collateralizes the rest of his share. The only asset Marion wouldn't let him touch is the trust from her mother's estate. And college money for the daughter. Everything else is in the account."

"You know this from the teenage daughter," Lomak said. "Real reliable."

"Not *from* her, *because* of her. I told you all this, several times. They have a DSL line in the house, separate from the phones. The girl's school has a website, that's how I made contact. Every time she left the computer on, I checked the Rosses' spread sheets and finances."

It was the same story Rohmer had told last month. And again at Brownie's, the place with the waitress. Lomak nodded, keeping his eyes closed. With someone like Rohmer, you had to keep track.

"And how's all this moolah end up in Costa Rica?"

"Wire transfer, very simple. The broker will wonder what's going on, but he has to do what Marion says. We'll have her send confirmation by the Net. She talks to him using my phone, he gets the confirmation online in his office. We'll be able to see it happen."

"Okay…" Eyes still closed, feeling gently rocked, Jerry folded his arms. "Real good. Now tell me, Louis, why does Ross do this? What makes her make the call?" He waited before looking over. Rohmer was staring at him, red in the face from windburn above the Papa Hemingway beard. "Tell me. What makes her? Say it."

"You do."

"Exactly, Louis, and don't forget it. That's why we're having this little meet 'n greet out here, getting some sun."

"Going to the Ross house was pointless," Rohmer said. "Risky."

"Yeah, well, you and me are coming from a different place on this. You got a money problem. Me…" Lomak shook his head. "Money alone won't cut it. I remember the Navy stockade in Manila real well, and I'm not doing any more serious time. That's what's called your hard time, Louis. Not just because some cunt lawyer snuffs my happy home. No, I believe justice will be well served when her crib joins that space station they put up."

He liked the idea. Eyes closed, Lomak saw what would be left of the Ross house on Monday afternoon, floating in space.

"We can go now," he said. "I wanted you and me to have this quality time, so no one forgets who needs who. It's me she's going to freak over when we have our defining moment. Way out here, Jerry Lomak. Got on my MichCon shirt for our big date, name on the pocket."

"I haven't forgotten." Eyes again closed, Lomak heard Rohmer move in his seat. "Just remember. Anything unnecessary works against us."

"Uh huh."

"Tonight, you follow in the utility. I'll make sure we all go fishing after dinner. When everyone leaves, you can go on board and check for phones. But give yourself plenty of daylight coming back. First thing tomorrow, we secure Charlie. Then you take the Stratos, and I stay at the house. The other women should make things easy on your end, especially the one in the wheelchair. Marion won't risk her safety."

Secure Charlie, he thought. What an asshole. Lomak said nothing, sunning himself. But now he had a mental picture of Rohmer. It was the same image from yesterday, in the motel room. Rohmer was alone in the plane, in one of the fancy shirts, the plane lifting slowly off the lake.

"This needs refinement." He turned slowly for effect. "Why do I see you alone in the plane, and me with my thumb up my ass on a houseboat?"

Rohmer took off the hat and smoothed his scalp. He looked out over the water and shook his head. "You see it because you don't trust me. We're almost done and you see me crossing you. You're not dumb, and you're right not to trust me."

"Fucking A I don't."

"That's fine. I don't like you and you don't like me. This happens in business. People don't have to be tight where mutual self-interest is involved."

Now he turned, smiling, little blue eyes wrinkled up with crow's feet. Like Doreen's before she got them done. "But you have insurance," he said. "So it doesn't matter. You know what I know. You also know if I left you, you'd have nothing to lose. In fifteen minutes there wouldn't be an airport in range that didn't know who I was and what happened. So, here we are, Jerry. Business as usual. In—" He looked at his watch "—less than thirty-six hours, we'll both be in Costa Rica. Very liberal banking hours. Instead of seeing me alone in the plane and you with your thumb up your ass, what you should try to see is this. You and me, together. At a bank officer's desk. Both signing for a joint account worth four million and change U.S. We split this account in half, say fuck you to each other, and go our separate ways. This is what you should see."

He turned the ignition key and revved the engine.

"My turn." Jerry got up and flexed his knees. "You drive like an old lady. Come on, move."

CHAPTER
19

"You think it's all cooking along just fine," Heather said. "You're juggling everything, and it's satisfying, it really is. The kids' schools and projects give you a sense of being in charge. You're in the house you wanted, you finally have it the way you want it. People on committees respect your opinions, and things *are* fine. It's real, you aren't lying to yourself."

Seated on the bow, Brenda had stopped fishing to listen. Heather didn't need much coaching to open up, though mini-bottles of vodka in her parka pocket were helping.

"But it's only good for so long," Heather said. "Then, it stops working. For me, it was the girls being gone, and now you find yourself thinking about them all the time. Envying your own children, because they're off doing God knows what, and you have no say in their lives. Your husband runs himself, who can blame him? How long has he been going out to the garage, to do whatever it is he does?"

Brenda nodded her best reinforcing nod. The nod had been developed back in her tabloid TV days, to keep crack addicts and scam artists talking during interviews.

"What I'm saying is, a life like mine makes you lose track of what's coming next. When it shows up, you're standing in the kitchen feeling jealous. Your kids, your husband, they're all moving away. Not *out*, necessarily, just away from you. You're standing at your nice new garden window in the kitchen, waving to them as the tide goes out."

One advantage to parkas was big pockets. Brenda studied the granite wall, hearing again the small *click* of another single-serving bottle being opened behind her. Heather had brought courage with her in this form—out the right pocket, down the hatch, into the left.

"Nothing like that's going to happen to you or Marion," she said. "When Carrie goes to college, Mar will pick up where she left off. She won't miss a beat."

"You know this for a fact?"

"Oh, she has her problems, I know that. Everyone does."

Heather threw another clumsy cast. Pleasantly tired and cool under hanging trees, Brenda was happy just working the trolling motor—down the wall and back, down and back.

"Why do you think Marion came here?" she asked.

"Drew won a raffle. Some charity thing. He was going to be in London, so she came instead."

"That's the how, not the why."

Brenda angled the trolling tiller, and the boat slowly nosed away from the wall. "She wanted to prove something to Carrie. That she's not a control freak. She told me she cut back her practice to be with Carrie. Except she turned into some kind of tiger mom. Carrie resents it. Drew saw it, too. She can't leave the kid alone, it's no joke. The trouble with being Marion Ross is, she's got this big brain and too much exposure to the nasty side of human nature. It's not a happy combination. Not when your kid's a nice, average girl who plays the flute so-so and just wants to be liked. What you see back there? Marion Ross soaking in a hot tub? Think hydrotherapy."

She turned on her seat. Heather was propped next to the motor, limply holding her fishing rod, thinking about it. "I'm doing the same thing with Brian Junior," She said. "He's my lifeline, the last one who needs me. I see the day when he won't. I'm making a mess of it."

"The hockey." Brenda waited for Heather to look at her. "Want to know what I think about that?"

"I'm not sure I do."

"Trust me, Heather, I'm a teddy bear. I think that's your safety valve. You go to every game and scream your lungs out. You drive to Chicago for the Black Hawks and go *really* ballistic. Brian Senior wonders what the hell's going on as you're yelling Kill! Kill! It's chaos, mayhem. There are no other parents in Chicago, so now you can go nuts over all the cross-checking. The fights. When it's over, you feel better."

Fishing rod loose in her hand, Heather turned away to face the wall. The woman's shoulders dropped, she looked defeated. No, she looked relieved. All the protests and coaxing before had been theater. Heather had wanted all along to fish and talk this way. Why else fill her pockets with junior-size bottles of Absolut?

"God, that's true," she said.

"Don't act like it's a revelation. I'm no wizard. It's obvious."

"It is to me, sort of. A revelation."

"I don't think so. You're bright and you know what's going on. So is Marion. You're angry, and you've painted yourself into a corner."

"I don't want my girls to be like me."

"Heather, changing gears is very hard. Believe me, I know. Marion told you some stories about her gonzo journalist friend. You formed an idea. You see me waking up to the sound of the Liberty Bell every morning. Hustling off to another fun episode of Brenda Starr, career journalist. I'm sorry, that's really simple-minded, and I'm not letting you get away with it. What I saw at your place—all right, it's too much of a good thing. I wanted to empty the trash basket in the middle of your living room. Something to break the spell."

"You should have."

"But I envied you, too. I envied what was there along with all the country-cute decoupage. Family is something only fools dismiss. But you need some fun. Some adventure. It doesn't have to be crazy, just different. I bet Brian Senior's waiting for a signal."

Small in her parka—*wanting* to be small—Heather looked at her again. "He said something?"

"Not really. We talked a little out in his shop. With you, it's hockey. With him, it's smoking and a table saw. I'm pretty sure he wants to come back inside."

"How do you mean?"

"I don't really know. I just bet he's tired of it, that's all. Making doodads out there. Sleighs and Amish gigs. There's nothing wrong with it, it's just not enough."

"I have no idea what to do."

"It hardly matters. Ski or something. Go bowling. Fish with him for real, instead of just putting up with it. And don't make him haul you back to shore when you have to pee. We could practice that right now."

Brenda slipped off the seat and stepped down into the boat. She moved to the gunwale facing the wall and unbuttoned her jeans.

"This is silly," Heather said, watching her.

"Why silly? I have to go and so do you. Come on." She worked the zipper and shucked down her jeans and panties. The tails of her flannel shirt hung halfway to her knees. She sat on the gunwale, still warm from the sun. "Come on, get over here, get in line."

Heather looked from her, out over the water. "We have no paper."

"Don't make excuses."

Still scanning the lake, Heather laid the rod carefully on the transom. She stood, peeled off her parka and dropped it on the seat, then backed to the side of the boat. She sat on the gunwale. Her gray sweatshirt was block-lettered with WORLD'S GREATEST MOM.

"The pants," Brenda said. "It's traditional to take them off."

Thinking a moment, she took a breath and began fumbling with the button, still looking out. She shucked her khakis, but kept her panties on. "I feel ridiculous." Very gingerly, she sat again on the gunwale, eyes on the lake.

"The underpants, Heather. Off."

"I'm working up to it." At last she stood, peeled them down and pulled the sweatshirt between her legs as she straightened. She looked quickly back to the lake, and now sat again carefully.

"Now we moon the wall and any fish under us." Brenda gripped the boat, scooted her butt out and got started. Heather was looking at her now, fascinated, amused. She again checked the lake for roving bands of Viking voyeurs. She did as Brenda had, and closed her eyes. A solid gurgle joined Brenda's, amplified by high granite.

"So *loud.*"

"You're making a statement." Over the sound, Brenda heard the faint growl of a motor. She saw Heather had not heard, eyes still closed. The motor stopped. Now Heather eased off the transom. She snatched up her panties and khakis and zipped the pants. Not yet finished herself, Brenda heard the reel, and now the rod flailed violently against the transom.

"Heather, get it! Grab it!"

"Oh God—"

"Set the hook, hurry up—"

Still not done, Brenda strained to finish as Heather lunged to the rod. It was bouncing on the transom, the line playing out. "Heather!" She grabbed the pole and yanked. "Go on, crank it—"

The drag ratchet was grinding. She fumbled to hold the rod, the tip arching, flexing. "Oh God, I can't—"

"Hold it, keep cranking—" At last Brenda finished. She came off the gunwale and moved between the seats. "That's it, you're doing fine—"

"It's so alive, it's so... I can't do this!"

"Loosen the drag." For no reason, Brenda felt a great rush, a wish. She reached over Heather's arms, loosened the reel's drag and stepped back. Something like this you hoped could actually mean something. Actually *be* a statement. She laughed and watched, rooting for Heather. Little Miss Muffet, sat on her tushy, peeing in the lake. Along came a fish.

"Please, Brenda... Take it, I can't hold it."

"Not a chance, that's your fish. Reel it in." She looked to the front and saw the landing net tucked under the cowling.

"I'm reeling, nothing's happening—Oh God, there it goes..."

"No, that's what the drag's for, Charlie showed us. That fish is working hard... Stay with it, the fish will tire. You're doing everything right." The line raked the water's surface. If she didn't lose it, they would need the net.

"Don't leave me!"

"I'm not going anywhere."

"Oh God, Brenda—" Gripping the rod above the reel, cranking and crying now, Heather sat heavily. She missed the gunwale and went down. The line sawed the boat's motor housing.

"Get up, you'll tangle it, get up!"

Brenda came with the net and grabbed Heather's sweatshirt. "Come on, up. Stand." She pulled and Heather scrambled to her feet, the rod bent low to the water. But still she was holding on, crying and laughing both now, and holding on.

CHAPTER

20

Grouped throughout the lake were small, forested islands like the ones outside Sullivan Bay. Some had beaches, others were rocky, with cliffs. The channel markers zigzagged through them. On one island they had spotted campers, a couple with a sky-blue tent and a red canoe. The couple had waved from a rocky slab, in shorts on a blanket. Aside from them and one party of fishermen, they had seen no one.

Then, perhaps a mile past the campers, half hidden on the north shore by the cove's land spit, Lomak spotted the white, humpbacked upper deck of the houseboat. When he pointed, Rohmer raised his binoculars, and Lomak cut back the throttle. He let Rohmer take the wheel, and as the boat slowed to a crawl, Lomak used the glasses. Once he figured out how to focus, he saw someone topside, in a hot tub. Someone else was sitting on the stern.

"I see two," he said. "Land this fucker, I can't draw a bead."

"It's them, no question."

Rohmer worked them toward the nearest island. He cut back the engine and they slowed. Again Jerry scanned the boat's upper deck, the bright disk clear but impossible to hold steady. Whoever it was now got up, wearing a cap. She had on a one-piece suit and climbed out of the hot tub. Now she had a towel. As she dried herself, from her general shape and movement he was sure it was Marion Ross.

He lowered the glasses and saw Rohmer was aiming for a stretch of beach. "I saw her."

"How many others?"

"Just her and one on the back." The Stratos slipped into the shadow of shore trees. Rohmer cut the engine and raised the motor. When the hull scraped bottom, he moved forward, jumped out and pulled the bow rope.

"We'll be able to check them without being seen," he said. "Bring the binoculars."

Lomak jumped to shore. "We should have a rifle. There's bears and snakes." He eyed the island's interior, then looked down at the beach. "What's those tracks?"

"Don't worry, nothing's here." Rohmer tossed the rope into the boat and took the lead, up the slope and into the trees. Lomak followed. The lake blinked and glinted; birds flew through slanting light. Something fell with a thud.

"What the fuck was that?"

"A rotten tree limb. Relax."

Rohmer swept through dried vines and scrub, the ground matted with pine needles. Nervous about snakes, Lomak kept his eyes on the ground. Now Rohmer stopped and looked out between trees. "Okay, this is directly opposite. Let me have the glasses." Lomak handed them over. Rohmer raised and adjusted them. After several seconds, he nodded. "You were right. Marion is topside. She's just going down now. The woman on the stern is in a wheelchair."

"Give 'em to me."

Rohmer handed them back. The bright lens swept over the foreshortened chop of dazzled water. Lomak adjusted—and there they were. Using the towel on her hair, Ross was now on

the lower deck, talking to the one in the wheelchair. The houseboat was in shadows, sun still glinting in the cove.

"Look to the right," Rohmer said. "Beyond the point."

He leaned against the nearest tree and tracked the lens
along the shoreline. Beyond the point, it grew dark. He traced
the rocky shore, went back and now saw the runabout.

"Got it?"

"The other two. What the fuck they doing?"

"Let me see—"

Lomak pushed him away. Now he laughed, holding the
glasses, braced against the tree. One of them was twisting
around, as though dancing. It was dark, but he saw she was
holding a rod. Had something on the line. The other—her
butt was bare. She was holding a landing net, leaning over.
Damn. Buns of steel. It excited him, the women with their
goodies hanging out, not knowing he could see.

"Show time," he said and laughed.

"What?"

He handed back the glasses. With the Stratos he wasn't
more than a couple minutes from shore. The channel markers would be easy to follow, and only Marion Ross knew who
he was. He backed away from Rohmer. "I got Schmidt's rifle
sight in the boat. Back in a minute."

Rohmer was now looking through the binoculars, smiling. "They're trying to net it."

Yeah, that's what they were doing. Lomak turned and ran,
retracing his movements, ducking under limbs. He saw himself moving at high speed in the boat, then slowing. The butt-
naked one would see and put her pants on. Be flustered. He
could tell from their clumsiness they would not know what to
do with the fish. *Hey ladies, what you got there?*

CHAPTER

21

"**I can't** hold it anymore, my arms."

"Yes you can, Heather. Can *do*. You're doing great."

Brenda had used every booster-club line she knew and was now down to self-help book titles. Again she readied the net. Twice she had reached down, but the fish, a long, snaky pike, had seen or sensed it and taken off.

"That's it," she said. "Keep the rod up…keep it taut."

"Why won't it just *leave*?" Forehead sweaty, Heather was still doing the right thing, holding the rod high. "I don't want it… I want it to *leave*."

"No, you don't."

Face flushed, Heather's eyes were locked on the water swirl above the pike. When it had been inches from the surface, they could see it—then nothing but the line raking out and back. Twice the northern had seemed done, like dead weight, until it neared the boat and again took off. Now, though, it looked to be well and truly finished. Brenda leaned again with the net, bracing her thighs on the gunwale. Thirty inches or more, the pike was thick in the middle. Spent now, it lolled at the end of the line. The Rapala trailed from the lower jaw.

"When I use the net, don't let go, keep the rod up. Ready?"

Heather nodded, breathing through her mouth. Brenda lowered the net in back of the pike. She held it with both hands, counted to three and swept up. The fish came to life. It thrashed above the water, the net handle jerking. It was heavy and violent, but she held it for several seconds. She motioned for Heather to step behind her, then brought the net over the boat and lowered it.

She stepped away as the fish battered the boat's carpet flooring. It was green and speckled, the eye enormous, jaw cruel. The thing moved as though hinged, back and forth. The force of it shook her, the metal boat booming like a marimba under mallets.

"Your fish," she said. "Congratulations."

Heather had backed away. Still holding the rod high, she was smiling and scared, face shiny.

"Tell me that wasn't a kick."

"I can hardly stand."

"Then sit. You're shift is over."

Heather eased herself against the transom. She dropped the rod and hung her hands between her legs. "How long will it take to die? It's big, it shouldn't die. I don't want it to."

"It's your fish," Brenda said. "It's up to you. Catch-and-release is considered very sporting, but if it were mine? First time out? I'd have it mounted. Stick it right up in the breakfast nook for the two Brians to see in the morning, when they have their Wheaties."

"What's catch-and-release?"

"Just what it says. If you're fishing just for sport, you get them in the boat to prove you can, then throw them back."

"Okay, that's what I want."

Heather nodded, arms heavy between her legs, staring at the northern. Brenda so wanted her to take it home. It mattered, it was her personal symbol, a memorial to an achievement rather than a trophy decoration. Her defense against garden gnomes. Heather raised the bottom of her World's Greatest Mom sweatshirt and wiped her face. The fish had stopped moving but flopped again, twisting in the net. The Rapala's treble hooks were now snagged in the netting.

She heard a boat and looked to the lake. It was coming from the western end of one of the small islands. During the struggle she had managed to pull on her panties. Now, she got her jeans and tugged them on. As the noise grew, it sounded like Charlie Schmidt's speedboat, but there might be lots of boats like his. She couldn't see the driver. The boat entered the channel, but only for a moment. Now it veered left and aimed for them.

"Who is it?" Heather shielded her eyes, hand shaking. "Is that Charlie?"

Maybe he had never gone home. Brenda shielded her own eyes. Maybe he'd stayed out here. To be sure they didn't get lost.

"A little help right now wouldn't hurt," Brenda said.

The fish flopped again. She looked down, seeing the mouth working, the eye a mirror. It was beautiful, dappled. Something worthy and tenacious that had lived under how many winters of frozen ice, surviving to spring thaw, to summer sun and cold pools, marshy coves. No, Heather shouldn't keep it. They were all tenderfoots, and not worthy of such a fish.

She looked again to the lake. The boat had neared and was slowing. Disappointed, she saw it was not Charlie Schmidt. Someone taller and younger stood behind the wheel. He wore sunglasses and was smiling, and as he neared, the motor's pitch dropped. Close now, still smiling, he reversed the engine. Heavy wash bellied under the boat.

"How you ladies doing? Catch something there?"

"A northern," Brenda called. "A good one. Beginner's luck."

The smile faded too quickly. "No shit."

"We boated it, but we want to release it. The hook's tangled."

"Huh." Floating close now, he raised up and looked down. "See what you mean." He turned off the engine and looked at Brenda, then Heather. He smiled again. "Might as well, they're slimy to clean. Full of bones." Perhaps it was the sunglasses that made him seem funny to her. Too casual, too familiar. It had also to do with his hair, a strange, off-white blond color, something from pop art.

"We have pliers," she said. "Maybe you could help get the lure out. I mean it when I say beginner's luck. We haven't a clue what we're doing."

"Yeah, I see that."

He moved to the front of a boat that looked just like Charlie Schmidt's, and threw them the bowline. Brenda caught it and pulled. He moved the sunglasses to the top of the weird hair. Hands on hips he stared at her, posing, letting her do the work of pulling them close. When the boats touched, he braced a hand, and vaulted. But something caught—he fell hard into the Lund.

"Son-of-a-*bitch*—"

His foot was still caught, twisting him at an odd angle. She saw his shoelace had snagged a cleat. She started for him. "Stay there—"

Pushing up on his free foot and hands, he yanked his leg. The lace broke. He stood now, angry, and saw his sunglasses on the boat's carpet. He bent and retrieved them. "Gimme the pliers."

She got Drew Ross's tackle box, and undid the clasps. Under the top tray were lures, hooks and sinkers, a package of leaders. She found a pair of needle pliers and held them out.

Still angry, watching his feet this time, he came from the front and took them. He pocketed the sunglasses and looked down at the pike. "How long's it been there?"

"A couple minutes."

He toed it. The fish pounded the boat, rising up, tail twisted in the netting. "Lively sucker." He knelt and hesitated.

"Can we help?"

He shook his head, put his left hand on the pike's thick midsection and pushed hard. It flopped again but he held it, brought the needle pliers to the mouth, and clamped them to the treble hook. Twisting, pulling, he began to work it free.

"I can't watch." Heather faced away.

"Yeah, it's in there good." He leaned closer, working the needle pliers. Watching him, Brenda realized he had never done this before. "It's the barbs in there." The pliers slipped off. He re-gripped them, and yanked hard.

"Tell me when it's over." Heather leaned over the water, holding herself. "Is it out yet?"

"No it's not out yet, lady." He yanked again and tore the hook free with a piece of the pike's lower jaw.

"Okay, good," Brenda said. "Thanks, we'll—"

He dropped the pliers and pinched the body of the lure to free it from the net.

"Look," she said, "let's just—"

Still holding down the fish, he fumbled with the lure. As he shook the Rapala to free it, a treble hook caught the back of his hand. Instinctively he released the fish to free the hook. The pike jumped. The head came down hard on his hand, and again.

"You motherfucker."

He said it calmly, part of an act. When he took away his left hand, Brenda saw the hooks there, drawing blood on pale skin. He shoved the fish down, still flopping, and replaced the hand with his knee. Holding it there, right hand in the net, he looked on the floor, and grabbed the needle pliers with his free hand. He raised them, held them over the eye and stabbed.

"Is it free yet?"

"Almost free now."

He shoved with the pliers, impaling the fish until the narrow head was pierced. Soon, the flopping slowed, but didn't stop. Knee still in place, he now worked to free the treble hook. At last it was out. He drew his hand from the net and stood holding it.

"See what that sucker did?" He was smiling at them, showing his wound, expecting them to admire it. "You can look now."

Heather turned, holding herself. She saw his hand, then the fish.

"Too bad," he said. "It happens. Want to keep it?"

She shook her head.

"We're staying in a houseboat." Brenda reached out and steadied his hand. She felt a grudging sense of obligation. "Follow us back, I'll bandage that."

"Nah, this is nothing. Little scratch helping the ladies. I'm late anyway."

"Well, thanks."

"Yeah. Just dump it for the coons and bears. Part of the big picture."

He moved to the front of the Lund, tore off the broken shoelace and dropped it before climbing carefully into the other boat. He wiped the bleeding hand on his pants, smearing red across his thigh, then stepped to the controls. Brenda undid the bowline and threw it to him.

"Later." He winked, got out his sunglasses and put them on, reached down and turned the key. Watching them, he threw the boat in reverse and backed away. The boat swung in a violent arc, and was soon moving out into the lake.

CHAPTER

22

"Any luck?"

"Yes and no," Brenda called as she guided the Lund toward the houseboat.

Tina closed her book and used the handrail to stand. Sonny began barking. He was onshore at the end of the inlet, thirty feet above the beach. Precarious-looking boulders rested there, on a flat outcropping. They looked intentionally placed, round and casting shadows. The whole arrangement of rocks, trees and barking dog formed a painting.

She corrected the boat a little, and cut the engine. Heather sat huddled in the passenger seat, any sense of triumph now gone from her face.

"It doesn't work that way," Tina called. "You caught something, or you didn't."

"Then the answer is yes. Heather did the deed."

When the Lund reached the transom she grabbed hold, feeling the boat shift as Heather came forward. This sense of motion added in some way to her wish to redeem the moment. Heather stepped off with the bowline, and Brenda went to the stern. She knelt beside the mangled fish.

"It was awful," Heather said, tying the rope.

"No, it wasn't. Most of it wasn't."

Brenda reached down and pulled out the needle pliers, then began freeing the pike from the net. "It was great. Heather stuck with it, wait'll you see."

"I thought I was going to pass out."

The fish was heavy, slimy. She had to grip it firmly to pull the damaged head free, then the tail. She turned it over. The left eye was glazed but unmarked. Maybe it could still be mounted. Once the nylon lacing was untangled, Brenda flopped the fish over. She scooped with both hands, rose with it and turned to show them, good eye up. The tail and head were draped at both ends, the belly slung between her hands. It was close to a yard long, as heavy as a well-fed beagle.

Tina whistled. "That's what my husband would call a lunker." She put out her hand.

Heather shook it and looked back at her fish. "Well, anyway, we *did* catch it."

"Where's Marion?"

"Marion! Out here!"

"We were just having a nice pee over the side when it hit," Brenda said.

"You don't have to tell that." Heather folded her arms, eyes on the pike. But there was a hint of grin in her eyes.

"Well, it's what happened. It's part of the folk tale. We were just doing like the guys when this thing takes off with her Rapala. She grabs the rod and starts cranking. It's all hers, I just watched."

She hefted the fish higher, pleased to see Heather was now smiling. That's what you can do, Brenda thought, arms growing weary. Something like this. Being bossy, getting people to do things. Elbowing your way into people's business. Sometimes, it turned out well. In the moment, feeling proud of this thing that was true about herself, she also understood it would likely mean she would not live well with men. Not for long. There would be more David Santerros, men with phones clamped to their heads, who smiled her way between calls and planes and meetings. Or weak men, happy to have someone else lead. She would like them all well enough, and they would be glad to know her. But probably not for very long. It's just that way, she decided, smelling the fish. Not a flaw or mistake, just the way things are.

"That's not how it was," Heather said. "Brenda told me everything, I just stood there."

The screen door opened. Marion came out holding a towel. "My God." The door flapped shut. Wiping her hands, after a moment, she came forward. "That's one damned big fish. I feel angler-challenged. Good for you, Brenda."

"Not me, Heather."

"*You* caught *that*?" Marion stared at Heather. "I get it, you're a ringer. You're a pro from the bass tour."

Good. Marion knew her cue and what to say.

"I'm not." Heather was obviously pleased. "It was beginner's luck."

"Yes, well, we're going to ice it and take it home," Marion said. "Brian has to see this. You can have it mounted. You can put it in the breakfast nook."

"I tried that," Brenda said. "She doesn't want to."

"I wanted it to live," Heather said. "Catch and release, they call it. That's what I wanted, but this guy killed it, he—"

"What guy?" Marion looked to Brenda. "Charlie?"

"No, just some guy. He tried to get the hook out, but it caught his hand."

"The fish bit him?"

"No, the lure. He didn't know what he was doing, he just wanted to impress us. He hooked himself trying to get the lure out. It made him angry."

"Very," Heather said. "Kill-something angry."

"Anyway, we have fish for dinner."

Arms aching, she shuffled with the fish, reached out and laid it on the bait box. The lid was fitted with a cutting board. "Now you have to clean it," she said. "Everyone has to clean her own catch."

Heather shook her head. "I can't. It wasn't supposed to die, it fought so hard. It's wrong."

"What would be wrong is wasting a fish like this one." Tina braced on the handrail, and worked her way to the cutting board. "I'll do it. You catch, I'll clean. I've done a few in my day. Someone get me a filet knife."

Brenda climbed back down into the Lund. She rinsed her hands over the side, knelt and opened Drew Ross's tackle box. The knife was in a leather scabbard. She stepped back up and laid it on the cutting board.

"This is good." Marion handed Tina the towel. "We'll have a choice of entrees, surf and turf."

Tina draped the towel over her arm, and reached for the knife. She drew it out and gently tested the blade against her thumb. Sonny had stopped barking. When Brenda looked, the dog was coming toward them, down the slope.

"I can't watch." Heather turned away and moved to the door.

"Come back," Brenda said. "First a picture. There has to be a record of this."

"Oh, I don't—"

"No, this is important."

Heather rolled her eyes but stepped back next to the bait box.

Brenda started up the ladder. "We have to have documentation, to bear witness to the alter ego of Heather Reese." She went up quickly. In the cabin, she got her point-and-shoot from her duffle bag and turned it on. A poster could be made of the photo. Heather Reese, Native Guide.

She went back down. They arranged themselves, and after many protests, Heather was at last persuaded to hold the fish. Making faces, almost dropping it, she stood between Tina and Marion. Brenda got behind the ladder. She rested the camera on what looked to be the right step, then checked them in the LCD panel.

"Perfect," she said, straightening. "This will be good. Everyone squeeze together."

"You have to be in it," Heather said.

She checked the image one last time, and set the timer. Carefully she took her hands away, came from behind the ladder and stood close to Tina. After a second, the shutter clicked. Everyone applauded. Heather turned and dropped the fish on the bait box, then knelt to rinse her hands. When done, she went inside and Marion followed.

Brenda turned back to see Tina steadying the fish. Now she placed the knife at the anus, and began sawing, tracing a neat incision up the white belly.

"Sharp enough?"

"Very sharp. A good knife."

"I can do it."

"No, it's therapeutic." Tina concentrated. "It's real, isn't it? Fish, pigs, little lambykins. We eat them every day. This is probably something we should see now and then, don't you think?"

"You're a vegetarian?"

"Pure carnivore. But I think there's something wrong about not knowing how all these little packages end up in the supermarket."

Fascinated and repelled, Brenda watched the knife's forward motion, the belly skin pushed and pulled, the pike's long jaw barbed with teeth.

"I never thought of it," she said.

"Why would you? Things being as they are lead me to some odd ruminations." Tina withdrew the knife. She looked over and smiled. "If we're going to eat everything that moves, we might at least have some respect."

"Have you had a good day?"

"I've had a great day, Brenda. One of the best in a long time. I'm truly grateful to be here."

"So am I."

"Yes. But probably not like me."

"No, not like you."

Very focused, Tina used the knife. "I think you saw what I came up here to do," she said quietly.

"Look, Tina—"

"It's all right, not to worry. I was being selfish. I thought this would make a good end. At some point you'd all be off fishing. Hiking. I'd get myself down into this beautiful brown water. Serve some useful purpose in the great scheme of things." She shook her head. Repositioning the fish, she worked the knife under the gill flap and began sawing. "Very selfish of me."

"Because of what it would mean for us." Brenda watched the knife, amazingly sharp, cutting laterally.

"Something like that. Romantic Wordsworthian nonsense about being 'rolled round in earth's diurnal course with rocks and stones and trees.' But it would never happen that way, would it? Even if I timed it for the end of the week, you'd still be tied up with police and medical examiners. I confess as well to aesthetic concerns. Dying out here would mean an autopsy. Some stranger doing to me pretty much what I'm doing to this fish. Weighing my organs with Musac in the background. It put me off."

"If you can have a day like this, why not more of them? As many as possible."

With some difficulty Tina now slid the fish forward and turned it over. She began sawing under the right gill, the pierced eye gray and mangled.

"Not likely," she said. "Look at that eye. My own are next. I can sense them starting to go. I can't walk Sonny anymore. Oh,

I roll down the block with him, but it's not fair. He deserves better. Heather would take good care of him, she loves that dog. No, first it will be big-print issues of the *Times,* and whatever books they do that way. Not probably my kind—best sellers, inspirational trash. Or Sonny and me in front of the Sony. Someone in to make meals. A version of Blanche Dubois and the kindness of strangers. Friends like Heather who more and more feel obligated. If Bert hadn't died, this might be a different story. He did, so that's it. My problem, not yours."

"Heather told me he left you."

"He did, and that hurt. He came back after two months, or would have. Heather chooses to forget that part. He came back, he said he was wrong, there was no life without our being together. I never blamed him. He wasn't a reader, he was very physical. Active. He died bringing boxes down from his apartment to the U-haul. The day he was moving back."

Tina worked the knife through bone to the cutting board. Now she pushed the severed head from the body, raised it by the lower jaw and flung it out into the water. She rolled the body back, raised the flap of severed flesh and began to clean it.

"Read me something."

She motioned with her head to the wheelchair. Brenda stepped to it and picked up the volume lying on the seat. *New and Selected Poems,* by Mary Oliver. She had read some Oliver in college, and turned it over. The poet sat before a beach, small craft at anchor behind her. She was dressed in a white sweatshirt and jeans. The day was bright, her hair windblown, eyes behind big glasses.

"I read a lot of poetry in college," Brenda said. "Not now, just what's in *The New Yorker.* I remember Oliver being very good. She doesn't look the type."

"She doesn't, does she? More like a jock than a poet. Read 'Peonies.'"

She opened to the table of contents, found the poem and leafed forward. She spread the book.

This morning the green fists of the peonies are getting ready
  to break my heart
    as the sun rises,
      as the sun strokes them with his old, buttery fingers

and they open——-
  pools of lace,
    white and pink——-
      and all day the black ants climb over them,

boring their deep and mysterious holes
  into the curls,
    craving the sweet sap,
      taking it away

to their dark, underground cities——-
  and all day
    under the shifty wind,
      as in a dance to the great wedding,

the flowers bend their bright bodies,
  and tip their fragrance to the air,
    and rise,
      their red stems holding

all that dampness and recklessness
  gladly and lightly,
    and there it is again—
      beauty the brave, the exemplary,
      blazing open.

Do you love this world?
  Do you cherish your humble and silky life?
  Do you adore the green grass, with its
    terror beneath?

Do you also hurry, half-dressed and barefoot, into the garden,
  and softly,
  and exclaiming of their dearness,
  fill your arms with the white and pink flowers,

with their honeyed heaviness, their lush trembling,
  their eagerness
  to be wild and perfect for a moment, before they are
    nothing forever?

She looked up. Tina's shoulders were bowed. The lowered sun shone bright on her wet hands as she scraped the pike's glossy vitals from the cavity. Brenda read the poem once more to herself. She looked out on the inlet. Everything you needed to know seemed here just now. Love and death, delight in a moment of beauty. Peonies and persons, a pike worthy of love, and all of it in the present. In the eyeblink before turning from something to nothing. It was as if the poem had been written for her, for them both to share, in this moment.

"Thank you, Tina. It seems perfect to me. A perfect poem."

"She's good, isn't she?"

"Yes. Thank you."

"Keep the book. Oliver gets some of the credit for changing my mind, and so do you. I want you to have it."

"Only if I can send a book to you."

Tina nodded. "As long as it's not a large-print vampire or zombie novel. Now I'm going to fillet this thing. I'll need a plate."

Closing the book, Brenda stepped next to her. She kissed Tina on the right temple. "One plate coming up."

◆◆◆◆◆

"**I had** no idea they fought so hard. It was like I could feel every move in my hands—"

Brenda eased the door shut, and stood in the passage. There was triumph in Heather's voice, floating from the lounge.

"At first it was very disturbing. Unnatural. Then it changed. I was telling Brenda I wanted to stop, but I didn't. Not really."

"You wanted to land it."

"I did. I felt guilty, but I wasn't going to stop, either."

"It's like that for me in court," Marion said. "Sometimes you know your client's guilty as hell, and *you* feel guilty. But it doesn't matter. You just charge ahead, you want to win."

Brenda smiled and moved down the passageway. Ahead, the oval table was set for dinner. A vase of plastic daffodils, discovered that morning at the back of a cupboard, now served as the centerpiece. Each stoneware dinner plate was topped with a peaked paper napkin, no doubt thanks to Heather and Martha Stewart. The wine glasses glinted. The waiting table, the poem she had just read, Tina's story, and Heather's—in the moment, Brenda felt an odd, profound respect for the makeshift scene before her. People seeking pleasure. Connection. Doing it against odds, in the unruly mix of days. She reached the lounge, and saw Marion cutting a cucumber over a wooden salad bowl.

Heather had the refrigerator open and looked over. "Is Tina finished with it?"

"Almost. She needs a plate."

Heather closed the door and opened an overhead cabinet. She brought down an oval platter. "It's my fish. At least I ought to be able to see it filleted."

Brenda stepped aside, and seconds later, the back door slapped shut.

"Nice work." Marion said. "Tell me what actually happened."

"That *is* what happened. I just wouldn't let her quit."

"What an accomplishment. The other—peeing off the boat—that's a huge leap. A triumph. You're in the wrong racket, Bren. In the next life, you can open a de-programming camp up here for uptight housewives. Your followers will be legion."

"Too much schmoozing and stroking. A little longer, and I'd have given her one upside the head. What can I do here?"

"The steaks are marinating in the fridge. You could give them a turn."

She got them out. Thinking of everything, Marion had brought a glass casserole dish. Brenda carried it to the counter and peeled back the tinfoil. Six delmonicos were stacked two deep, brown with teriyaki sauce.

"I don't see any garlic."

"It's teriyaki."

"Marion, get with the program, these are men coming to dinner. Don't you watch TV? The ads for beef always show men loading steaks with garlic."

"Well, load them up, the garlic's right here. We're keeping this simple and heavy. Shrimp cocktail, twice-baked potatoes with sour cream and butter, salad and pie. And rolls. They're in the dry-ice chest. You could get those out."

After using the press and adding garlic to the steaks, Brenda wiped her hands and stepped to the door wall. Outside, Sonny was looking up hopefully. He was covered with burrs, legs wet with sand.

She slowly eased open the door—"No, you don't—" and slipped through. Blocking the way, she grabbed Sonny's collar and tugged. "Not tonight, off you go. You'll get yours later." Tail banging chaises, he backed from her, turned and trotted out along the plank. He stopped and looked back, one final mute appeal. Brenda shooed him again, then knelt and opened the chest. She found a package of brown 'n serve rolls, went back in and closed the door wall.

"Speaking of skills…" Marion was holding up a measuring cup, pouring olive oil. "Is my jury-selection radar getting rusty, or did something register when Charlie was here?"

"You need to get back to full-time work. You're losing it."

"Am I?" Marion cocked an eyebrow, still pouring. "We were being very attentive, Brenda. We were being very anxious to learn everything the man had to say."

"Were we?" She peeled back the cellophane on the package of rolls. "And could this not mean that we would rather fish than parboil all afternoon in a hot tub?"

"Yes, Brenda, it most certainly could." Marion was now employing her fake, unctuous lawyer voice. "We just thought the great *skill* with which you took instruction on casting and boat handling demonstrated an exceptionally keen level of interest. That's all."

"We did, did we?"

"Yes. 'Your Honor'—" Marion set down the olive oil and got the bottle of vinegar "—Permission to treat Miss Contay as a hostile witness. Permission granted." She uncapped the bottle and poured. "Were you or were you not, Miss Contay, even last night, on a strange road in the middle of nowhere, especially attentive to Mr. Schmidt? Long before any prospects for fishing surfaced, did you not hand him the tire iron with a certain—what shall we call it—familiarity?"

"I'm glad you're enjoying yourself," Brenda said. "All right, he has a definite field-and-stream charm."

"I'm not arguing."

"He's also a nice guy."

"You know this already?" Marion finished pouring and set down the vinegar bottle. "You have great confidence in first impressions."

"I try not to, but there it is. If I were on trial, I think I'd want Charlie Schmidt on the jury. But if you want familiar, you should meet the klutz who 'helped' with Heather's fish."

"She said he made her nervous."

"There was something about him, I felt it, too. But it could have just been the circumstances. We were both peeing, then all at once Heather's fishing rod starts jumping all over. I was so much on Heather's case I forgot to put my jeans on. Then I hear someone coming. No, I take that back, he *was* weird. Looked weird. Acted like he knew us. He came over from one of the islands, straight over, as though he'd seen us. Mr. He-man coming to help the struggling women."

"A local?"

"No idea. He had a boat like Charlie's. He made this move, jumping into our boat like he knew what he was doing, and fell on his ass." Brenda laughed. "Very comical. It messed up his big scene."

Marion nodded. "Believe me, I know the type."

"Yes," Brenda said. "I'm sure you do."

CHAPTER

23

Rohmer had said to wait an hour, then to follow in the utility.

Lomak glanced at his watch, then back to the laptop. He was seated on the couch with the joystick. The computer was open on the coffee table, the game *METEOROIDS*. You were on this alien planet, and protected yourself by blasting incoming meteors. When you ran out of laser juice, you escaped in the space module to the Federated Defense Fleet.

The gauze bandage on his hand made it hard to work the joystick. When he wrapped the wound, Schmidt had said he should have a tetanus shot. It was the women, Lomak explained. They messed me up. Got in my way when I was working the lure out of the pike.

"Shit—"

His blaster stopped firing. He worked the joystick, dodged another flying rock, and hustled behind boulders. A flaming ball came down. In the instant before it smashed his ship, the screen flashed *ACTIVATE DEFLECTOR SHIELD!* Too late.

He hit QUIT and clicked off the computer. On the sofa next to him rested a plate of roast beef stew. He took up the plate, sat back and resumed eating. Dinty Moore. Better than last night's chili, but Rohmer and Indian Joe, no canned food for them.

"Four women," he said, eating. "Asking and fetching all evening. If you was there, you'd be pitching in, too. Right, Doreen?"

Fetching, smiling. Laughing at their jokes. He saw Doreen bringing Charlie Schmidt more short ribs from the slow cooker, one of his own favorites. All because he changed a fucking tire. It angered him, being the one they should thank. Two women playing fisherman, not knowing how to find their ass with both hands, even when it was hanging out for the world to see.

Finished with the stew, he put the plate on the table and sat back, hands behind his head. Louis was full of plans. What you had to do was make sure he didn't screw you at the end. He would have backup ideas, "contingency plans" he would call them. It meant you had to think ahead.

But it was hard. Lomak closed his eyes to concentrate. He remembered Rohmer's call in March, after Rohmer had read a *New York Times* story on women lawyers. "I knew Marion Ross in college," he said. "It's not fair what happened to you, and I have a business proposition you might want to consider."

Using the daughter's school chat room, Rohmer had hacked into the Ross's computer. He had learned the Rosses were preparing to invest heavily in an English financial-planning company. Rohmer's own plan was to carjack Marion Ross in Detroit, and force her to transfer the money to an offshore account. But when Rohmer learned Marion Ross was going fishing in the Boundary Waters, he had changed the plan. "This is perfect, I know someone with a place there. It's cut off, completely remote."

Before coming back that afternoon, they had taken the Stratos to Kettle Falls. Rohmer kept repeating the plan, pointing to landmarks. His biggest concern was cell phones, that the women might be able to call for help before he and Lomak were in the air. He was sure Charlie would take them all to Johnson Bay, leaving the houseboat empty.

"He could screw me there," Lomak said. "Except he knows what that would mean."

But did he know? Lomak opened his eyes, facing the painting over the fireplace. He closed them. After the wire transfer, that's when Rohmer would pull whatever shit he had in mind. He was supposed to fly to the falls and pick up Lomak. Then they were gone. Home free, on their way to Costa Rica.

He again opened his eyes and studied the Indian above the fireplace. But if Rohmer left alone, it was game over. Except that would mean Lomak no longer had anything to lose. Exactly. The idea made him feel better. "Nothing to lose, nothing to lose—"

That was it. Problem solved. He had nothing to lose, because he would have a phone. Police would know how to intercept Rohmer's plane. How to track him. "Do right, we be tight," Lomak said. "Otherwise, it's hard time for you, Louis. Up here in some frozen joint, some mean-mother Hershey highwaymen running a train on your sorry ass. Hah!"

He liked that a lot, and now remembered seeing the red-head bare-assed through the binoculars. Buns of steel, cute. Something like Doreen, or the waitress in Brownie's. He got up and moved quickly to the bathroom. Lomak snapped on the light and looked at himself, seeing the waitress coming with her tray of drinks. Bouncing. Late twenties, maybe thirty. He saw her leaning down with the tray, giving him a good look, then looking straight at him. *Damn,* he thought. Jerry Vale's younger brother strikes again.

He clicked off the bathroom light and stepped out. *Holy shit—*

Lomak stood motionless. The bedroom door opposite hung open. The room's window curtain was tied back, and now the glass blinked with the last downward dip and disappearance of something below the window frame. He was sure of it. A rack of antlers, a buck. It was still there, bowed below the window. Eating. Not forty feet from where he stood.

The curtain was open, window closed. No scent would come from the house. He crept out of alignment with the window. If the buck raised up and saw any flicker of movement inside—goodbye.

In the cedar chest outside his own bedroom, that's where Schmidt kept his guns. A Browning over-and-under, a Remington 30-0-6. He had taken the scope sight, it was still in the Stratos.

He didn't need it, not at this range.

Carefully he pulled off his Reeboks, set them down and padded over the floor's heavy planks. He opened the chest and lifted out the deer rifle. Boxes of ammunition were stacked along the side. He opened one, got out three rounds and carefully chambered them.

He stood and thought about it. The door wall in the kitchen was open. But step outside, even if you did it perfect, the buck would hear or smell you. You could maybe crawl in the bedroom and get a shot off through the closed window. Or it might come around the front. Every second made him more nervous, a chance slipping away. To kill the buck would mean something. Prove his luck, assure the future.

He decided on the bedroom and moved carefully, watching his stocking feet. At the entry Lomak pressed against the wall. It would be best to have the rifle ready, to take the shot from the open entry. He counted to himself before rolling left—but in the corner of his right eye, he now saw the buck's head slip across the kitchen's open door wall. Slowly, head down and browsing, it was crossing not fifteen feet below the porch slab.

A gift. Confirmation everything would work out. Lomak raised the rifle and sighted for the heart. He squeezed slowly—never pull, that was a problem he had, but not here, not today. Because this was a sign. Everything was going to work, the whole plan a lock—

The buck raised up. Lomak pulled.

He knew in the rifle's dead-heavy report it was wrong. Reflexively he fired again at nothing. His ears rang.

He ran to the kitchen and out the open door wall, tumbled off the slab, now out on the lawn. Maybe he heard it running, and turned. Defeated, rifle raised and breathing through his mouth, he stared into thick trees behind Schmidt's pole barn. No buck, no moving branches or sign it had ever been there. Everything was at rest. A perfect shot. Impossible to miss.

Anything could spook them, and looking over the raised rifle at the still-shiny pole barn, Lomak was now sure a bright glint from the barn's new metal had done it.

Movement. He spun with the raised rifle and was sighting on a man at the back of Schmidt's pickup. *You,* he thought. Not the pole barn, *you* spooked my kill.

He fired.

The shot echoed out behind him, over the lake. Ears ringing, Lomak lowered the rifle, watching as the man, standing at the back of Schmidt's pickup, reached to steady himself on the truck's tailgate. Something, papers, fell from his right hand. He let go of the tailgate and dropped.

"Aw fuck—"

The man bowed his head and landed on his knees. Slowly, he fell on his side.

Lomak ran forward. "See, I thought you was a buck—" Sharp twigs and stones jabbed through his socks. Holding the rifle, limping, he shook his head. Goddamn hunter, no orange on him, coming out of nowhere.

He reached whoever it was, curled in a ball. "You hurt?" He walked around to see the face. "Hey, an accident, what the fuck? This is private property, come up here, no orange on you, don't say nothing."

Then Lomak remembered it was not hunting season. He bent down. "Okay, now, let me think, how you doin'? Talk to me, where you hit?" He waited. "Where you from, around here? You know Schmidt?"

Nothing.

Standing quickly, he walked to the end of the truck and came back. Bad news, out of nowhere. He stared down. The man was dressed in brown pants and shirt. He was old in the face, with gray stubble, a John Deere cap still on his head. "Come on, pop, you ain't hurt bad, talk to me."

After a minute, he reached down and pushed the shoulder. "Aw fuck." He pulled on the twill shirt and heard a breath, a sigh. The body seemed to deflate. He pulled hard this time, turning him over. Knees still folded, the man lay twisted at the waist, looking up. A stain with a hole in the shirt was spreading six inches above his belt. "What is the *matter* with you? Come up here, say nothing, fuck around, piss people off. How'm I supposed to know? You tell *me.*"

One goddamn thing after another.

Lars Nielson was stenciled on the shirt pocket. That was the neighbor up the road, where Rohmer had gone for the outboard. A perfect shot, absolutely through the heart. It was an accident, but…in some way, it was like the rifle had known something. Missed the deer, but was still hunting. Like the rifle knew the first two rounds had to clear the rifle barrel before the killshot.

He stood. So, when it was fired, the killshot—whatever was out there…there you go. A done deal. He looked around and listened. Trees, birds. No one was coming. What you could do, you could pull it out in the woods, behind the shed. Then cover it with leaves. Like they did in Westerns. Cover your tracks with a branch. Broom out the footprints, check everything for blood and heel marks.

He looked to the plane, the utility boat, and remembered what he was supposed to do. Everything was on him, all the shit details. He looked down again at the body. Next to the man's outstretched right hand lay envelopes and fliers, and a shrink-wrapped sample of toothpaste. Bringing Schmidt his mail. Colgate Tartar Control.

He set the Remington against the truck, reached down and grabbed the free hand. He began pulling Nielson off the gravel. When he reached the trees, he backpedaled faster. It was easier now, over matted needles. They pricked his stocking feet, and as Lomak dragged, he again saw himself inside, sighting the rifle. His right hand was bandaged, the gauze pink where the wound had soaked through. It was tender and swollen, so his trigger was stiff.

Exactly, he thought, dragging the body. That's why you pulled and didn't squeeze. With an injured, stiff hand, what could he do? Something was always getting in the way.

Always because of women.

CHAPTER

24

By four-thirty, Heather had finished with the lounge. She collected her sponges and roll of paper towels, then looked around approvingly. "You can tell men cleaned it," she said. "It was filthy. I'll give the upstairs bath a quicky once-over." She grabbed the Glass Plus off the dining table and bumped down the passageway.

"Washing windows," Brenda whispered. "It's a boat, for God's sake."

Marion shook her head. They were working side by side in the galley. The stern door slapped shut.

"To her, it's home," Marion said. "I bet she follows Brian around with a Dust Buster."

"I thought she was loosening up."

"Oh, she is. You accomplished great things out there. Try this." Marion raised a spoon of cocktail sauce.

Brenda tasted. "More horseradish."

Arranged on the counter were lowball glasses that would serve for the shrimp cocktail. Brenda had baked the potatoes, dug them out and mashed them with grated cheddar and chopped onion. She began stuffing the skins.

"You mean Heather's back in familiar territory," she said. "Back in control."

"Something like that. Back where she feels safe."

"She told me she was agoraphobic."

"That may be true. Or borderline. I don't think she and Brian go anywhere. If it *is* true, it took real courage for her to make this trip." Marion added more horseradish to her sauce. She stirred and tried it. "Okay, all systems go. Your potatoes look terrific. I'm going up to change. I'll try to disarm Heather of her bucket."

"What's it going to be? The Balenciaga, or the Halston?"

"The L.L.Bean." Marion rinsed her hands and tore off paper toweling. "This is working for me, too. I've had only six urges to call Carrie since lunch. Four more days may do the trick."

"I thought you might've patched through by radio while we were gone."

"I did think of it. Carrie's actually level-headed, but her friend Brittany? Very devious. I think the mother's getting ready to dump husband number two. She was reassuring on the phone. I've met her, but not before leaving. Do you think they could've pulled a fast one? Mommy's off somewhere, and they're playing *Risky Business*?"

"Don't do it, Mar. Leave it."

"I know, I know."

Marion finished wiping her hands and dropped the towel in the basket under the sink. "I guess that does it." She stepped around Brenda and crossed to the end of the counter. The liquor bottles and an ice bucket waited with more glasses. She dropped ice into a tumbler, got the unopened bottle of Cutty Sark and began working off the cap. "You?"

"Later."

"It must be the air out here," Marion said, pouring. "I drank two big vodka tonics in the hot tub. To avoid patching a call to Carrie. That much to drink usually puts me away, but I hardly felt a thing."

Brenda smiled and pressed another dollop of potato into its jacket. "You boiled it off. You can keep watch up there, and tell us when they're coming."

Marion topped up her drink with water and left. A minute later, the potatoes were ready to go. Brenda arranged them on a cookie sheet for second baking. Finished, she looked to the bow. Outside the glass door wall, Sonny lay sprawled on one of the chaises, dirty paws over the side. He was looking at her, sad-eyed and exiled with a bowl of Alpo.

The stern door opened and banged shut. "My work detail's finished," Tina called. "Time for the rum ration." She rolled down the passage and came to a stop. "I found a hose and swabbed the deck. Heather's topside, washing chairs."

"One rum ration coming up." Brenda stepped into the galley. "What's your poison?"

"Do I see maraschino cherries? Sweet vermouth? Scotch? I'd like a Rob Roy with a cherry." She waved toward the dog. "And a beer chaser for the guy in the brig."

"Sonny drinks beer?"

"Bert corrupted him. When they watched football, Bert would drink beer and pour some in a bowl. Sonny's a regular guy now."

Brenda began mixing the Rob Roy. "Marion thinks Heather's borderline phobic. About leaving the house." She handed the drink to Tina and got out a beer. "Is that true?"

"Thank you." Tina sipped. "I think it's possible. She gets nervous when we go out for a walk. Riding in cars doesn't seem a problem. Or hockey rinks."

Brenda found a bowl and crossed to the door wall. The dog jumped from the chaise, tail working as she opened the bottle and poured. When she cracked the panel, Sonny's nose shoved through. She reached through, set down the bowl and closed the door. The dog stared at her.

"I spoil him rotten," Tina said. "He's not used to limits."

"So I see. Go on—" Brenda motioned before the glass. The dog looked down and began drinking. "Does he get tight?"

"He snores. By the fourth quarter, they'd have a duet going. It's the sort of thing I miss most." Tina sipped her drink. "This is just right, thank you. My doctor tells me no, but he tells me lots of things. Diet, exercise. Vitamin supplements. He can't do a damned thing for me, but soldiers on in the most professional way. Aren't you drinking?"

"Later," Brenda said. "I operate on one kidney. A little wine, and I start wearing lamp shades."

"I see." Tina held the drink in her lap. "Does it scare you, having just the one?"

"Not now. These days, it works something like the poem we read. You have to know how good things are out there. Having one kidney helps keep me on my toes a little more. Smelling the peonies. Like you remembering your husband. The funny, touching things, like snoring a duet with the dog. I think losing a kidney made me more aware that way."

Tina drank and held the glass in her palm. "I'm sorry you live in Michigan."

"Milwaukee's not so far."

"It isn't, is it?"

"Not at all."

♦♦♦♦♦

Ten minutes later Brenda was topside, going through her duffle bag when Marion called "They're here!"

She looked out and saw the boat coming. The weather had held, still cloudless. The sun was lower now, but dazzlingly bright on the water.

She turned back to her bag, wondering what Charlie Schmidt liked seeing houseboat women wear. No, better to go with what *she* liked. Green was always good with her eyes and hair, but just now that struck her as trying too hard. She got out her black cashmere turtleneck, pulled it on, then looked at herself in the mirror above the cabin's tin sink.

She smiled at herself, amused by the foolishness of her interest in Charlie Schmidt. Still, she was pleased with the color in her face, cheekbones other women said they envied. She hoped he wouldn't notice how pointy and narrow her nose was. It had been "done" twice in high school, when she had hated everything about herself.

She folded down the sweater's neck, stepped quickly through the passage and out onto the deck. Marion was at the railing, watching the boat approach. Charlie was standing at the wheel, his buddy next to him. The friend wore a khaki hat, and had a beard. He looked the part of someone who flew his own plane. Both men waved, and as they neared, Charlie cut the engine. Brenda and Marion moved to the ladder and went down. Heather and Tina came out as the boat nosed forward.

"Hi there," Marion called. "Right on time."

The Lund and the canoe were tied up alongside, leaving the stern open. Schmidt angled in slowly. His friend leaned and caught hold, looping the bowline around a cleat. He waited for Charlie to secure the stern line, turned back and smiled.

"Welcome." Marion waited as the two stepped on board.

"Well, here we are." Charlie took off his cap and smoothed his hair. "Louis, this is Marion—"

Hand on top of his head, looking at her, he laughed. "Help me out here, please, Marion."

"I'm Marion Ross," she said, and held out her hand. "Glad you could join us."

Hesitating for some reason, taking off his hat and steadying his glasses as he looked at her, Charlie's friend at last stepped forward and shook her hand.

"I'll be damned," he said, still shaking. "Unbelievable."

Smiling herself now, Marion raised her eyebrows. She looked to Brenda and back.

"You don't recognize me?" He laughed and let go to rub his bald head. "And why would you?"

"Uh oh." Brenda looked to Tina and Heather. "Get ready, everybody. I think we have a recognition scene in the making."

"Don't tell me." Marion went on looking at him, the mental Rolodex at work. A client? Law school, or an art gallery owner? Marion's hobby was pottery, and she was good.

"Five seconds more," he said. "Larry, Moe, but definitely not Curly." Still smiling, he looked to Charlie, and back. "Time's up."

"You have to forgive me." Marion shook her head, studying him. "This is happening more often. I need a clue, please give me something."

"Albion." Marion nodded, her college wheels working. "Albion and Paris."

Now her hand went to her mouth, eyes wide. "*Louis.* Louis Rohmer—"

She went to him and they hugged, turning together, Marion laughing with relief. "My God, Louis…out here."

It was fun to watch. Marion, the competent professional, the *maestro* lady lawyer, suddenly at a loss. Finally, she let go. Still wide-eyed, she held him at arm's length, studying him. "This…it's too much, I have to sit down." She looked quickly at Heather. "Who cooked this up, you?"

Wide-eyed herself, Heather shook her head. "Not me, I promise. But I remember you, Louis." They shook hands. "You did magic tricks, you were Mr. Magic. You were good, too, there were talent shows. I remember seeing you."

He reached up to her ear, and held his closed fist in front of her face. He opened it, holding a fifty-cent piece. Everyone laughed. Even Charlie was half smiling, looking a little lost.

"So *long*," Marion said. "So many years. What…twenty-two? Three? This—" She took him by the arm and turned with him to face the others. "—was a serious romance."

"Trouble, I see trouble." Brenda winked at Charlie, working to include him. "Shipboard reunions, look out."

Genuinely pleased to see him now, Marion again hugged Louis. When done, she turned to them, arm over his shoulder. "We're not going to bore you with this much longer."

"Oh, yes you are." Brenda opened the door and motioned everyone forward. "Drinks and then dinner, so the rest of us have something to do. After you." Tina wheeled through, and all followed, talking at once. Charlie brought up the rear.

"How'd you do today?" he asked.

"One lunker," she said. "It's on the menu."

"No kidding. What on?"

"A Rapala, twelve-pound test. We did everything you said."

"You used the trolling motor?"

"I was born to troll."

"I'll charge it for you later. You look…I see you got some sun."

"Instant freckles."

He smiled and held her gaze a moment, then went in. She followed, easing the door shut. Seeing his broad back moving ahead, hearing voices, she felt ready now for a glass of wine. Ready to *troll*, she thought, smiling at herself and following.

CHAPTER

25

"**Hah hah...** Yeah, that's good, yuck it up."

Another burst of laughter issued from the houseboat. Lomak stood concealed by trees, on the hill in front of the boat. The sun had dropped. Now, the cove was a mirror filled with tall pines. On the houseboat's stern, heat waves still rose from the two grills. One for fish, one for steak. Each time the breeze shifted, he smelled garlic and teriyaki.

It made his mouth water. He remembered the steak Diane they served at Mario's. Duke and Pilar. When Doreen got high on wine, she laughed just like that, the way they were doing with Rohmer and Schmidt. For nights out, she always went to the salon and got little pictures painted on her nails.

He trained the binoculars on the empty upper deck, and again down to the bow's door wall. A plank was in place for going ashore. With his back braced against a tree, Lomak could partially see them inside, at the table. They had cleared the dishes. Now they were finishing up with the single malt Scotch Schmidt had brought as a gift. Rohmer was starting another card trick. The dog sat outside the door wall, looking in.

He had taken care of business at Schmidt's. Buried the accident, found a rake on the porch. By the time he finished, everything looked normal. Then the channel passage in the aluminum utility. It had been easy getting here, not so easy climbing the hill in cowboy boots. After breaking the lace on his Reeboks, the boots were all he had.

He lowered the binoculars, uncapped another beer and drank. "Ooh, ah," he said, mimicking the voices below. Again, the patter of applause echoed out over the inlet. "Cut the amateur hour, Rohmer, you're wasting daylight."

He screwed the beer bottle into sandy soil between his feet, straightened and raised the binoculars. As though they had heard him, all of them were now pushing up from the table. Rohmer's last card trick still lay on the cloth.

"Yeah, yeah—" Here they came, out the back, the wheelchair first. "Now we see if she stays or goes."

The others followed. Schmidt jumped into the Stratos, talking as Rohmer stepped forward and nodded—*okay, good, that will work*—nodding again. Now Rohmer ducked under the canopy. A second later his bald head reappeared on the starboard catwalk. Untying the Lund, he jumped in and shoved free. He bent down, came up with a canoe paddle and began maneuvering around the stern. Still in his own boat, Schmidt was pulling the Stratos clear of the transom. When Rohmer got the Lund alongside, the women knelt to hold it close. As Schmidt jumped back on deck, the cripple shoved up from her chair and grabbed the handrail. He came to her— more words, laughter. He picked her up, and stepped down onto the houseboat's transom. He paused a moment, checking to see the others were holding it close. Now he stepped into the Lund and set the woman in the passenger seat.

More clapping. Lomak got his beer and drank, watching as Schmidt helped Ross down, then the other woman from that afternoon. Not the redhead, the timid one. "Right on, Charlie," he said, watching. "Go with Red." Now Schmidt jumped back on the houseboat and turned. He used his foot to shove them free. A few seconds passed before Rohmer started the motor. Once back in his own boat, Schmidt helped the redhead step down. She went to the bow, untied the line and shoved off. The big Stratos motor came to life.

"That's good. Everyone go see Indian Joe's favorite fishin' hole, have a ball."

He watched the two boats moving slowly toward the mouth of the cove. His bandaged hand throbbed as he steadied the binoculars. He remembered falling into the Lund, the treble hook catching him. It was why he had taken the third shot with the Remington, jumpy and off message from the bandage. People said that on TV, politicians—off message.

When both boats had cleared the cove, Lomak finished the beer, then started down the slope. Blinkered through trees trunks, he saw the two boats slip from sight behind the land spit. Now the motors whined higher, heading out. He kept moving down, slipping in the boots, lurching between trees.

He thought again of the waitress from Brownie's, in a bikini this time, joining him in the houseboat's hot tub. Kicking back, taking in the evening. If it was clear tonight, Schmidt had said they might see the northern lights, some kind of show the sky put on over the north pole. From solar particles, he said, shit like that. Sliding down the sandy incline, Lomak saw himself and the waitress in the hot tub looking up, seeing fireworks. The air would be cool, the water hot, little Jacuzzi jets working on his back.

The trees grew farther apart as he neared the base of the hill. He came down onto the beach and stopped to listen. The two boats now sounded far off, still fading. He crossed the sand to the swaybacked plank that served as a ramp.

The dog barked, and Lomak stopped. It was watching him from the bow, front paws on the end of the plank. "Hey Fido, what's up?" The dog barked again, tail going. Jerry waited, clucking, patting his leg. "Come on, check it out, I'm cool—"

Pleased, he watched the golden retriever trot down the board. It understood. The thing with old man Nielson, that had been an accident. Bad luck. The dog reached him, sniffed his pant leg and looked up. He patted the dog's head, feeling vindicated. "Go on, we're buddies—" He waved. "Lead the way, show me your house." The dog turned and trotted back to the glass door wall.

As he followed, Lomak saw the outside screen was closed, but the glass door wall had been left open a foot, for fresh air. He stepped to it, looked in. Captain's chairs were pulled away from the table, Rohmer's card trick still there. He looked down at the dog. It was whining now, wanting in. It had been Lomak's plan to work along the catwalk and enter from the stern. But the retriever's paws and belly were caked with sand and burrs. If it got in and was there when they returned, anything out of place would be blamed on Fido.

"You tired of this lockout shit?"

The dog barked.

Lomak knelt and ran his hand over the screen. It was stretched in places, kicked accidentally. He felt a snag. "Okay, see, here's our story. They leave you out here with junk food when they're chowing down on the good stuff. Then…" He pushed on the snag, increasing the pressure until his good hand broke through. When he drew it out, the dog shoved its nose in. Lomak tore the screen vertically. Now the retriever shouldered aside the sliding glass door and slipped inside.

Lomak pulled the screen back and entered. The dog was prowling, smelling the rug. "Let's check out the bedrooms."

He moved down the passage. Four cabins, two bathrooms. All the curtains were pulled back, there was still plenty of light. With the dog banging around his legs, he inspected the two occupied cabins. Clothes and undies, packages of Handiwipes. He opened all the cabinets and closets, looking for phones or two-way radios, laptops, palm pilots. Finding

none, he checked the bathrooms, the lounge—down between
the sofa cushions, the window sills, the galley and chart cupboards under the controls.

He went then out the back, up to the sun deck. Reenter-
ing, he looked in the first cabin, seeing the redhead's clothes
from the afternoon. With them on her bunk was a book. He
stepped in and picked it up. The picture on the back showed
a woman with glasses. Poems. Maybe Red was a lesbo. Fishing, hopping up and down, showing off her ass to another
woman. He dropped the book, knelt and rummaged through
her duffle.

Bingo, a phone.

He studied it, trying to figure out how to get it apart, to
get to the battery. He could just stomp it, but she might notice
before tomorrow. Finally he found indentations on the back,
for pressing and sliding off the cover.

He cradled the phone in his bandaged palm and pressed
gently. Then with more pressure until it hurt. He took the
phone in his good hand, raised it to his mouth, caught a corner
of the cover in his teeth and pulled.

It gave with a snap that made him drop the phone. The
battery popped out and went flying.

Cheap Chinese crap. He got down on all fours, looking,
feeling. "Where the fuck are you?" He was wasting precious
daylight, and feared driving the boat after dark. At last he
found the battery, and stood. Lomak pocketed it, then slid
the phone's cover back in place. He knelt and shoved the
phone deep in Brenda's duffle bag, stood and crossed to the
cabin opposite.

Ross's. Her smell. For two days he had smelled her scent
in court. Seated behind her table, he watched her leaning and
whispering to Doreen, patting her arm. On the second day, they
had called him, made him swear and sit, looking out at Doreen's
aunt and sister. Both were wearing sweatshirts with HANG IN

THERE DOREEN. Every time Marion Ross came close—bringing printouts and receipts, pointing and asking if this was his signature—a cloud of scent rolled over him.

He looked through her things—designer jeans and sweaters, a cashmere robe from Neiman Marcus. Paid for by people she fucked over, like himself. Everything had the smell. He had to fight the urge to pee in her bag, to drop his pants and squeeze out some actual shit for her to find. Or burn the houseboat. Why not? An accident from the grills, a fire.

No. Stay on message. Her life from now on, *that* would be shit.

Lomak finished the search. There were no other phones, and no laptops on the houseboat. He went back down and returned to the lounge. The dog lay on the floor, sand marking the clean rug, muzzle between its paws. On the counter rested a plate wrapped in tinfoil. He stepped over and raised it to his face. Teriaki. A steak they hadn't eaten.

"This one must be mine." He peeled back the wrapping, lifted out the steak and dropped the foil. He took a bite, watching as the dog got up and began licking the foil. "They locked you out. You were pissed."

He took another bite, and moved to the door wall.

CHAPTER

26

"**Tina got** one!"

Marion's voice carried over the water with perfect clarity, along with the ratchet noise of a spinning reel being cranked. Brenda looked up from her own line. A hundred yards from Charlie's boat, the Lund was anchored at the end of the bay. Tina was working hard in her seat.

"Go, Tina!" she yelled.

It was six-thirty, utterly still. Shouts and words of encouragement crossed the placid water with sharp precision. Trees rose on all sides, black against the setting sun's copper light. Simplified this way, the moment held a static magic.

"That's four for them and three for us." She cranked her reel, seated on the forward seat. "What's going on?"

"Welcome to fishing. When they're hungry, this is what you get."

Charlie cast again, standing at the back, cigar between his teeth. Rohmer had brought the cigars, saying they would keep off no-see-ums. He claimed that currents in the Pacific had made for a warm winter and early hatch. Everyone but Heather was puffing. As she cranked, smoke rose from Brenda's own cigar, a blue, sweet-scented rope.

"I do believe this is just about as good as it gets," she said. "I'm sold."

A splash. She looked again—more shouting. Ripples were fanning out from the Lund. She raised her lure and turned to face Charlie. Watching him fish was part of the moment's magic. It made you understand both the conservation of energy, and the meaning of *it's all in the wrist*. Each cast he made formed a simple, fluid gesture. The force of it was evident only in how far the lure traveled before it hit the water, a distance out of all proportion to the effort used.

Still a little high from wine, she set her rod on the bow and sat back. He had brought beer. She took a sip from her bottle, puffed her cigar, and sighed.

"Tired?"

"In the best way," she said. "I wish we could cue the sun to give us another couple hours."

"That's no good."

"I mean it. I want this to go on as long as possible."

The rod whipped again and Charlie's Rapala sailed out. "No, it's better this way."

"Why better? This is perfection."

He cranked slowly. "If you could cue the light and weather, you wouldn't like it. The point's the luck, don't you think? This kind of day, at this time of year isn't supposed to happen. It's better as a found thing."

He was right, a gift from Mother Nature. "Speaking of found things," she said, "how about your buddy and Marion?"

"Yeah, like it was planned. But such things happen."

"Have you known him long?"

"We aren't really friends." Charlie had lowered his voice. Every sound seemed amplified here. Unreal. He looked out toward the Lund. "To be honest, I kind of wish he hadn't called." He turned back to her. "We met in Mexico, shared a fishing charter. He phoned three weeks ago. Said he had some problems, did I want to do some fishing."

"What kind of problems?"

"Money, investments. He took a big hit in the stock market. Used real estate to collateralize a margin call on a stock he bought last year. A lot of it. When it tanked, he lost the property." Charlie shook his head. "I told him to come on, take his mind off it. Then he shows up with some guy that works for him. I'm glad he didn't want to come tonight."

"How so?"

Charlie tapped his cigar over the side, put it back in his mouth and set his rod next to the engine. "Just a strange guy. Bitter. He got himself in some kind of trouble. Louis didn't give me details, but he's up for sentencing this week or next. Then his lady dumps him, and, yeah, that's too bad. But I own rental properties, and I've hired guys like him. People that did time. Roofers, rough carpentry. Sometimes it works out, but this guy…. He's looking at jail time, and gets the chance to come up here for a few days. If it was me, I'd try to have some fun. Not Jerry Rizzo. He comes all this way to feel sorry for himself. You could mope back home, that's what I want to tell him."

"He has weird hair?"

Charlie nodded.

"Heather and I met him this afternoon. When she caught the northern."

"He and Louis were out in my boat."

"I thought it looked like yours, same guy. He was alone at the time." Smoking her cigar, seeing Louis Rohmer getting the net ready for Tina's catch, she described what had happened.

"Yeah, that's the guy," Charlie said. "Jerry Rizzo. I bandaged his hand. I thought Louis might've brought him along to check out property up here, but that's not it."

"Did you think there was something funny at dinner?"

"All that college stuff? It came off sort of fake to me."

"Twenty-some years," Brenda said softly. "He talked like no one else was there, it embarrassed me. We're all nodding away, a captive audience. He didn't seem to notice."

"Yeah, I think you could say Louis is pretty much thinking just about Louis."

"I mean, it was, what? A year they were together? Fine, first love, everyone remembers that. But enough's enough. It's not like a marriage."

Wreathed in smoke, Charlie said nothing, and Brenda felt another wave of pointless attraction. It had grown all through dinner, but now, here, it no longer seemed pointless. He held the cigar before his mouth and looked at her, as he had when passing plates. Pouring wine. Lowering his voice next to her, intimacy between them at a crowded table. When she got up for clean forks for the pie, she had grazed his shoulder with her left breast. Intentionally? She wasn't sure, but Brenda had felt it right down into her midsection, and below. She'd seen that he, too, felt something.

"You mean my wife, Lillie," he said.

"Yes."

"No, it's not like me. Make that twenty-eight years, not one."

"This place must be all memory for you."

She was sure now it had been wrong to bring up marriage. A misstep. It would lead Charlie Schmidt to old thoughts of sadness and loss. To memories that would wipe away the chemistry between them. Resigned, feeling selfish, she breathed deeply. But once you were in, you were in, and she drew on the cigar.

"Did she like it here? I can't think she didn't."

"We were real good together," he said. "She hated the bugs, liked to swim. Whatever it did for her, she was mostly here for me and Andy. Our son. He's twenty-four. There are two older girls, twins, Patty and Laura. Both married. They aren't much younger than you."

"They come up?"

"Andy still does." He waved at his boat. "That's what this thing's for, tearing ass all over. He has a business keeps him out of trouble now. Plus his girl wants him home. That's why I said yes to Louis, to get some use out of it. I'm pretty much alone up here. Pretty much alone in Milwaukee, for that matter."

Clear enough. No lady back in town, riding shotgun in his truck. Facing him, she sipped her beer and puffed the cigar.

"How about yourself, Brenda?"

"You don't want to know, Charlie."

"Try me."

"Maybe some other time, not here. This is a beautiful place. My story doesn't fit the decor."

He regarded her a moment, looked away and flicked his cigar toward the shore. It hit the water with a hiss. "You're right, not here. Not tonight. I'm an old guy, lots of mileage, but I'm very attracted to you. Here and now, which I think you know. I'm sure my son could tell me all about it, a wild and crazy guy."

"Back in the day."

"You too? Wild and crazy?"

"Mileage like you wouldn't believe," she said. "Mad as a hatter, and glad it's over." She had said it to reassure him, and now felt ridiculous. The painted woman rehabbed. But it had the virtue of being true. She *was* glad it was over, and she hoped he saw she meant it.

"I want to take you someplace," he said. "The weather's not predictable. You got lucky today, but that could be the end of it. It's something you should see."

"Do we have time?" She looked up. The sky was now a darker blue, the moon a gray disk, almost full.

"It's not far. I'll get you back safe."

She believed he would, and climbed down from the bow. She fixed her lure to the top guide on the rod as he secured his own. "See you later!" he called to the Lund. "Back soon!"

Voices called in answer. She returned the waves and lowered herself into the passenger seat. Take me for a ride, she thought facing forward, ready to go most anywhere with Charlie Schmidt.

◆◆◆◆◆

At full throttle on calm water, the Stratos flew. The motor was deafening. Holding on, exhilarated, she narrowed her eyes against the wind. Yes, a boat bought for a son. She thought she knew just how it would feel to be eighteen or twenty with him on the thing. Hair whipping, laughing each time the hull came down hard. She liked the idea, the father taking over the son's role. Charlie Schmidt, widower, out on a date with some red-head that took a shine to him. Showing her what the Stratos could do. Taking her for a ride.

In what was left of the evening, small islands came and went, the shoreline a blur. She felt him pat her arm, and looked where he pointed. Ahead, something off to the left was floating, perhaps a log. The engine dropped suddenly to a growl, and the hull slumped forward. As they dipped in the backwash, she kept her eyes on whatever it was, seeing now the size of it, a huge head with antlers, the neck coming up, sinking back.

"Cue the moose," he said. "A bull. No boat for him."

They chugged closer and passed, the head pushing up and forward, not turning. "What's he doing?"

"Whatever he wants," Charlie said. "He owns the place."

She shook her head, amazed by the size of it, the nose and muzzle, donkey ears flapping. She wondered how much more of it must be down there, hooves working. Once they passed it, the motor revved again, throwing her back. She saw he was pleased. Her hands were freezing, and she shoved them between her legs.

"Too much? Want to go back?"

She shook her head.

Now, just ahead she saw they were nearing the opposite shore, and what must be the falls. The shoreline curved inward to form something like a separate pool. It was perfectly calm. A long dock extended from the left, and to the right, floats separated the pool from the spillway's final path before Kettle Falls.

Again the boat slowed. Charlie angled them toward the dock. The pilings were whitewashed, the sheds too, stark before pines. Meeting the pier and curving up out of sight ran a gravel road. As they slowed to trolling speed, she heard a steady, muffled thud.

"It sounds big," she said.

"Big enough."

He spun the wheel, then put the engine in neutral. For a moment she was scared, feeling the hull taken by the current, moving with the water's will. No barrier stood before them, nothing but floats. This was no whitewater torrent, or rafting thrill seeker's kick. It was something different, and she stood to see.

Level with the lake, a hundred feet of cement wall extended from either shore. Centered between the walls was the spillway, perhaps fifty feet across. Over the lip, like a bronze cylinder in constant motion, fell the lake.

Charlie again put the Stratos in gear, moved closer to shore, and levered to neutral. He would keep the engine running until they were secure. Relax, she thought. This is something people here do all the time. Brenda went forward and prepared to catch a piling. In the seconds that followed, she listened to the thud of the falls. Felt lulled by the sensual roll of bronze water falling off into nothing—she couldn't see beyond the lip.

She got ready. The current eddied around the dock's pilings. Now they were there, and she grabbed one. Charlie jumped to the dock, tied the bowline, then the stern. He held out his hand and pulled her up. For a second she felt dizzy, feet and legs trembling from the memory of the boat's powerful motion. This gave way to vibration underfoot, a tremor many feet below that survived as a thin shock where she stood.

"I can feel it," she said. "Where to now?"

He held out his hand, and she took it. Their boat shoes moved in unison on the hollow dock. They reached the gravel path and started up.

"This goes to the hotel," he said. "It's not open for guests yet, but the bar should be, later in the week. The damned floor's so warped, one end is two feet lower than the rest. They use cinder blocks to level the pool table."

She felt her frozen hand being warmed in his. "Lots of tall tales," she said.

"Yeah. Lots of beer, lots of lies."

Where the main road passed up into trees, a dirt path branched to the right. They took this, and now climbed in silence through the dim light of the forest. Still exhilarated, smelling leaf mold and pine, Brenda felt expectant. A girl on a first date. It should be funny to her, but wasn't. Walking uphill, feeling the work of it in her thighs, she saw herself in the Chevy Suburban, all at once focused on David Santerro.

She wondered now exactly how many first dates she'd had. Very few had survived in her memory as more than a face or gesture, or perhaps a single phrase. Here and there, the chain had been broken by real attachments, connections that ended slowly and painfully. The long goodbye, leading eventually to boredom or contempt. But the sudden goodbyes—the few men she'd been moved by who left her quickly, for whatever or whomever—those men had carried off something of herself. In the aftermath, seeking distractions, she had known herself to be smaller in some permanent way. Diminished. When this happened, she declared war on hope. And knew that eventually, when she won that war, she would be lost.

Feeling his hand tighten slightly in hers, she felt herself withdraw from him.

"Watch your step—"

She tripped and recovered, holding on, darkness concealing tree roots. Brenda glanced at him and down at her feet. His face looked lost in thought. In memory. Like Marion after her fax from Drew. Charlie was with her right now, his wife Lillie. Up here again, for Charlie and their son. A swimmer. In it for the long haul.

No. He was just scared. On familiar ground, but not with her. *She's no kid, but she's too young*—that's how he would see her. But she wasn't, she stopped, and pulled him back.

When he turned, still holding his hand she moved into him, drew his arm into the small of her back and kissed him. He answered and pressed into her, cradled her head and kissed her for real. He tasted of cigar. She relaxed. At least she'd learned something from all that experience. Learned how a kiss tells you about people, this one full of wanting, desire, a very good kiss.

But she didn't want him to know too much. Not yet. Feeling his erection, she lowered her head. Lost, eyes closed, he blinked and stood away, holding her hands.

"Maybe we should go back," he said

"Is that what you want?"

"No."

Again he led the way. He kept her hand, moving faster, up the incline. The falls had been there all the time but now grew loud, the trail winding. Ahead, light penetrated the gloom—and this *was* funny to her. Something from movies.

A moment flooded with stock images of desire—pounding water, beaches, emerging from dark tunnels into sunlight. One scene of pop-culture ecstasy after another. Watching her feet, she thought of Louis Rohmer. It had been that way with him, all through dinner. An account of romance, punctuated with heavy-handed irony. There we were, he said. Marion and me in Paris, on the Alexandre Trois Bridge. In the rain, saying good-bye. All that was missing was a soundtrack. At that, everyone laughed, and Charlie had pushed away from the table. End of romance, he said. Time for Johnson Bay.

The trail leveled. They stepped from the trees and now faced an observation site, a concrete slab fitted with wooden rails. He drew her forward and they walked to the end of it, cantilevered over the falls.

Looking down, she held back her hair and watched. Smooth where it left the spillway, water fell in static freefall for forty or fifty feet. There, it slammed down on massive slabs, boulders, upended trees. Beyond the point of impact, water roiled and eddied for another fifty feet before fanning out into a new lake. This one, too, was dotted by islands. Brenda looked back down at the falls. Feeling the force of it in her thighs, she was no longer amused.

He was saying something. She looked at him, shook her head and waited, this time closing her own eyes, then feeling his mouth, tasting tobacco, stirred by the press of his groin. She reached down and pulled at his belt, then let him do it, let go and looked at him as she unbuttoned her jeans. She shucked them down with her panties—she was doing this a lot today—kicked free, and waited for him. He did the same and stepped again to her, smiling now, amused himself. He shoved her gently into the apex of the railing, and she raised her right foot to the lower rung, high enough. Pulling him by the shirt, she spat into her palm, warm from his hand, and held it out. He spat into it and she grabbed his penis, worked the wetness, then guided him.

How did we get here?

She was feeling him now, the rhythm of it, still thinking her question, thinking she would have to go back to the nail on the road. Perhaps clear back to the Mesabi Iron Range. All the movies she wanted, it wouldn't matter. Not when *push* came to *shove*. She held on, being raised by him and helping, smelling him, his shirt and soap, Charlie Schmidt all cleaned up to come see her.

And so you did, she thought, holding on. Indeed you did.

CHAPTER
27

"How'd you people do?"

"They knew when you left," Rohmer called. "They stopped hitting right after."

Marion stood next to him on the upper deck, looking down as Charlie slowed the Stratos. Brenda waved from her seat, relieved to be back. As Rohmer started down the ladder, she turned to Charlie. "How about a nightcap? One for the road."

"Better not, getting late. But you should take advantage—" He looked up. "It's still clear. The temp's dropped pretty good. We'll get clouds soon, maybe some rain. But in the next couple hours you might see something."

"Northern lights?"

He nodded, looking at her one last time before putting on a different self for others.

She, too, made ready, glad that windburn would explain her glow. He brought the Stratos alongside the houseboat and held it until she was on the deck. Still topside, Marion watched as Rohmer stepped into the Stratos and took Brenda's seat. He put on his hat and looked up.

"It was great, Marion. Thank you."

"Yes, Louis, you take care of yourself. Charlie, what can I say?" She blew him a kiss. "I'm not ever going to forget Johnson Bay. It was… You know what it was."

"You're not done here," he said. "Mica Bay, Lost Bay. Lots of things you ladies are going to see. Brenda and I checked out Kettle Falls, you'll like it. I'll call Gus, he'll know when the hotel's open. Sometime this week. We'll do that too."

He took his cap from the control panel. As he put it on he winked at Brenda, the peak concealing his eyes from others. She smiled and waved as the boat backed off. Quickly she climbed the ladder and joined Marion at the railing. They watched the speedboat pass out into the lake.

Hands in the pockets of her windbreaker, she felt the box of cigarettes. "What are Heather and Tina up to?"

"Very tired. Reading or asleep."

Brenda got the Marlboros out and lit one.

"Sonny's in quarantine outside," Marion said. "He got in while we were gone. Tore a hole in the screen. I don't suppose you're going to tell me anything."

"What's to tell? We went for a ride." Brenda leaned on the railing, smoking, watching the Stratos. It angled right, and began moving west.

"Okay, that's fine. But I know what I know."

"And a rose is a rose is a rose," Brenda said. "What's this, a deposition? *I'm* not the one with the old beau who comes calling twenty-plus years later. "

"God…" Hands on the railing, looking out, Marion shook her head. She had pulled on the fishermen's knit sweater and was again wearing the captain's hat. "What can I say? I tell you, people stay themselves forever. This self-help nonsense about change? Forget it. He lost his hair and grew a beard, but Louis Rohmer has *not* moved on. It's too bad."

"Charlie said he lost a lot of money in real estate and the stock market."

Again Marion shook her head. "Somehow that figures. Magic tricks and gambling on the stock market go together."

The Stratos now slipped from view, behind the cove's hill. "But you did have a thing with him. He didn't make it up."

"Oh, it happened. Actually I was nuts about him. For about a year. He was funny and a very good actor."

"And now he's neither."

"No," Marion said, looking out and smiling. "But it was serious enough. I thought we'd get married. He had a car, we'd go to Chicago. That's how I ended up in art school there. I was a year ahead of him, he came to visit every weekend. I remember he wrote great letters. I must've told him that, he asked if I'd kept them." Marion looked at Brenda. "Do you believe that? The ego? He clutched his heart when I said no. Said he'd kept mine, which you know has to be bullshit. Give me one of those."

"No way," Brenda said. "You don't smoke."

"Neither do you. In college I smoked like there was no tomorrow. This is college night."

Brenda got them out, gave her one, and lit it. Marion leaned again and inhaled. She coughed and banged her chest.

"So this was serious," Brenda said. "You thought you'd get married. What happened?"

Marion was still banging her chest. "I made the mistake of pressing him on it. I really did want to get married. You know me, I was no hippy. I ironed my hair and smoked pot, but I was actually straight as they come. He wasn't the first. I'd had this summer fling with a Frenchman my junior year abroad. That was the glitch for him, I'd been to Europe and he hadn't. Louis said he wanted to go, too. First. To sow his wild oats. That didn't work for me—my guy says he loves me, but he wants to go to Europe and screw around first? It got me thinking."

"So you dumped him."

Marion inhaled and coughed again. "Not right away. We fought about his going to Europe, but we were still together when he left. We wrote. Then, in art school I met this guy. A painter. If I had a 'wild phase,' that was it. I suppose I was punishing Louis, at least in part. So my painter and I, *we* went to Europe. On nothing. He had just enough to buy a used motorcycle. The guy took off, and I ended up an au-pair for a French couple with a little girl. Mademoiselle Renee Tremont. All dressed up like a Laura Ashley ad, with her American nanny in the Luxembourg Gardens. In Paris. You remember Paris."

"The bridge and the rain."

"Yeah, he didn't make it up. God…" Half smiling, Marion leaned on the railing, lost in memory. "I must be suffering from dementia. Or I'm a very superficial person. I haven't thought about any of this in years."

"As they say, 'Get a life,'" Brenda said. "You got one."

"Anyway, I laid it all on Louis, there on the Alexandre Trois Bridge. Told him we were finished, and that was pretty much it for me. I went back. Started living in New York. I saw all these artists waiting tables like me. Driving limos. I realized being an artist was better as an idea than a life's pursuit—that's how I decided on law school. Frankly, I can't say I've thought of the painter or Louis Rohmer more than half a dozen times in the last decade. Usually, when I got something from Albion College asking for money."

Brenda put her cigarette out in the ashtray fitted to the railing. She looked up into the night sky. "What did you say to him up here?"

"Oh, you know. Boilerplate about job and family. Hell, if he'd ever grown up, we could've had a good time tonight. Reminisced. Thank God for the fishing, that shut him down for a couple hours. Just before you got here, I told him it would be better if he didn't come back. I said he was making me uncomfortable. He was, too, Bren. He knew about Drew and me. Carrie and Jay."

"Maybe from the alumni magazine?"

"Probably. But it was still creepy." Marion put out her cigarette. "Louis the Thespian. The magician. "Oh, look—" She grabbed Brenda's sleeve and pointed up. "Turn out the lights, I'll get the downstairs."

She moved to the ladder and started down. Brenda stepped to the upper-deck entrance. She reached inside, clicked off the outside lights, and returned to the railing. Seconds later, the lights below blinked out over the water. There they were now, above the lake, Aurora Borealis. Dim but visible, they seemed to flicker. As Marion came back up the ladder, the lights moved in a sweep. It was as though they traveled themselves, independently, not as reflections.

"See them?"

"Yes."

Marion stepped next to her. "Tina's already in bed. Heather said she's too tired." Together in silence they watched the night sky. It was another gift. A coda to the day.

"They change," Marion said. "Look at the colors."

"It's like Christmas. They're festive."

After a minute, they positioned two chaises to face north, and stretched out. Leaning back, both looked up, cold and captured. "Amazing." Marion clucked her tongue.

"I thought they'd just blink, but they dodge."

"They roam."

"Heather and Tina really should be up for this."

"Don't go down, you'll break the spell. The same way you and Charlie took all the fish to Kettle Falls." Marion laughed. "Know what Louis said to me? Something just like that. He said he doubted I ever realized *he* was responsible for my good life."

"Don't you love the way men make everything happen?"

"He said he was sure the two of us would've been miserable together. Ergo, by going to Europe, *he*, Louis Rohmer paved the way for a better tomorrow for me."

"What a fool."

"Another magic trick. That's when I told him not to come back."

CHAPTER

28

They both rode standing, in order to spot the channel markers by moonlight.

Schmidt again saw her on the lookout point. She was saying something. They were doing it next to the falls, impossible to hear. She was laughing.

He smiled, and again focused on the glossy lake in front of the bow. How much time had passed? You are one foolish old fart, he thought.

But he knew that thinking this way—*old fart*—was a kind of buffer. To keep from thinking that what happened meant anything. To keep it small.

It wasn't. Every time he saw her kicking out of her pants, spitting into her hand and holding it out to him, he felt himself getting hard. And when they were at it, laughing, slapping at an early hatch of no-see-ums and going like crazy, lost in it but not, looking at each other, there was no joke about it for her, either.

Unless he had it all wrong. Unless he really *was* an old fart, seeing what he wanted to see.

Rohmer stood beside him, watching for drifting logs or something swimming. She was right about him, and Charlie adjusted the wheel. Louis was fake. Going on about Marion Baxter, using her maiden name. It had made Charlie think of Lillie, giving up her name for his. That was something that didn't happen much now, women's lib and the rest of it.

Steering, watching the channel, he felt a pang of betrayal. He saw Lillie in her hospital room, just before he had brought her home for good. He'd felt something like that before, but much less strong. Just a sense of being disloyal, when he had gone out with the two divorcees, last year. But it was not the same this time. First one, then the other had gone to dinner with him, and taken him home. Both had been family friends, both of them generous and meaning their interest in him. Looking for some connection in this world.

Who wasn't? With both women, there had been no feelings of shame or guilt. That was because he had not been able to think about them in any terms other than disappointment. Theirs, too, in both women's faces, when they realized by the third or fourth time with him that there *was* no connection. Nothing but sex, shared space, and talk of children.

This was different.

◆◆◆◆◆

You go on ahead." Louis finished tying the stern line and stood. "I want to check with International Falls on tomorrow's weather." He crossed the dock, sat, and grasped one of the plane's wing struts.

"Louis, before I go up—"

"I'll save you the trouble, Schmidt." Beard white in the darkness, Rohmer stepped onto the wing's pontoon and turned, holding the strut. "It hasn't worked out, that's all. My fault. Jerry and I will be leaving tomorrow. I'll tell him. I very much appreciate the hospitality, and don't want to leave on a bad note."

"Thank you, Louis, that's good. I think—"

"No, I won't call, don't worry. A clean break is better. But I have one last favor."

"Name it." Schmidt felt grateful. Louis Rohmer understood how it was.

"I won't be back, but this place—it's something I want to remember. I'd like to take your boat first thing in the morning. Take a final cast or two before we leave. Alone."

"It's yours, Louis." He reached in his jeans pocket, crossed to Rohmer and handed him the ring of keys. "Who knows? Maybe the big one's waiting on you."

"Right, who knows? Be up in a minute."

Rohmer pocketed the keys and swung up under the wing to the cockpit. Schmidt turned away. He felt better and moved quickly up the dock. It always troubled him, having to fire guys who kept calling in sick Mondays and Fridays. Guys who drank their lunch and left jobs half finished, tenants calling to complain. Always they had a reason, sometimes good ones. It didn't matter. Let it go, and they took advantage. Pushed their luck until you had no choice. This was like that, but Louis understood.

He climbed the grassy incline, glad not to hear music. What kind did she like? It was something to find out. What movies, night or morning person? Sports? Andy had made him try in-line skates last summer, laughing his ass off, watching the old man veer and flap his arms, out of control in an empty parking lot. Crazy new stuff every week, skateboards, parasailing. It made you feel old. He hoped he wouldn't have to look clumsy in front of her, past his prime, trying to keep up. Up here, that wouldn't happen. But elsewhere, in what you could call the real world—that was something else.

He was getting way ahead of himself again.

He neared the porch slab and remembered the ladder still in place, screens in the shed. He would put them up tomorrow, after they left. Now seeing Rizzo inside, feeling happy, he pulled open the door wall, stepped in and shoved it closed. Jerry was on the couch, cleaning his boots. He looked up a second, and went back to working the rag.

"Want a beer?"

"Yeah, why not?"

Schmidt got them out, opened them and crossed to the table.

Jerry took his and nodded. "Fun with the ladies?"

"It was good." He felt tired now, wanting his bed. "Nice boots."

"Justins. Fucked 'em up checking out the woods. You got a shitload of deer ticks up here."

"You got bit?"

"Three of 'em," he said working the rag. "Took me half an hour to find a needle and dig the fuckers out."

A walking disaster. Schmidt drank, watching him. It was just as well he was going. Rizzo might already have tetanus or Lyme disease. His socks were dirty, jeans rolled up on both legs, Band-Aids in place. How you got bitten by deer ticks when you were wearing cowboy boots he couldn't figure. That, he supposed, was just Jerry.

"Okay, then, I'm turning in."

"Where's Louis? He get lucky with the dollies?"

"Out in the plane."

Rizzo smiled. He stuck his hand in the other boot and raised it.

"I think he wants to leave tomorrow," Charlie said.

"I bet he does."

"Make sure you don't forget anything."

"I won't, nighty night."

Easy enough. Schmidt moved into his bedroom, smelling cedar and the camphor odor of moth balls. He snapped on the light and closed the door. Turning, he now saw the closet door was open. His wife's sewing basket rested on the floor, between pairs of old shoes. Rizzo. Looking for a needle to dig out deer ticks. It irritated him, the idea of someone like Rizzo shoving through his wife's things.

He bent down, replaced the wicker lid and put the basket back on the top shelf. He drank his beer, looking at the shelf. Stacked there were plastic storage bags for sweaters and spare blankets, extra life preservers. Schmidt looked at them another moment, identifying textures and colors. He stepped back and finished the beer. On the closet floor rested shoes in pairs, some of them Lillie's—tidy, ordered, painful to him on the shiny, polyurethaned floor.

He closed the closet, undressed, and snapped off the light.

CHAPTER
29

MONDAY, MAY 7

Rain on the roof woke her.

She lay on her back, listening a minute before working her arm up from the sleeping bag. 6:50. No time seemed to have passed since saying goodnight to Marion and turning out the light. It was still dark outside, sunrise just underway. Only the patter of light rain separated then from now.

Cocooned in the semi-dark, she saw Charlie Schmidt's profile in the copper glow of Johnson Bay. Saw and heard the whir of his cast, the plop of the lure. She imagined him awake in his own bed at the other end of the lake. In a cabin smelling of wood and mildew—she smiled. He would be pleased with himself, stretched out on his bed and playing it back. Getting lucky with someone younger. One movie cliche after another—crashing falls, sudden lust, towering pines.

Focused now on the cabin's ceiling, she knew such efforts to deflate what had happened would fail. But she had to try. Because of the sudden disappointment that came from wondering whether, as the two men made their way back to his house, Charlie Schmidt had told Louis Rohmer about Kettle

Falls. It was his right, his experience. But it was painful to think of him out on the lake at night, in his boat and talking loud over the motor, giving Louis a play-by-play.

He was strange to look at, Louis Rohmer. Startling. Theatrical. Bald head fringed with prematurely white hair that blended into the white beard. Pink skin and periwinkle Santa's eyes behind rimless glasses. Sharp nose, small, full mouth. Rohmer's features somehow projected intelligence without serious thought to go with it. Magic, not judgment. She remembered his careful, tidy hands dealing cards. *He asked me if I realized how much my good life depended on his going to Europe.*

Funny little man. Brenda listened to the rain. Louis Rhomer was not physically little, but he seemed so in memory. Seemed like someone who didn't fit as a friend of Charlie Schmidt's. She could imagine a chance encounter leading to polite exchanges, nothing else. They were too different. Maybe it was just the male-bonding thing, cars and sports. For men, sports gear and games represented a sort of social Switzerland. Neutral ground where they could kill time and make deals. But that would be all there was between them.

She was pretty sure Charlie hadn't talked about her.

But if she were fair, what, really, would it mean if he had? What difference, if she liked him for her own reasons? If she was attracted and thought him graceful, observant, able to lead without pushing? No. It would still mean quite a bit. But one thing she felt sure of: Today or tomorrow, if she asked Charlie Schmidt about it, he would give her a straight answer.

The rain was slowing, and for no reason she now remembered the canoe. That would be *her* Switzerland. Before the morning got invaded by meals and words. You couldn't know what the days ahead would bring. This might be the only chance to commune with the place.

She unzipped her bag, swung out and quickly put on her Levis. Rummaging in the duffle, she found clean socks, her heavy sweater. New yellow foul-weather gear hung on the door, purchased last week from Eddie Bauer for just this moment.

She dressed, grabbed the rain gear, shoved into her boat shoes and stepped from the cabin. The door opposite hung open, Marion a speed bump under her dark green down comforter. Brenda moved down the passage and let herself out. Standing under the deck canopy, she studied the cove, gray and motionless. Opposite the houseboat, ground fog floated in trees on the bluff.

She stepped into the overalls and pulled up the shoulder straps. Now the parka. She crossed to the ladder and went down. The stern was white and shiny, everything rinsed. Rohmer had tied up the Lund on the starboard side. She opened the equipment locker and got her rod before crossing to the port side.

Clicking came from the closed back door. When she looked, Sonny was on his hind legs, smiling at her, paws braced on the glass. Heather stood behind him, and Brenda smiled. So near and yet so far, she thought. The door opened and Sonny banged out.

"Good morning." Heather held open the door, balancing a steaming mug. "God, it's cold. You look ready for anything."

"I'm taking the canoe."

"Now? Alone?"

"Why not?"

"I don't know." Heather took a sip. "Isn't it dangerous? The water must be freezing."

"There's no wind. I'll take a float cushion."

"Even so. Don't you want some coffee first?"

She didn't, but Heather still held the door. She stepped in, seeing Tina's door was closed. Brenda pulled off the parka hood and followed down the passage. She smelled cinnamon, but would stick to her plan. No coffee klatch this morning, she was on vacation in the north woods. In the lounge, she got the carafe from the Mr. Coffee and poured. Heather stepped behind the sink and opened the oven.

"Sarah Lee. Ready in another five minutes."

"When I get back." Brenda drank too fast and scalded her mouth.

"You guys must've been up pretty late." Heather closed the oven door. "I was exhausted. I slept well, though. Fishing is *work*. I hope Charlie comes back and takes us again to Johnson Bay."

"Me too."

"His friend, though. Louis…"

"They aren't really friends," Brenda said, instantly annoyed with herself for defending Charlie Schmidt. But she wanted to. She drank more carefully. "I think Rohmer invited himself here, and Charlie said yes. That's all."

"Last night?"

"Coming to Minnesota, the whole thing. Once someone's staying with you, you can't just leave him home."

"I suppose not. Listen…" Heather came around the counter. "Didn't you think that whole thing at dinner was weird?"

"Not so much weird as forced. Stagey."

Heather nodded *exactly*, waiting for more.

After a moment, Brenda said, "He's a type, that's all."

"How do you mean?" Watching her intently, Heather was in her element now, trading gossip in a cozy breakfast nook with a neighbor, after the hubbies had gone to work. "I was out of school a year. That's when he and Marion started dating. I don't remember him much, only the magic tricks."

"I just mean he's an identifiable type," Brenda said. "Aren't we all."

Sonny barked outside. Heather's expectant expression slipped away. Replacing it was her little-girl-lost look. No, not today, Brenda thought. No personal-growth moments, not now.

"You mean me," Heather said. "Betty Crocker watering the vodka."

"I mean everyone. We're types, that's all. Marion, me. Tina."

"*Tina*? She's unique. At least I never met anyone like her."

Sonny stopped barking. "It's not a criticism. You're different, I'm different. Marion, Louis Rohmer."

"How in God's name is Tina a type?" Heather was back in full gossip mode. "I'm serious, how do you get that? Does it come from being a journalist?"

"Could be. Interviewing people, seeing likenesses. Anyway, she's smart, educated, flinty." Brenda drank more coffee. "I bet she's very environmentally knowledgeable. Liberal in her politics and religion, if she has any. If it weren't for MS, I bet she'd be out marching against soft money in politics, or in support of Planned Parenthood."

Heather frowned, thinking about it. "I guess she would be. That makes her a type?"

"A very good one. The flinty, no-nonsense, educated, politically correct, elderly tree-hugging liberal type."

"And this Louis Rohmer. What type is he?"

No you don't, Brenda thought. "Later, Heather." She downed what was left in her mug and set it on the counter. "I want to nose around before it starts raining again."

She started up the passage. One good thing about someone of Heather's *type* was that she would never ask to come along in a canoe on a cold, wet morning. Through the door, she saw the dog was seated on the transom, looking out. Several gulls had landed in the cove. She pushed out, got her fishing rod and stepped to the Lund. She knelt and grabbed a floatation seat cushion, then moved to the port side. Edging along the catwalk, she settled her rod in the canoe, dropped the cushion on the back seat and untied the rope. She shoved the gunwale with her foot, and the canoe floated away. Heather stepped out as Brenda drew the rope to the stern. The canoe's ribbed belly held perhaps two inches of water.

"Please get me the hand pump in the locker."

"What's it look like?"

"A bicycle pump. On the bottom shelf."

Heather opened the locker and got it out. On her knees, Brenda hung the hose over the canoe. She began working the handle. Each suck was followed by a sigh.

"What type am I?"

Still pumping, Brenda looked over her shoulder. The type that needs constant reassurance, she thought. But there it was, in the woman's body language and eyes. After less than seventy-two hours, Heather Reese wanted her approval.

"The kind that makes a big difference in the life of someone with MS," Brenda said. "The kind that surprises others, including herself. Someone," she added with mock gravity, "who pees off the sides of boats."

Heather ignored the joke. "I hope you're right. I admire her so much. She's my lifeline, she takes me seriously. I don't know what I'd do without her."

"I'm sure it cuts both ways."

The sucking sounded different. When she lifted out the pump, Sonny jumped from the transom into the canoe. It bobbed from his weight as the dog looked up at her, ready to go.

"I guess you have company whether you want it or not," Heather said.

"Okay, sport, here we go—" Brenda untied the rope. She stepped into the canoe, sat, and used the paddle to push off. Heather waved. She waved back, and began to paddle.

CHAPTER

30

Charlie Schmidt rarely remembered his dreams. When he did, they were so uninteresting he always kept them to himself. Dreams about bowling, for Christ's sake.

Before the cancer, his wife Lillie had dreamed in color. Night-after-night dramas, derring-do escapes and pursuits she recounted the following morning over cereal, always in an offhand manner. She stopped telling them after the diagnosis. Schmidt had supposed life with him must be boring for her—hence, the nightly suspense movie. His life, by his own modest standards, was interesting enough to not require such visits from the unconscious. Or, as he often suspected, he was just too thick to remember them.

But he did dream Sunday night, and woke with traces of himself struggling and slipping high up on a ladder. Then came voices.

He opened his eyes in the curtained darkness. Rohmer was talking to someone, but not to Jerry Rizzo. Gus Gustofson? No, to John Nielson, Lars Nielson's younger son. It would have to do with local business, or lake conditions. A broken water or power line. Last winter, a moose, a bull with five-foot rack had crossed the frozen lake and lumbered up the Nielsons' drive. He had browsed his way to the hay bales around the house, used for insulation. Everyone inside had watched as the moose proceeded to kick down the support holding up the Nielsons' electric power line. The house had gone dark, the moose then shambling off and down to the lake.

It would be something like that, so Schmidt pulled back the covers and snapped on the bedside light. He got his jeans from the chair and pulled them on, then his work shirt.

When he opened the door, Jerry Rizzo was sitting opposite on a kitchen chair, sighting a rifle at him. The Remington. He put a finger to his lips and back on the trigger.

"He don't wander off, ay?"

"Anyone would be worried," Rohmer said, at the door. "I wish I could help. Like I say, Charlie's not here. He spent the night on a houseboat with friends. As soon as he gets back I'll have him call."

"Houseboat?"

"Right. With friends. I was with them for dinner, I came back alone with the boat. They'll be bringing him here sometime this morning."

Rizzo nodded at this, still aiming at Schmidt's forehead. Whatever was happening, Schmidt knew calling out would get himself killed, then John Nielson.

"You see my father, ask him to call, ay? He don't leave like this."

"I will—and listen, when he comes in, have him call. Charlie will want to know."

"I'll do that."

"Okay, then…"

Seconds passed, boots crossed gravel. The door closed. Keeping the gun on him, Rizzo now motioned for him to come out of the bedroom. Schmidt stepped forward and looked to the front. Rohmer stood before the cafe curtain, looking out the window. He stayed there a full minute.

When he turned, he put his hands in his pockets. "I'm sorry, Charlie. I had it worked out differently."

"What are we talking about here, Louis?" Schmidt looked back at the Remington.

"Nothing that concerns you. I mean directly. We'll be gone soon."

"What's with the rifle?"

"He means you don't have to do nothing," Rizzo said. "It's your day off, a man of leisure."

"Where's Lars Nielson?"

"Wherever he went. Porking squaws. Cooking up white lightning. You tell me."

When Schmidt glanced again, Rohmer was looking at his watch. He crossed from the window and moved behind Rizzo, to the coffee table. A laptop rested there, screen up. Rohmer closed it. "We should get started."

"And Indian Joe?"

He slotted the computer in the soft case and tucked it under his arm. "I don't like it. Violating the laws of hospitality is not what I had in mind."

"Because you had something else planned," Schmidt said.

Rohmer nodded, looking solemn, needing to act out some apology. "That's right. Something that didn't require this step."

"What step is that?"

"Well, I guess, now we'll have to tie you up. In a way that insures you'll be found soon, but not too soon."

Rizzo cradled the rifle and reached under his chair. The toolbox was there. He shoved it in front of him and opened the lid. "Louis means some time before deer season." He took out a roll of duct tape and flipped it underhand. Rohmer caught it. Rizzo stood and nodded. "Sit, Charlie. Hands in back."

He thought a moment, the two of them now forming a single unit. They were following some plan that had to be changed. For no reason, this fact convinced him Lars Nielson was dead.

Only the touch he now felt, a firm, steady pressure of the rifle's muzzle at the base of his neck, saved him from bolting.

He sat clumsily in the straight chair and reached his hands behind the back. The tape rasped. It was the most familiar, prosaic of sounds, the kind of thing he dreamed about. Wrist to wrist, the tape was wound round, rasping. It was being worked in circles, up his arm a few inches, and back again, pulling the hair. He could feel his arteries pulsing on the thin inside skin of his wrists, strapped together.

"This will be good." Standing in front, Rizzo rested the rifle on his shoulder. "Right like this, in the chair."

Rohmer tore off the tape. "We leave him here, then? Like this?"

"Jesus, Louis. If you violate the man's hospitality, do it right. No, not here. Too many visitors. We're going to make Indian Joe into a mummy with this tape. Sitting in his chair, out in his new pole barn."

He pushed Schmidt's head down and pulled his bound arms up over the back of the chair. Now he pulled him to his feet. "Bring the chair." Cradling the rifle, he moved, holding Schmidt's elbow. At the front door Rizzo looked above the cafe curtain, then opened the door and led him out. "You got his keys?"

Carrying the kitchen chair, Rohmer passed and trotted ahead. At the pole barn, he got out the key ring and began sorting through. He tried one, then another.

"Come on, Louis. Hustle."

He fumbled another into the big Yale lock, and this one turned. He slid the doors apart, grabbed the chair and stepped inside. Rizzo followed with Schmidt.

"The light is—" He stopped himself. Real good, he thought. Tell them where the switch is, help everybody out.

"The light will be over near the workbench, right?"

Rizzo crossed, pleased with himself, enjoying being in charge. He found the switch and clicked it. Three bulbs came on, strung from a cable looped over roof struts. He stepped to the door and rolled it shut. Facing into the barn, Schmidt now saw John Nielson's pickup, parked where he normally kept his own. Rizzo had found the extra keys last night, to hide the truck. He was surveying the barn, the rifle in the crook of his arm.

"Man, look at all the toys." He nodded approval. "Very nice, didn't notice yesterday. Got your SnoCats, your jet skis. A float boat. What's that, a backhoe? What the fuck you want that for?"

"It's Nielson's," Schmidt said. "Maybe he'll need it today and come back."

"Uh huh. Shit, even a tractor. You use that to haul out the dock. I had a service do mine. Snow blower, got your cultivator." He looked to Schmidt, then up to the struts. Two-by-six headers ran between support poles. "I don't have the visitor etiquette problem like Louis," he said, still looking up. "We need to deal with this in greater detail. Have a seat."

Rohmer brought the chair and Schmidt sat. The floor was dirt. If they were going to let him live, if they left him here alone, even taped he could do something. Dig, make noise. The rain had ended. If Nielson's son came back, he would hear.

"I see the wheels turning." Rizzo walked now to the back of the barn, kicking dirt. He stopped next to the truck, before the two snowmobiles. He studied them a moment, reached out and pushed one. Now he stepped to the pair of jet skis and did the same. "These are pretty light." He pushed again, and the machine rocked. "Yeah, these are better, less solid. Okay, problem solved."

Louis waited next to the chair. He didn't know about such things, it was why he'd brought help. Rizzo came back and pulled Schmidt to his feet. He walked him to the jet skis and stopped. "Bring the chair."

Louis followed with it.

"Okay, sit like before, Charlie. Lean forward—that's it, arms over the back.... Good. Now, Louis, you shine with the tape. Very nice technique. What I want you to do, I want you to tape Indian Joe, so him and this chair are one thing. Like a mummy. Legs and feet, chest—all around, so he's really stuck there. Then, we're going to put Charlie up on these jet skis. Balanced between them. And Charlie will have some rope around his neck. See how it works?"

Rizzo glanced from Rohmer to Schmidt. "You don't get it?" He shook his head. "This is from *Once upon a Time in the West*, a classic. Neither of you seen it? Great spaghetti Western. Too long, but a classic. The bad guy, Henry Fonda, makes this kid support his brother on his shoulders. Charles Bronson is the kid. Fonda makes his brother stand on Bronson's shoulders. All fucking day. And the brother has this noose around his neck—get it? Fall down, you hang your brother."

Seeing the movie scene in his head, half smiling, Rizzo now remembered where he was. "Okay, maybe you could say a little corny. But a good idea for this situation. See, Charlie, you won't want to move, sitting on the chair. On these shaky jet skis. But you won't have nothing like the load Bronson had. You'll be sitting down. Nothing to do but keep still. Do that, you'll be back in the hospitality business real soon. Move, or any shit like that, big mistake."

"I think—"

"Yeah, that's fine, Louis. You think while you get moving on the tape. Oh, and Louis? Something else. The plane."

"What about it?"

"You're waiting for my call, then setting down at Kettle Falls."

"Of course."

"It makes me nervous."

"That's because you think I won't show up. I told you, Jerry. I can't go without you. Leave you, and everyone will know where I am. Crossing you would cut me off. That's your guarantee."

"No, Louis. What's the diff they know where you are? They can't extradite your ass from Costa Rica. Can't send Nazi hunters to haul your ass back to Tel Aviv. I think the plane doesn't leave until I drive Charlie's boat back here. Then you and me take off together. Say around noon, or a little before."

Rohmer opened his mouth, then closed it. He looked down at Schmidt. After a moment he raised the roll of tape, and stepped behind the chair.

CHAPTER

31

From his stately, seated position, Sonny turned to look at his galley slave. No doubt Tina talked to him a lot. Paddle suspended, Brenda listened as the sound of her stroke sank in the heavy air. Now it came back from the sheer wall on her right.

"Know what's going on here?" Still looking over his shoulder, Sonny waited. "I'm practicing. Only one time since summer camp I canoed. I'm rusty. The one time was not a fun experience. This is a training session for Charlie Schmidt. So he won't think I'm a klutz with a paddle. Do you believe that?"

The dog faced forward. He raised his head to receive the rich olfactory world that galley slaves would never know.

Brenda's earlier canoe experience dated from the story that had made her briefly famous. Five years earlier, taking off without permission from her TV station, she had gone to Micronesia. Someone from college had died on an atoll, a Peace Corps Volunteer. Sick of her work in tabloid TV, she'd gone out to learn what happened. Desert islands, a tuna trawler that snagged on a reef, two weeks drifting without food. The story had become *Blue Sky Six,* her one claim to fame.

Your big whistle-blower moment, she thought. Your fifteen minutes. The book had won a Pulitzer. The film rights had
been sold, freeing her from television, but the movie would
never be made. She'd sunk from sight too soon. A one-trick
pony, a flavor-of-the-month. She had felt relieved when her
fifteen minutes were over.

Shoulders pleasantly weary, warm now, she raised her binoculars to pull off the yellow rain parka. She folded it, shoved
it under her seat, then hung the glasses around her neck and
took up the paddle. Again she dug water, fanning the blade to
keep straight.

Gray and still, the lake spread beyond the golden retriever's head.

A mile or more to the south, the opposite shore rose from
the lake as a stark Norse landscape. It was uncompromising,
beautiful. A lake and landscape with no interest in pleasing
anything or anyone. Such an image did not figure in any file
footage, or calendar. Cold air met the warmth of Brenda's face
as she shoved forward. Her breath was visible. Only bird calls
and her paddle strokes broke the silence.

She remembered Heather's butt over the side, and smiled.
A summer here, away from her house, and maybe Heather
Reese could be more free. As they had fished, little bits and
pieces had given Brenda clues. A mother who never said or did
anything. Who cooked every meal in the basement, to keep
the kitchen "clean for visitors." Little Heather getting a college
scholarship, but breaking down and having to take a year off
before graduating. This perhaps was why she had said yes to
the first man who proposed. It was probably wrong to think
she knew so much so soon, but Brenda thought she was close
to the truth.

She stroked with the paddle and studied the dark granite
wall on her right. It rose like a fortress, sinister in the sunless
morning. The temperature had dropped about thirty degrees

from yesterday's high. But the contrast, that was part of the pleasure. The risk. Somewhere behind the islands was Kettle Falls, and all the lake's slow current was destined, fated to reach it. In the passage of time the water would be drawn there, gaining speed, flowing first under a static pool, until it reached the spillway and dropped to Rainy Lake, in a different country.

Sonny eyed a hawk, tracking its passage overhead. Brenda looked back out at the lake. Freed by the canoe's motion, she now concentrated on Marion. If they weren't friends, she might call Marion Ross manipulative. Controlling. It was in her essence, something like the fate of water and Kettle Falls. A gift-curse that was driving away her daughter Carrie. So, she made a promise, gave up her cell phone, and would struggle all week.

On her right, the granite wall now sloped with the gradual curve of land. Brenda stroked with the paddle, following the curve. In the next seconds she cruised past tumbled rock. At some point, water had frozen in small fissures and exploded the stone. A hundred yards farther up, this gave way to sand beach.

Sonny was now on all fours, tail going, ready for shore leave.

"Good idea, let's take a hike."

She angled the canoe closer, away from fallen trees in the shallows. Somewhere was the rush of water, hidden. This shoreline would put her on the far side of the houseboat. That was her mission. Climb the hill to see it from above. If it wasn't too far or steep, she would walk down with Sonny and have some Sarah Lee before coming back for the canoe.

"This is good, don't you think?"

She back-paddled and came about. Sonny's tail was still working, the dog turning to her every few seconds. Seeing rippled sand below, she sat far back for maximum leverage and dug deep. The canoe scraped on the sand. Again, the dog looked to her.

"Permission to go ashore, go on—"

He stepped up onto the front seat, composed himself, and jumped. Brenda laid the paddle flat and worked forward. She hopped out and beached the canoe as Sonny nosed his way up the slope. He peed as she pulled on her rain parka, then shambled back.

Tying the hood, she heard a motor. It was familiar to her now. She listened to the uh*huh* uh*huh* as the hull rose and fell. She judged it a good way off, Charlie Schmidt's fancy Stratos. She looked at her watch—9:30. He was in a hurry to get the day underway. She liked the idea and thought to wait for him, to wave.

No, that would be needy.

She moved quickly up the beach, into the slope of woods. Rich with spongy pine needles, the ground rose sharply. Ahead, Sonny was tacking left and right, busy now. She began working her way between trunks scaled with lichen. Many felled trees lay like pick-up-sticks, a broken herringbone that made her work. The binoculars thumped her chest.

"Look at this, working my ass off to see the guy."

She slipped and broke the fall with her hands, pushed up, brushed her palms and continued. The angle of incline was now sharper, the forest floor slick. Crows cawed. Soon, Charlie would leave the channel and enter the cove. He would have a plan—Mica Bay, Lost Bay. The place with beaver dams.

It would be a test for him, too. He would be alone this time, with no Louis Rohmer to make him look good by comparison. Just Charlie Schmidt, hung out to dry with four women.

CHAPTER

32

Lomak felt pumped and confident. It was great like this, even in the cold. Cold was good, it got the juices flowing.

"Indian Joe, man, right out of *The Mummy*."

He laughed, flexing his knees as the Stratos lunged over shallow swells. He pulled his cap down hard, again seeing Schmidt in the barn, up on the two jet skis. Wrapped like that in duct tape, he looked like a real mummy. A piece of sculpture.

"A work of art, man—"

It had come to him spontaneously, what to do with Schmidt. Anybody told you movies weren't educational, they knew nothing. He closed his eyes, feeling the big outboard's vibration, hands on the wheel. Except here, Charles Bronson would not be coming back to settle scores. In this new version, Duke Wayne goes to Costa Rica with two mil and buys himself...

He opened his eyes. Whatever he wants, Lomak thought.

He liked standing at the wheel, knowing this was how it should be, not sitting.

"Stand up, take it like a man—"

He split a pair of buoys doing fifty and looked back at the rooster tail. Facing forward, he felt energized, in charge. He saw himself in a Jacuzzi at night, with a Bud—no, a Heinekin. It was Costa Rica, and coming toward him in the aubergine dress, looking ashamed and wanting forgiveness was Doreen. She was holding a plate of her short ribs, his favorite, trying to make amends.

Ahead, on the north shore, the houseboat's upper deck showed above the cove's land spit. He turned the wheel, bending his knees, liking how the boat did what he told it to. They would have them in Costa Rica, Stratos boats just like this one. If they didn't, he'd have one shipped. Get the whole deal. The motor and cover with the stitched logo. The trailer. Or maybe not. It was ocean there, Atlantic one side, Pacific the other. So out there, they would have something even better, made for reefs and swamps. Whatever.

He didn't like swamps. That was the Philippines, the fucking Navy. Filthy, stinking country. Garbage. Pollution. Snakes coming out your ass in the countryside. He hated snakes.

Did they have them in Costa Rica? Or Crocodiles? Those suckers, in the Pacific they ate actual people. Cruised the mangrove swamps, tipped over canoes. He had seen a canoe moments ago, pulled up on the beach. Some tree hugger dicking around in the woods. Not a problem.

He thought ahead, now seeing the stern of the houseboat. For the first time Lomak considered what should follow. It was better not to think too much, to let it happen, trust the moment's vibe. The only thing for sure, he had to separate the women. Two and two, easier to handle. Two with him to Kettle Falls, two left on the boat. Women talked, so what you had to do, you had to shut them down. Up front, right away. Otherwise, it went on, time got used up—yadda yadda yadda. His ETA for reaching Kettle Falls was 10:10, forty minutes.

He looked down at the poncho on the passenger seat. Wrapped inside were the cell phone and laptop. Rohmer had said weather didn't matter. Rain or shine, the wireless network would work. Plus, a backup phone and computer were stashed in the bow, just in case. It was the kind of technical shit Rohmer was good at. You had to give him that, how he got into the Rosses' brokerage account through the daughter's school chat room, on the Internet. How he managed to lift everything off the Rosses' home computer. You had to give him that. Anything else, forget about it. A pussy, a wuss. He had not seemed surprised about the plane, understanding where he was at, needing Jerry Lomak to take charge.

As he neared the cove, the stern of the houseboat came into full view. He throttled back, the Stratos sank. Someone was outside, one of the two from yesterday. Not the redhead, the shy one. Her and Ross would go with him to Kettle Falls. All that money winging off with a few key clicks. Bye bye, money, he thought. Bon voyage. But something was needed first. To straighten them up, show them he was serious.

The woman was drinking coffee, watching him over the mug. Coffee would be good, but later. He waved, feeling a strong wish to drag Marion Ross at full speed, all the way to Kettle Falls. The shy one half raised her hand. He fought down his rage. It was important not to hurt Ross, but he saw her now, in the Oakland County courtroom pointing at him— *intimidation, exploitation, preying on a helpless woman*—

Mind games for the jury.

Lomak guided the boat, smiling for the woman. When all he'd done was give Doreen Taylor some direction. But he would not touch a hair on Marion fucking Ross's head. Not touching her would show Ross how wrong she had been about him. Fucking lady lawyer, thinking, *presuming* she knew him.

"How you doin'?"

He waved again. She put the coffee down on the rail and stepped back, holding herself. No, we aren't fishing today, Lomak thought. He put the throttle in neutral, then reverse. He jumped forward as the boat neared the transom.

"Charlie?"

When he looked up, Marion Ross was standing topside on the sun deck, looking down. "My God—"

Hand to his chest, still looking up as her face changed, Lomak staggered. "It's a dream. *Star Trek*, Han Solo, some shit like that—'Beam me up, Scotty,' I can't believe it—"

She took a step back, eyes on him.

"Here's a dream for you, Marion. Don't go far." Quickly he jumped to the transom with the bowline. He wound it over a cleat and faced the shy woman. "Hello again." Still hugging herself, confused, she looked to the door. "You still up there, Marion? Talk to me, Baby."

"What do you want?"

"Well, I want a cabbage patch doll and a mountain bike just like Carrie's and my very own allowance." He crossed to the woman, unlatched the railing gate and swung it open. "Marion? Hello?" He turned quickly, grabbed her sweatshirt with both hands and threw her. She screamed. It was just like Doreen at the cottage, for fun. She cleared the transom and hit the water on her back.

"No!"

Here Ross came, down the ladder as the woman splashed and screamed. Lomak looked again to the stern. "Lady, for Christ's sake, it's four feet deep." Thrashing in near-freezing water, losing her footing, she heaved for breath. He turned to Ross who was down now, looking out. "Well, shit, Marion, she'll freeze. Help her. Get a rope, *do* something."

He threw open the door and moved down the passage. Staring at him as he came, the old one was at the far end, in her wheelchair. He smelled cinnamon. "Hello there, don't get up, it's just the help. Where's the redhead, upstairs?"

She shook her head as he stepped into the lounge. "She took the canoe."

On the table were plates and mugs, half a coffee cake, a knife. He stepped to it and cut himself a piece, hearing shouts outside, thumping on the hull. "Coffee?"

Her hands were folded, a lap robe over her legs. She nodded and he turned, seeing the Mr. Coffee. He crossed behind the counter, opened a cupboard and found a mug, poured from the carafe. He blew on the coffee and drank.

"Decaf? What's the problem, everyone *tense* out here?" He sipped again, facing her. Her chest rose and fell but she held his gaze. "You aren't scared. Why not?"

"Should I be?"

"Probably not."

"What did you do? What happened?"

"Polar bear initiation."

"What do you want?"

"A popular question. If this is decaf, not bad."

He set it down, hearing the door open. Crying and thumping filled the passage. He stuck his head around the corner. The shy one was just inside, hopping, doing a dance, teeth chattering. Ross now followed.

"A blanket, Marion," he called. "Come on, pick up the pace, she's freezing."

He watched Ross duck into the nearest cabin, heard bedding torn from a mattress. She backed out into the narrow passage, arms full. She threw a blanket over the woman's head, a second around her shoulders. The woman kept dancing, crying. A little cold water, Lomak thought. Give me a break. But it had worked. He could see it when she now raised her face, terrified. Ross, rubbing the woman with the blanket, seemed lost, frightened.

He crossed to the front of the lounge, to the chrome wheel and instruments. Pulling down hard with both hands, he tore off the thin veneer housing, exposing wires. He took clippers from his hip pocket and cut them, then tested the ignition and horn, the radio. All dead. He walked to the port side and tapped the window. Glass, not plastic. What else? Their boat, the Lund. He would take the keys before leaving, but fire was a possibility. He had checked for phones and flares last night. The cripple would not be able to manage, but the redhead? She was off somewhere, with the canoe. She would be back eventually.

"Okay, conference time," he said. "Officers' mess. Everyone fall in."

One more thing was needed, to set the hook. Marion came up the passage, eyes not leaving his, trying to figure it out. The other stayed where she was, near the door. She was whimpering now, baby-doll whining without tears.

Just like Doreen in court, it irritated him. "Shut that off right now and get in here."

Huddled under the blankets, she shuffled forward. Marion stepped aside for her. When the woman stopped, he looked down at the cripple. "Please move yourself up next to the door wall."

"Don't hurt her, Jerry, this doesn't—"

"You aren't listening, Marion. I said 'please.'"

The best thing about all this, right now, was Ross with nothing to say, having to wait and see what was coming. No brief or new evidence. No recently located forklift driver from MichCon to give testimony. Nothing. He looked back down as the cripple released the wheel brake and rolled backward.

"That's good, thanks a bunch." Houseboats were mobile homes. Floating trailers with junk fittings. He stepped to the end of the dining table, lifted and moved it against the wall. "Well, come on, Marion—"

Hands in her pockets, she took them out and stepped hesitantly to the table. After a moment she lifted her end and moved it even with his, under the window. She stepped back, watching him. The captain's chairs now stood alone on the blue shag carpet. It was crap like the family-room junk Doreen had owned, before the renovations. Each chair had a swivel base with chromed legs. He reached down to the nearest chair, and gripped the armrests. With his back to the table, he hefted the chair to his chest, lunged forward, and threw it. Glass shattered, chair and window collapsed as one, falling out. The chair caught a moment on the boat's catwalk, then fell. It made a dull smack on the water. Silence filled the room as cold air floated through the opening.

"Oh God, no, he'll kill us—"

The swimmer. She was falling apart, and he wished the redhead were here. She would be easier to handle, less stupid.

"Please, Jerry, Tina has MS. This is no good."

"Marion, you're absolutely right. All gather 'round, here we go."

He stood with his back to the empty window frame, waiting until Ross had stepped next to the old woman. He looked down at her. "It's Tina, right? Hi. MS, degeneration of the nervous system, with no cure. Not yet, maybe down the line. Who knows, maybe in time, you think? Anyway, I would guess that cold, like we have here now, it can't be good for you. We're going to leave you blankets, and you might get the heater going. But what you really need, Tina, is a nice, warm room. Which you will get, I would think, pretty soon. That is, if everyone does right in the next thirty to forty minutes. Marion here and me, we go way back. And if *she* does right, Marion will be able to tell you all about it later."

He looked at the shy one. "Name?"

"What you did, for no reason—"

"*Name.*"

"Heather."

"Heather, of course. That was a nice northern last night, to go with the steak. Surf and turf. I know you're still shook up, but it was necessary. To sort of speed things up. What you need to do, Heather, you should change clothes as fast as you can and dress warm. Marion, you should go topside and get your coat, your hat and mittens, and you should do it right now. While Tina and I wait here. Speed is of the essence, as they say—and don't bother with the phone in the redhead's duffle. It doesn't work." He looked at his watch. "Sixty seconds. Go."

"We aren't doing anything," Marion said. "Not until you tell me what you want."

He continued looking at his watch.

"I'll do what you want, just leave them out of it."

He dropped his arm, and put his hands behind his back.

"Please, Jerry—"

He sighed and looked again at his watch.

Marion now turned Heather by the shoulders. "Put something on, your parka, go on—" She moved with her, down the passage. The woman was shuffling, crying again. At the first cabin she went in. Ross moved to the back door and hesitated.

"Thirty seconds."

She threw it open and he heard her scuffing up the ladder. When the upper deck creaked, he looked down at Tina. "She's always the one in charge. This is new to her, I'll give her an extra half minute."

"You're someone she tried in court."

He smiled at her. Tina, you could tell, was smart. Illness had made her less fearful and he liked her for it. It was the right attitude.

"Essentially correct," he said. "She threw me under the bus to defend my ex-lady. She did it with lies and innuendo, and she got my old lady off with nothing. With probation. It was wrong and she has to pay." He looked down the hall. "Hey! Heather! Chop chop, the boat's leaving—" He looked back down, feeling more cold air coming from the empty window. "And bring some blankets for Tina here!"

"Won't what you're doing make it worse?"

"For me? Why the fuck would I come all this way to make it worse?"

"I heard the boat. I thought you were Charlie Schmidt."

"Good ear, Tina. It's Charlie's."

"You know him. Did you—"

"Nah, we're tight, Charlie and me. That would be dumping on the laws of hospitality. He's fine, if he doesn't get antsy. He won't, he's a solid dude. Everything will be cool."

She looked away, thinking. "The man with the beard."

"Right again, Tina. Smart lady. Louis is definitely part of the package. The MS does not appear to be messing up your higher-order mental activity. Hurry up, Heather! Got a plane to catch!"

He listened to her crying, heard a zipper. The thin deck overhead thumped. He looked around, to the couch littered with glass, and saw a broom resting in the corner. He got it and banged the ceiling. Dropping it, Lomak now saw a magazine. It was lying face down on the sofa. He shook off broken glass and brought it close.

"Jesus—"

It was amazing to him, as though he were in the new addition, picking one of Doreen's magazines off the chair before sitting down. Lomak stepped next to Tina and held it for her to see, tapping the page. "Now this, this is exactly the sort of thing Doreen's into. Made me crazy. *Look* at this shit. It isn't yours, right?"

"No."

"Of course not. Where's the dog?"

"With Brenda."

"The redhead. Okay, now, Tina, you're intelligent. I see that. Now, I want you to tell me what you think of this." She was studying his face, but now looked down. The magazine was a catalog of Christmas novelties. Lomak had it open to a page of what were called Pet Pleasers.

"Right here, this one—" He tapped the page. "What do you think?"

Sad now, Tina looked away.

"Exactly," he said. "Who would do it? Little antlers with bells you strap on your cat's head." He leafed to a new page. "Aw, God, look at this, Tina. A fucking halo. That's your dog, right? The golden?"

She said nothing, still facing away.

"You wouldn't do it to him—Shit, look at this, a fucking bow tie on a German shepherd. Look at the poor fucker, Tina. He *knows* it's humiliating, you can see it."

He lowered the magazine. Did she get it? Probably not. Even the smart ones you could take only so far. That sort of shit had been all over the house—little toys and ornaments, something called Precious Moments in a curio case, twenty or more figurines. Then, at Christmas, there were Disney ornaments and these itty bitty pottery deals, Snow Babies. She loved all that shit and he had bought it for her, getting a kick out of watching her tear open the packages. Just like a kid. She believed it meant he loved her. Duke and Pilar.

Hair lank, face flushed, Heather came now from the cabin, holding blankets. She looked small in a gray parka, staring at him. He pointed to Tina, and as she came forward, the roof creaked overhead. "Wrap her up good."

She knelt and began snugging the blankets around Tina's hips.

"Is this yours?" He held out the catalog.

Tina squeezed the woman's hand as Heather stood. She nodded.

"It's your lucky day," he said. "If I seen this before, you'd still be doing laps."

The door slapped shut. Ross came up the passage, dressed in a striped wool coat, Hudson's Bay.

"Lots of blankets," he said. "Everybody all bundled up for our trip."

She crossed to Tina, bent and held her hands.

"Yeah yeah, that's nice, Tina's doing fine. You listening?"

Ross took a deep breath and straightened. She turned to him. Fear was still there, but less so.

"Got your gloves?"

"I can't do what you want without knowing—"

"*Gloves?*"

"Yes."

"Good. You're in the steno pool today, going to do some typing. Anyone have to pee? Kids and women always have to go before leaving. No? Okay, Marion, you and Heather are coming with me. Tina stays here. And Tina, this is important. This Brenda, the redhead with the canoe? When she comes back, tell her where we're going. Kettle Falls. It's not far. Plus, it's a very still day. Any loud sound, any fire or shit like that, I'll know about it. Now, you don't want that, because all this good-neighbor shit with coats and blankets, that will be over the second I hear or see anything. Marion Ross and Heather Pet Pleasers will die. Absolutely that is what will happen. So, you need to be sure this Brenda understands. Big responsibility, Tina. Life or death, dig? A couple hours we're talking, not more. Then we fly out of here, and everything's hunky dory. So...."

He motioned to the passage. "After you."

CHAPTER

33

"Daddy? Hey Dad!"

John Nielson stepped down from his truck, listening as he looked from his father's house to the barn. It was possible dad's own pickup had broken down. If so, he would go by boat to meet the wrecker. But when he turned to the lake, both runabouts were hanging motionless in the boathouse.

He started for the front door. The walkway was made of broken cement, from a construction site. His father was well known for making use of others' cast-offs. The house itself had been finished with reclaimed brick, and John remembered helping unload the truck. The yard on this side was decorated with his mother's lawn ornaments. Disney characters and life-size deer she'd given names to.

On his right as he neared the house, slightly tilted, stood the shrine they'd set up for her. That had been in the last year of her illness. It gave his mother comfort, standing at the window with her rosary, looking out at it. The Virgin's head was bowed over praying hands, cowled beneath the half-buried, pale blue bathtub they had salvaged after the Nolands' cottage burned.

He reached the front door, and pushed in. "Daddy?"

Wiping his feet, listening, he moved quickly through the tidy, never-used front room to the back. The TV room lay open, littered with bachelor neglect. He looked in his father's bedroom, then snapped on the light in the bathroom. The heart medicine bottle stood on the toilet tank. Turning away, he went quickly back through the house. He slammed the door and trotted for the barn.

"Hey Dad!"

Lars Nielson took his pills when he thought to. He also carried nitroglycerin tablets, but ignored anything the doctors said about diet. Eggs in the morning, meat at every meal.

John reached the barn, and saw the padlock was open. The last thing daddy did before bed was lock it. John shoved aside the corrugated panel, stepped in and snapped on the lights. Spread out over the dirt floor were a dozen or more lawn mowers waiting for tune-ups. Racks of outboards rested beside the workbench. He walked between them, checked behind the riding mower, the pontoon raft, the portable dock.

Still worried, he turned and faced the barn's open panel. Beyond his truck, the lake lay gray and motionless. He stood a moment, retracing his morning search. The front door opened at Charlie Schmidt's, the stranger with the beard smiling. *Your father? No. If he came last night we were out, Charlie's not here—*

The thing wrong with it was Charlie Schmidt spending the night with friends. On a houseboat. Only one houseboat was out on the lake, the big one used for company meetings. Four women, Gus had said Friday, at the landing. They had won some raffle, and were coming up tomorrow. Also, since Lillie Schmidt's death, Charlie complained he slept poorly. He said loons now woke him, or wind rattling his windows. He liked his own place and routines, it didn't figure. Plus, he had people with him at his own place. Guests.

Again John saw the man standing in the half-open door-way, his pink face and white beard. Like you did to get rid of someone. A neighbor coming, saying who he was—what you did, you stepped out, or invited him in. Except there wouldn't be any need. Because Charlie Schmidt would be there, looking after his guests.

CHAPTER

34

The front door scraped, followed by the crunch of gravel. Just one person was crossing the turn-around.

The lock rattled. Whatever Rohmer and Rizzo were doing, they had changed their minds. They would do something different with him now. Whatever it was, it had to do with Marion Ross. With both of them winding the duct tape, passing it front-to-back between them, each time Rizzo mentioned her, Rohmer shut him up. But Rizzo's hands had smelled of last night's dinner, teriyaki and garlic. So Rizzo had gone on the houseboat, after they left for Johnson Bay.

His eyelids fluttered, lashes stuck to adhesive. The metal panel rolled aside.

"I'm really sorry, Charlie. This is wrong."

Rohmer. The panel rolled shut. Shoes moved and stopped. "It won't mean much, but this would not be happening if I had my way. Bringing Lomak was a mistake, he's probably certifiable. By the way, that's his name, Jerry Lomak, not Rizzo. I told him to use Rizzo, to make him think it mattered, which it doesn't. Friday night he murdered his girlfriend, I just found out. It was on the *Detroit Free Press* website. Now that he's gone, at least I can check on you."

Schmidt felt more humiliated than scared. After truss-
ing him up from head to foot, they had raised the chair and
balanced the legs between a pair of jet skis. His neck was in
a noose, tied to a cross beam. It was from some film Rizzo—
Lomak—remembered.

Alone, he had been scared, at first. But what had served
best to keep Schmidt motionless on the chair was knowing
that if he coughed, or forgot about the noose, the only thing
people would ever remember was *how* they found him. Nothing else would ever figure. That's why he'd stayed motionless.
Otherwise, for years in every tavern—in The Red Fern, the
Dew Drop Inn and Lindner's at the Landing—that's what
would be said of him. How Charlie Schmidt had bought it,
taped up and ready for UPS, hanging like a piñata.

Rohmer was dragging something metallic—the aluminum
stepladder. *Lomak murdered his girlfriend*—that now registered.

He broke open the ladder and snapped the safety
hinge in place. Louis Rohmer was cautious, safety-minded.
Schmidt remembered them walking up to Rohmer's place in
Cabo San Lucas. Louis had kept his wallet in his front pants
pocket, his hand on it, wary of thieves. Now, as he mounted
the ladder, Schmidt could hear his breathing. Smelled after-
shave. He felt hands on the noose, felt it loosen. Now the
hands stopped working. Rohmer let out a breath and the
metal ladder creaked.

"I don't know, Charlie. No, I don't think I can do it."

Rohmer moved carefully down the ladder. "Sorry, but
you're in good shape, and not stupid. You might figure something out. I thought to take the noose off, but who knows what
you might dream up? You'll be all right like this. One of the
Nielsons will be along later today. You'll miss lunch, that's all.
I brought along a really nice '95 Pommard. It's on the counter,
next to the sink."

Rohmer carried the ladder several steps and set it down. "I'll leave this open for whoever comes. Lomak should be in custody in a couple hours. He doesn't know the area. He can take off in your boat, but where to? Unless the fool leaves the channel, your Stratos should be all right. Anyway, you're insured. But if he's dumb enough to come back here, I don't know. You see what I'm dealing with. He doesn't know how to think, Charlie, it's that simple. It makes him hard to read. I'll take your rifles, he might decide to play cowboy. Marion will explain."

Something was scratched, Schmidt smelled sulphur. "I saw this piece...last winter...in the *Times*—"

Now came the pungent odor of cigar smoke. "— on lady lawyers. It described one of Marion's cases. The one with friend Lomak. This was when my drug stock went down the tubes. I guess that was just the gambler in me. Like setting up a magic trick. But after, I saw I'd have to leave New York. Parting words, Charlie—"

He rolled open the door panel. "Do *not* screw around with the market in bio-medical research. Wireless technology? Broadband? By all means. What I'm doing here would be impossible without it. There'll be some consolidation, but once that shakes out, definitely consider taking a position in wireless."

The panel rumbled again.

"It's even possible you and I might meet down the road. Who knows, maybe in Cuba. The fishing must be incredible there, they'll open it up in a few years. The Cubans would refuse extradition, I'm sure. If you deck me in Havana, who could blame you? There should be time before I leave, I'll come back and check on you. You're a decent guy, Charlie. I wish you well."

The door slid shut. They had wound the tape in double layers, starting with the head, sealing his eyes. But the ears had caused a flap, a partial opening. It was true. Blind, you heard everything better. He angled his head as Rohmer's footsteps receded.

But he was not going back to the house. The footsteps continued up the gravel drive, alongside the house. Rohmer would now be moving down the lawn, going to the lake, the plane.

Hot under the tape, but also chilly in the unheated barn, he saw Brenda Contay at Kettle Falls. She was on the dock—not with him but with Rizzo, shouting at him until he struck her in the mouth. *Don't do it, he killed someone.* She went down, blood coming from her small, sharp nose, eyes wary. Why did he see that?

But Schmidt believed she would not go to pieces. She would keep her head, pick her moment.

CHAPTER

35

She almost fell, but again caught herself. Brenda straightened, and continued up the slope. Sonny ran ahead, tracking a scent. It was hard work. Each time she thought the crest was just ahead, she faced another gully full of fallen trees. They looked to her like pick-up-sticks.

The Stratos. She stopped and straightened.

The big motor had come to life in the cove. He was leaving. Coming to look for her. She stood listening, liking the idea of Charlie Schmidt on reconnaissance, cruising along the shoreline in search of the canoe. He would spot it, shut down the outboard, call her name. The engine sound continued pushing out into the lake.

As she started again up the incline, once more Sonny appeared. He was thirty or more feet in front, looking down at her and panting.

"Yeah yeah. You're better at this, good for you."

She kept trudging, at last getting the hang of it. The best part had been stopping to rest, pleasantly fatigued, smelling leaf mold and pine. She had a sense in those moments that something was calling on her to meet a challenge. To realize some potential.

The outboard engine revved higher, still heading out. And this being called on to meet a challenge, she thought. Does it have to do with Charlie Schmidt?

Ridiculous. It was just a moment of being alone.

She labored on, pushing down on her knee with each step. Would it still be there after you died, this moment of challenge? Like a ghost or spirit that had come into the world when you did, still waiting to be born after you were gone?

Still hearing the motor receding, pushing her way up, she continued to hold the thought. The idea intrigued her. That a moment might have a life all its own. A chance, a possibility. On constant alert for you to intersect with it. Waiting for you to journey here or somewhere, then stop. And if you did stop, if you brought the dormant thought to life, it might change you. Even at thirty-three.

Shoving on weary knees, she wondered what the moment was, and what it wanted from her. Brenda breathed through her mouth. It wouldn't be anything stagey or big. She thought it would be something like salt. Something necessary out of all proportion to its size and weight. Like Charlie Schmidt's graceful casts. What, then?

Trudging, thinking, Brenda wanted to get it right, this moment that was waiting for her. She stopped again, and this time closed her eyes. Immediately came peonies. They were hanging limp after rain, in her mother's garden. In pink and white clusters, they were interspersed among leafy hosta plants, irises, day lilies. It was a favorite memory, but long forgotten. Just after a rain, she thought. In late May or early June. She could smell them in the moisture-laden air, the heavy blooms bowed on the lawn, needing to be cut and brought in for their fifteen minutes of fame, on mantel or dining table. Mary Oliver had spoken of peonies, of their eagerness to be perfect for a moment, before they were nothing. If you could feel perfected, if you were now and then able to meet the world with a sense of rightness and perfection, then knowing you would one day be nothing forever would not matter so much.

She opened her eyes and resumed walking. The ground flattened at last. Feeling relief in her weary legs, she sighed and moved more quickly. Soon, the slope tipped down. Ahead, a natural path had been formed by runoff. She followed it, bracing on shagged bark, lurching as the boat's engine ran steady on her right. Kettle Falls, maybe Charlie was taking the others to show it to them. A quick trip there and back—it would give her time to shower. She felt no jealousy, still warm in the pleasure of her mother's garden, knowing she would soon see Charlie Schmidt.

Sonny drew her attention. He was pawing at something, in a small clearing. He lay down now, waiting for her. She reached him, seeing how granite table rock had formed a stretch of bare slope, a natural campsite. Below, the houseboat roof stood white and blinkered through tree trunks. Looking out beyond birch trees, she saw the wake of the Stratos moving away. She raised the binoculars and steadied them. Heather and Marion were crouching in the bow, holding on as the boat neared the islands. Back to her in the bright lens, Charlie stood at the wheel.

She lowered the glasses, and now saw empty bottles. They lay on a point where someone had sat looking out. Beck's. That was the brand Charlie had brought last night, to Johnson Bay. She stepped to the bottles and picked one up. The label was new, not faded.

Dropping the bottle, she moved to the end of the point and looked down. Her field of vision was filled by the houseboat. The empties were someone else's, because Charlie Schmidt wouldn't leave his trash like this. Still, it intrigued her, the thought of him coming up here, watching. Being curious. She smiled at the idea, how it changed him. Made him different. Made him mildly suspect, not so completely a pet-ting-the-dog good guy.

"Come on, time for breakfast."

As she started down, the dog loped past. Just below was the plank board, the drooping tie-up ropes. In the water on her right, something was bobbing. She stopped, and slid. Sat down hard. When she stopped sliding, she looked again, see-ing the padded captain's chair floating in the space between houseboat and shore.

Movement—she watched Sonny trot along the plank, onto the bow. He passed between deck chairs and stood before the door wall, tail working.

She began scuttling down, crab-like, feet first, risking fall-ing. The chair in the water, the Stratos leaving at high speed—

In another minute it would make sense, something where it didn't belong would gain its place. Fire, maybe. A cigarette, a match. Better a ruined chair than a boat fire.

Jeans wet and slippery, Brenda scrambled to her feet. She ducked under the port tie-up rope and quickly bounced along the plank. She pulled open the door wall, Sonny slipped in and she followed.

But it didn't make sense. The dining table had been moved, with coffee mugs, the Sarah Lee. She looked to the broken window. Glass littered the couch. "Heather? Tina?"

She faced the hall, and heard a voice outside, at the back. She dropped the binoculars on the littered couch, then ran down the hall. As she pushed out, Sonny banged past her. Tina was in the Lund, looking up. The dog whined.

"Did you bring a phone?"

"I have Marion's, in my—"

"No good, he broke it."

"What happened?" Tina was still in her flannel night-gown. It was wet, the sleeves clinging to her arms.

"The man from yesterday, with the fish. He followed Marion here from Michigan. He's someone she sent to jail. He took her and Heather to Kettle Falls."

"Why?"

"I'm not sure, but Louis Rohmer is part of it, whatever it is. They have a plan to steal from Marion, I don't know how. He cut the ship-to-shore, the horn. He said the falls aren't far away, he'd be able to see or hear anything I did. He said if that happened he'd kill them."

"God, Tina, what are you doing? How the hell did you get out there?"

"It took some planning." Tina squeezed water out of her sleeve. "Bert had a boat, he kept an extra set of keys in the bait tank. In a baggie. I thought Heather's husband might do the same, but so far no luck. I knew you'd be back at some point."

Brenda stepped to the catwalk, and down into the Lund. She reached with both hands and circled Tina's forearm. "You're freezing."

"Cold, not freezing. Come on, help me look—" She pointed. "Go check up front, I couldn't get there." Whining, wanting Tina, the dog now jumped and landed in front of the outboard.

Brenda let go. She folded open the hinged windshield and moved to the bow. A cowling covered it.

"Where's the canoe? No, Sonny, sit—"

"I left it to walk." She dropped to her knees and bent to feel under the cowling. "What happened?"

"I thought maybe you could paddle out and spot some-one. Fishermen or campers. There must be game wardens."

Feeling where she couldn't see, Brenda looked back.

Tina was feeling under the windshield. "He came in Charlie's boat. Someone from a court case. He threw Heather off the stern, to shake us up. It worked."

"Casual? Too familiar?"

"Yes."

"Funny hair."

"The same guy. "He came here for her, he was spooky. Chatty."

"In Charlie's boat."

Tina stopped feeling for keys and straightened. Her face was gray, hair matted. Sonny nuzzled her elbow and she stroked him. "No, Brenda. Whatever this is, Charlie's not part of it. Absolutely not."

The beer bottles. "Someone stops and fixes a tire…" Brenda felt now along the underside on the left. "The next day, there he is, showing us the sights."

"Don't, Brenda. How could he know we'd have a flat?"

"It doesn't matter. He followed, he waited for something. Anything would do. A flat, teaching us to fish, helping you with the wheelchair—"

"No, Brenda. It's the friend. This Rohmer."

"Fine. How does the friend get here except with Schmidt's help?"

"We don't even know it's Charlie's boat. There must be dozens like it."

True, why believe the worst? Fear is why, Brenda thought, feeling along unpainted aluminum. An absence of faith. Wanting something when reason says it makes no sense.

Convinced she would find no keys, she shoved up on weary legs. She stepped to Tina, reached down and again felt her arm.

"I don't think I can get you back up," she said. "Not by myself. You're very cold."

"I'm fine."

"I'll get blankets."

"It's all right. You went for a ride last night. To these falls."

"Charlie and me."

"Is he telling the truth, the man? From out in the lake, could he see if we tried to signal?"

"I don't know, it was dark. Halfway back we could see the houseboat lights."

"Then we shouldn't risk a signal."

"It was after dark."

Brenda raised a leg to the boat's gunwale, shoved up and stepped on deck. She went back inside, moved into the second unused cabin and began snatching blankets and sheets from the top bunk. Then the lower. Arms full she backed out and pushed through the door. She looked at the grills, the propane tanks. She had no idea what to do with them. She turned back, watched her step, then jumped down. She began wrapping Tina in blankets. It might be possible to get her back, but it would be risky. If she could do it, Brenda might then load the Lund for a fire—clothes, cushions—set it going, then shove it out into the cove.

"You're sure Marion's phone doesn't work."

"That's what he said. He made her go up and get her coat, I'm sure she checked it. I think he came here last night, when we were fishing. He said...what was it? He said she had to be warm, she was in the steno pool. Typing. That's good, thank you."

Brenda straightened and looked around. Tina sneezed, still stroking the dog.

"Did you check the bait tanks and rod cases?"

"Yes, I did. Nothing."

Hidden by islands, someone on the far side was not likely to see smoke. But then she thought of him smashing the fish's head, something small tripping a switch, setting him off.

"Charlie didn't know." She looked down at Tina. "I'm sure of it. This person stole the boat. He came here for a specific purpose. He forced Marion and Heather to go with him, to split us up."

"If he needs her, he's not going to hurt her," Brenda said. "It must be related to her husband's deal. He's in London, all their assets are at some broker's."

She looked out at the cove. It was flat and gray, the day windless. "Do you think, between us, we can get you back on the houseboat?"

"Yes."

"Then that's what we'll do."

"He was playing a part," Tina said. "There was something loose about it. Unconcerned. I was in here when he tied up. I heard him call 'Hi,' then Heather screaming. He threw her in, just like that, without warning."

She looked down at Sonny, kept stroking his head. "He came here for something. Whatever it is, if he gets what he came for—"

"What, Tina?"

She looked up, stroking, and shook her head.

CHAPTER

36

Nielson left his truck on the road and walked in. When he reached the bend where Charlie Schmidt's drive curved around big boulders, he could see the house.

Charlie kept things up. He had his gravel graded every couple years, trimmed back his trees. Painted. He had been a pallbearer at mom's funeral, driving up from Milwaukee. Summers, if you needed help taking down a tree or putting in a dock, you could call Charlie Schmidt.

Crows were at it off to his right, loud behind the pole barn. They were coming down through the trees, flying back up. Looking again to the house, Nielson came to a stop where the gravel broadened into the turnaround. Schmidt's truck still stood parked before the barn's closed doors. Starting forward, he looked once more to the barn, and here, too, the lock was undone. Like daddy's. Not broken, just open.

He crossed the turnaround to the house, stepped up and knocked. The sound fell hollow inside. He waited several seconds before trying the handle. The door opened.

"Charlie?"

He entered and crossed the big room, glancing left and right. The bedrooms were open, all four empty. Stepping around the hearth furniture, he moved to the kitchen door wall. Down on the dock, someone was sitting in an Adirondack chair, facing the lake, and Nielson now saw it was the friend with the beard. He was bowed over, concentrating. The plane bobbed on his right, Charlie's utility on the left. In the utility, next to the motor, Nielson saw rifles.

If you went out on the water with guns, a park ranger stopping to check your fishing license would give you serious trouble. Charlie would tell that to anyone staying with him. The old man missing, and Charlie nowhere. With his company here, his truck here.

Nielson turned away, and moved to the first bedroom. Snapping on the overhead, he saw the quilt Lillie Schmidt had shown him once, bought at some auction. Everything looked normal. Deciding to talk again to the man on the dock, he snapped off the light.

But snapped it on again. Lined up on the floor next to the bed were boat shoes. It was all Charlie ever wore, brown Topsiders. Where would he go without his shoes?

Nielson again checked the man on the dock—still there—returned to the front entrance, and stepped out. He moved to Schmidt's pickup, glanced in and saw no keys. Quickly he crossed to the pole barn and eased open one of the panels. The wedge of light expanded, revealing something shiny, silver. It was on a chair, like a mummy. He stepped inside. "Daddy?" The figure moved slightly, and now Nielson saw the chair was balanced on Schmidt's jet skis. The rope with a noose hung loosely from the person wrapped in tape. Shoeless feet hung between the skis.

"Charlie."

Now Nielson saw his father's pickup. He thought to look inside, but moved behind the jet skis. He stopped a moment to study the skis, then the noose. It had been pulled loose, not cinched. He stepped back, to the workbench. A broom rested next to the vise. He got it and looked around, saw a leaf rake in the corner, and retrieved it. Back behind the jet skis, Nielson gripped rake and broom. He raised both handles.

"Okay, Charlie, this is me. Don't move."

Carefully, he lifted the noose, working it up over where Schmidt's nose would be, until he had it free of the head. Once it hung loose he dropped the broom and rake, slipped quickly between the skis, opened his arms and wrapped them around man and chair. Nielson lifted and stepped back, smelling adhesive. He set down the chair.

Schmidt made a sound, but sat motionless.

"Yeah, Charlie, just wait."

He knelt, looked for some place to start, and now began working his way around the chair on his haunches. The tape looked seamless, a hundred feet of it or more. Nielson stood and moved back to Schmidt's workbench. Tools hung from hooks. He remembered the open door, crossed and closed it, returned in the dark, found the light switch. A tin-shaded bulb shone above the bench. Drill bits, screwdrivers, wood planes—

Tin snips.

He got them down, moved back and knelt. He raised the heavy scissors to the small gap where the ear would be, but stopped. The head was too tightly bound. He knelt and studied the feet. Cutting along the leg and tearing up would be best. Nielson worked the inside blade under the taut base, where naked foot met ankle. He clipped, and the tape split. He snipped again, dropped the shears, grabbed with both hands and ripped up. The tape tore along the side, up one width of double strapping. Clipping and pulling, he separated tape, up to the knee. He continued, snipping and tearing, but stopped. Schmidt's thigh and calf were exposed.

"You okay? I cut your pants—"

Schmidt again made the sound.

"Okay, sit still."

Nielson re-gripped the tear. The tape separated with a ragged sound, revealing Charlie's belt and flannel shirt. Snipping and pulling, he worked along the bound arm, the shirt staying intact. Once his right hand was free, Charlie tore at the tape over his belly. At the ridge of the shoulder, Nielson was able to snip to the neck. Again he stopped.

"Can you pull it—" Feeling with his free hand, Schmidt fumbled to the point of separation. Working his thumb under, he pulled, made a small lip on the tape and leaned away. Nielson could now insert the tin snips. He cut and tore again, several times, until Charlie's neck was exposed. It was blotchy, lined with adhesive.

"Thank—"

Again he sat still while Nielson snipped, up the side of the head, into the hair. Charlie reached again with his free right hand, and pulled. Drawn by adhesive, his face followed. Nielson helped, seeing tape matted with hair. He tore back and away, peeling with both hands, pulling out hair until thick strapping hung off the back of Schmidt's head.

He stood abruptly, the chair with him. But he waited patiently, straddling his legs as Nielson forced loose the husk-like wrapping. It was furred with shirt flannel, head and body hair. At last it was possible to grip the kitchen chair for added leverage. With Schmidt's legs braced, he pulled. Charlie tore free. Nielson dropped chair and husk.

"The one with the beard is on the dock," he said.

"There's two. The other has my boat."

"How do you want to do it?"

Schmidt was studying his sliced right pant leg. It hung open, up to his hip.

"You seen my old man?"

Schmidt looked up, turned and faced the pickup. He shook his head. "It has to do with four women on one of Gustofson's houseboats." He twisted his neck and rubbed his face. Wiped his hands on the shirt. "You keep a rifle in your truck?"

"It's out on the road, I walked in. I went in your place, I seen the guy out on the dock. There's rifles in your utility."

"Get the one in your pickup. Come back and make sure he doesn't leave. John, if you see him moving to take the utility or the plane, stop him. Your boats are in the water?"

"Just crank one of 'em down."

"The other guy is bad news, these women don't know he's coming. I've been to the tie-up site, I'll go there. You call Gustofson from my house. Tell him to phone Lester Gertz. Unless he moves to leave, don't let the guy on the dock know you're here."

"Why not take him now?"

"He has a cell phone, they're working together. If the guy with my boat is waiting on a call and doesn't get it...I don't know. It's better they think I'm still in here."

John pointed at the rope, and Charlie glanced up. "Yeah."

"Lester's thirty minutes from here."

Charlie touched his face, and only now did Nielson see Schmidt's left eyebrow was gone. "Let's go." He walked quickly to Lars Neilson's pickup and looked in. "The keys are here, John, we'll find him."

He quickly crossed the dirt floor to the work table, got down and went under. He came out holding a worn pair of leather dress shoes spattered with paint. Charlie dropped the shoes, shoved into them and moved toward the entrance.

CHAPTER
37

They had left the islands, and were now in sight of Kettle Falls.

On shore, where the dock met the road to the hotel, ground fog was lifting out of the trees. It was rising up, drawn by the dim morning fireball. In the last few minutes, it had burned a hole through the eastern sky.

Still huddled in the bow, the women were facing forward. Lomak eased back the throttle. "Going to be nice later, Marion. Sunny."

She looked back and stared at him, then faced forward. She put an arm around the shy one. That's right, Lomak thought. You bond, do the sister thing. In the minutes it had taken to cross the lake, something had happened in his head. Like a discovery, he had seen it was all really going to happen—the transfer, the plane, all of it.

In a way, it made him feel generous. Forgiving. What made things different—steering the boat through cold air and now seeing the flat platter of motionless water ahead—was suddenly understanding that until this moment he had not actually believed it would happen. Months of bad luck and too many fuckups by other people had made him lose confidence.

You had to buh*leeve*. Lomak aimed now for the long pier. That's how they said it on the bible-thumper cable shows—you got to buh*leeve*. Enough bad luck and you started thinking like a loser. But he wasn't a loser, and he would forgive Doreen—hell, with someone like that, you almost had to. They relied on others to think for them—himself, Marion Ross. Doreen would cry and thank him, then get in next to him in the Jacuzzi, in Costa Rica.

As he throttled back, the spillway slipped into view. He had to think ahead. Leave the shy one in the boat. Tie up, but let it drift off the front of the dock. In front of the spillway. That way, Marion Ross wouldn't try some crisis-management bullshit—bargaining, negotiating. Someone like that you *never* forgot, or forgave. She was tricky, smart with words. But with her buddy out there, being pulled by the current in front of the falls, Ross would do the transfer without a lot of lawyer crappola.

"Hey, why not?" he called. "Make the most of your day when we're done. Throw in a line this afternoon, Marion. Fire up the hot tub, catch some rays. You're on vacation, right?"

This time, Ross didn't turn. Exactly, she had nothing to say. It made him want to tell her about her house blowing up in a few hours.

No, he was sure of what Ross's face would look like. He still remembered it from court, something she did with her nostrils. Like customers coming down to the basement when he was snaking out a sewer line. Smelling soggy toilet paper and sewage, they got that same look. Or diapers. Amazing how many people soaked diapers in the toilet, then forgot and flushed. Crazy fucking people. Then they called him to snake it for them. If he told Ross about her house blowing up, she would give him that same bad-smell look. *I'm not surprised,* the look would say. *It's what I'd expect from pond scum like you, a bottom feeder—*

That's what she had called him in court. A bottom feeder praying on a helpless woman. Lomak eased the throttle back still more. The boat slowed to a crawl. Remembering the moment, he was angry again. Then, later, out in the corridor during a recess, he remembered sitting on a bench with coffee. She'd passed with Doreen, speaking so only he could hear. *Pond scum.* Then she'd gone back inside, all super-professional. My client this, my client that, may it please the court. When Louis Rohmer had called, the memory was still fresh.

He took a deep breath and let it out. He had to be cool.

He put the throttle in neutral. After some seconds, the boat was taken by the current. The bow glided toward the long dock.

"Well, shit, ladies, all hands on deck. Get ready up there."

Ross looked back, still holding the shy one.

"The bow line, hurry up."

She let go and edged up to grab the rope.

"Not the anchor, the bow line. Pay attention to what you're doing…that's it."

You had to stay on them, otherwise they lost concentration. And it wasn't just the dumb ones like Doreen, the ones with a slow-boat-to-China brain, it was all of them—smart, dumb, it was something about their wiring, how they were put together.

Lomak looked left, to the shoreline. The road to the hotel rose steeply. A trail branched to the right, then disappeared into a ridge. He thought it must lead to the falls on the far side. There were no signs of life. If he saw people—fishermen or hotel staff—Rohmer had said to execute the transfer, then go back to one of the islands and leave the women there. He saw now that it would not be necessary.

Ten feet from the dock, he reengaged the clutch, spun the wheel. Now he returned to neutral and waited. Pulled by the current, the boat came alongside the pilings. Lomak grabbed one and drew the Stratos close. He got the canvas sack with the laptop and phones, turned off the ignition and jumped up onto the dock. Marion looked up, holding the bow rope. He knelt and took it from her, then held out his hand.

"Come on, take it—" She took his hand, and he pulled her up. "Sit over there."

Weathered wooden benches had been nailed to the plank deck. He turned back to the second woman. She had stopped crying and now looked sullen, resentful. Still thinking about her bath, he thought. What a big old nasty man you are.

"What's the matter, Heather, don't you like me? Come on, the swim was just to get your attention, lighten up."

She looked away.

"Okay, you want to pout, that's your business." Holding the rope, he used his foot to shove the boat. It floated off from the dock.

"No! What are you—"

Ross came off the bench, following him as he walked along the dock, holding the bow line. The shy one was crying again, doing the little hop from earlier, staring at the spillway. When the boat cleared the last piling, the bow swung sharply as the current pulled the line.

Serious pressure drew on the rope in Lomak's hands.

He felt the boat's weight in his arms. The yellow nylon rope seemed to stretch with the force of the heavy fiberglass Stratus and motor. Not a good idea. Needing all his strength, he pulled, then ducked and slipped the rope over his shoulder. He leaned. Braced and bent at the knees, Lomak struggled to recover the boat. Not easy, a bad idea.

Ross was next to him. "Let me help."

"Get your fucking hands off and sit down. Do what I say, or I let this fucker go."

Hunched forward, the rope cutting his shoulder, he stared at her until she backed away. Once she sat, he pulled. Very

BARRY KNISTER

slowly, he was able to bring the boat back. First to the pier, then around the end piling, on the safe lake side. Quickly he tied the bow and stern lines without looking at either woman. It had seemed a good idea, putting the shy one out there a few yards from the spillway, to keep Ross focused. Strong fucking current, an honest mistake.

The woman in the boat had hold of a piling. Without letting go, she raised a leg to the gunwale—frightened, anxious to be on shore.

"Stay in the boat."

She took her foot down, looking up.

"You seen what can happen just now. That's what I wanted you to see, so we have cooperation."

"Please—"

She was sobbing now, out of control, going to pieces. A song, *I Fall To Pieces*, Patsy Cline. Jerry glanced over his shoulder. From her expression he saw Ross understood the rope thing had not gone as planned. And there were the nostrils, like people coming down as he worked in their basements.

"What is it, Jerry?" Marion crossed her arms. "What now? We're here, you want something. Let's get on with it."

"We'll get on with it when I say, Marion, so shut your fucking mouth."

Lomak had a strong impulse to throw her off the dock. Right now, right here, into the smooth, whalebacked brown glide of fast-moving current just beyond the dock. She was taking over the show, giving orders. What was the expression she'd used so often in court? *Let's go, let's go, Mr. Lomak, we haven't got all day.* Incredible bitch of a woman. But you had to keep yourself on track. Keep focused. Couldn't let them knock you off message. That's what politicians called it on TV, staying on message.

The one in the boat was whimpering. When he looked, she was slumped now on the passenger seat, rocking. He reached down, got the canvas bag and carried it to the bench. He ripped open the Velcro and set the bag next to Ross before sitting.

Practiced and efficient from Rohmer's many rehearsals, he took out the laptop, clicked it on, and got out the two cell phones. Efficiently handling the phones and computer brought a sense of recovery from the mishap with the boat. He used the wireless laptop to log on, waited, then tapped out the online e-mail address of the Rosses' broker. Waiting again, Lomak readied the two cell phones. He tapped out Rohmer's number. Louis answered.

"Yeah, we're at the falls."

"I was starting to worry." Rohmer was an uptight old woman, a pussy. "You were going to call from the houseboat."

"I'm calling now, Louis. Let's rock."

"Put Marion on."

He handed her the phone and leaned to hear.

"Marion? You there?"

"It won't work, Louis."

"What's that, Marion? What won't work?"

"Whatever this is. It's too bizarre. Just let it go before someone gets hurt."

"Actually, it *will* work. You can thank wireless technology, and the hotel's hot spot. As soon as we're done talking, Jerry will call your broker in Birmingham, Michigan. You'll be speaking on one line and sending him an e-mail sell order with the laptop. He'll have questions, but you're good at those. Plus, the e-mail sell order will be right in front of him. What's he going to do, Marion, say no to you? You and Drew share a joint account, his-and-her everything. That means you can do this solo. I'll know everything happened when I dial up your home PC and check your Merrill Lynch account. When the transfer's effected, it'll register on your account. It should be slightly more than four million, not less. Then I'll know it's in my offshore account."

"How—"

"Carrie. Her high-school chat room. Starting in March. That's how I learned about your big deal, and everything started falling in place. Especially when she talked about you going to the Boundary Waters. Don't worry, I never actually chatted with her, she's fine. Having fun with crazy Brittany—that's what she calls her. She's a cute kid, your daughter, I can tell. Nice kid. You should ease up with her, Marion."

Ross looked dazed. Seeing her this way filled Lomak with a sense of triumph.

"Okay, that's it," Rohmer said. "As Jerry says, time to rock. You take care now."

Still watching her face, Lomak took the phone. She'd been broadsided, down for the count. Ross sat staring past him as he tapped out the broker's number from the card in his hand. Printed below the phone number, in bold letters was BANCO REAL, and the account number in Costa Rica. Nine digits. He handed back the phone and held up the card for her to see.

"Good morning, this is Merrill Lynch, Mr. Aronson's office."

"Hello, Toni. Marion Ross."

"Well, hi, how you doing?"

"Let me talk to Leonard, please."

"Just a sec."

Lomak glanced down to the boat. The shy one was watching. Her eyes were red, face blotchy.

"Marion, good morning."

"Yes, Leonard, something's come up."

"Everything A-OK with your deal?"

"Change of plans, Leonard—" She looked at Lomak. "Drew needs to do this through some arrangement offshore. He called last night."

"I don't—"

"Neither do I, but that's how it has to be. And right now, that's all he had time to tell me. Something to do with the British end. I'm going to give you an account at—" she glanced at the card "—Banco Real, Costa Rica."

"Marion, I don't—"

"Leonard, I can't talk here. Even if I could, I wouldn't be able to give you the details. All I know is, we have to do this right now. Got a pen? Banco Real, and the following number."

She pronounced each digit slowly. Lomak listened to the broker repeat them, then silence. He signaled for her to cup her phone. It pleased him very much, seeing her do as told. All that money, from people like him paying her ticket, setting her up like she was.

"Tell him you're sending the order by e-mail for record-keeping," Lomak said. "To confirm the order."

That's what Rohmer had said to tell her. She uncupped the phone. As she repeated this to the broker, Lomak steadied the laptop on his knees. But thought about it. No, he would make her do it. He placed the keyboard on her knees.

"Ready?" She was looking at him, but now faced down and began typing, pecking with one hand.

"I wish you'd tell me a little more," the broker said. "Drew never—"

"I know. We'll both find out more later. Ready?"

"Just a second... All right, I'm booting it up...I have it. This leaves you...eleven-five and change in the vacation account. Sure you want to do this?"

"No, Leonard, I'm not sure. But I have to. That's all I can tell you."

"All right, you're the boss... That's it, transferred."

"Thank you."

"I—"

"Talk to you later." She pushed the button.

Lomak took the phone and tapped Rohmer's number. "Jerry?"

"Hey, Louis. We have a 'Go,' we have ignition."

"Terrific. Say *feenee*."

"What's that?"

"French. It means, we're done."

"Yeah, well, get ready. I'll be there in twenty minutes."

"Understood, I'll warm up the plane."

"If I see that fucker take off, I make a call."

"Understood, not to worry."

Rohmer hung up. Ross had her arms folded again and was looking at him. He took away the laptop and felt a rush of satisfaction. Of mastery and completion. Now Ross looked to the boat, and Lomak realized he had never really believed it would happen. He had lacked confidence, seen himself along just for the ride, to take Ross over some jumps, as she had done to him.

He stood. For emphasis, he dropped the laptop off the dock. It hit with a satisfying slap, and now he saw a half-full six pack of beer. It was resting under Schmidt's seat in the Stratos. There was plenty of time, and he slipped the phone into his shirt pocket. "Hand me that—" He motioned to Heather. "Right there, under the seat." She looked, saw the beer, and handed it up. Three left, perfect. He took the carton. Five minutes, ten, it didn't matter now.

"This is good," he said. "A toast. Heather?" He raised his eyebrows, holding out one of the bottles as she stared up at him from the boat. He turned. "Marion? No? Sure?" He set down the carton, carried the bottle to the nearest pier post and snapped off the cap with his palm. Getting the cap off on his first try was like an exclamation point. A high-five.

CHAPTER

38

Charlie slammed John's pickup in gear. The tires spit gravel as it moved from the road's shoulder to asphalt.

Cradling his Remington, Nielson turned away and began jogging back along the gravel path. Soon he reached the big boulders, and again became conscious of crows off to his right. They were coming down in threes and fours, disappearing behind the pole barn, flying up. From the moment of seeing his father's truck in Schmidt's pole barn, working to free Charlie and hearing the crows outside, he'd known Daddy was gone. In a few seconds he would find what was waiting.

He reached the barn, trotted along the corrugated wall, then stopped at the back. Three spooked birds flew up to a pine bow, but others stayed where they were. They were big and black, a crowd of them working on it, stabbing down.

Running now, watching them scatter and fly up, he reached the place and saw the boots. He did not need to see more, did not want to see. Laying the rifle on the leaf-strewn body, he grabbed the feet and began dragging, but stopped, feeling the weight of his father, his stiffness. It was wrong this way. Disrespectful.

Facing away, he set down the feet. Most of the leaves covering the body had been scratched away. Averting his eyes but still seeing, aware that some of the crows were already strutting close again, he knelt at his father's side. He lay the rifle on his father's chest, then worked his hands under. He lifted, balancing the rifle.

So light, his father. Small all his life, but tough. Good people, a good man.

Crying, Nielson carried the stiffened body followed by birds. He turned on them and they scattered, but did not leave. He carried his father to the back of the barn, along the wall. With his elbow he opened the panel. He stepped to the pickup truck, got the passenger door loose, then worked it open with his hip. He cradled his father with one arm, leaned the rifle against the truck, then worked Lars Nielson's stiff body into the passenger seat. He looked away as he did this, as much as he could, but the torn, soft flesh of the face, eyes gone… That was the way crows did with anything, you couldn't blame them, it was their nature, how they lived.

He looked around for some kind of covering. For modesty, respect. In the crack of light, a drop cloth hung from a nail next to the pegboard. He got it and came back, shook it out. But stopped. It was wrong, sitting him up like that in the truck, with a tarp over him.

He went to the back and unhinged the truck's deck, returned to the cab and gathered up the body. He carried it and laid it gently, then jumped onto the truck bed and did his best to straighten his father's stiff corpse. He got down, brought the tarp and spread it neatly over the body.

Finished, Nielson got the rifle. He stepped outside, remembered the crows, and gently slid closed the panel. He crossed the drive. At the house he went to double-time, glancing in windows. Nielson stopped, thought he heard something. After a moment, he now moved to the end of the house, and looked.

Below the greensward, the man was still seated on the dock. He would not be able to hear anything at this distance.

Nielson moved forward, down the lawn about twenty feet. He dropped to his knees with the rifle, then lay flat on his stomach. Fort Leonard Wood, boot camp. Some things you never forgot. Body and elbows forming a tripod, he sighted the rifle at the man in the chair.

On the breeze he heard the voice, saw the phone held to his ear. More than a minute passed. The man nodded, said something more, nodded. He was done. A leather satchel lay open next to his chair. He dropped in the phone, stood and stretched before moving to the plane.

In that moment Nielson relaxed his grip. Seen briefly in profile, the man seemed a total stranger. The beard was gone, a tweed coat added. No, it was him, the same man in the door-way that morning. Nielson again sighted, holding the man's back steady in the rifle's scope, watching as he stepped down onto the plane's pontoon. He saw through the bright lens that the angle of the plane's cabin would leave him a clear shot. He sighted lower, seeing the man in the circle of light working open the cockpit door. He hauled himself up, disappeared a second and reappeared inside.

The door hung open. He was not leaving.

After another moment he came out and down, hold-ing something. A small case for eyeglasses or sunglasses. He stuffed them in his inside jacket pocket, Nielson seeing that the man was now wearing a turtleneck. Back on the dock, cap off, he ran a hand over his bald head, pulled the cap back on. He smoothed both hands over his pink face, then grabbed up the bag, and stepped down carefully into Schmidt's utility. The rifles still rested next to the outboard motor.

Nielson sighted from the rifles to the man. He was now lighting a cigar. Just like that, John Nielson thought. Just like that. Once he had it going, the man sat and turned on his seat to adjust the choke. He pulled the rope, and the motor came to life in a cough of blue smoke. He reduced the choke, stood now and stepped forward, undid the bowline, shoved free. He returned and sat, hand on the tiller. The boat moved slowly from shore.

Just like that.

Nielson heard crows. It wasn't likely this one had done it. You could tell by looking at him—soft hands and pink face, the beard making him look friendly this morning, standing in the doorway. Smiling. Had he shaved it off, or was it fake? Sighting on the man's motionless back as the boat chugged casually, Nielson thought again of his mother at the window with her rosary. A strange thing to think right now, squinting into the scope, the man's back in the cross hairs, cigar smoke trailing and the Canadian shoreline opposite. He was getting ready to kill someone, no question, but it was like his conscience was watching. Not to tell him something, just to be there, his mother at the window in her robe, looking out at the bathtub in the ground, the Virgin at prayer, a friend.

He focused, steadied, and fired. The man bucked forward, head snapping back. Nielson lowered the rifle and stood, seeing him sit several seconds before he pitched forward. Something had knocked the motor's tiller. The utility began a slow arc to the right.

Now he would call. Nielson stood, turned and started up the lawn.

CHAPTER

39

"Rohmer won't be there."

"Is that a fact, Marion?"

Lomak sipped his beer. Ross was still seated next to him with her arms crossed. Now she crossed her legs.

"Why would he stay?" she said. "He has the money, the plane. What's he need you for?"

"He doesn't, Marion. Not anymore. But I know his flight plan." He took a sheet of paper from his breast pocket and wagged it in her face. "This is the number for the air-control tower in International Falls. He leaves, he's toast. The family that plays together stays together." He stuffed the paper back in his shirt and drank again.

She did the thing with her nostrils, foot bouncing. "Let's just listen. He said he was going to warm up the plane, let's listen for it."

He listened, aware that was what Ross wanted. He hated her again, that face, the wagging foot. In a minute he'd finish his beer, then throw her off the dock.

He stepped again to the Stratos. The shy one was seated again, holding herself and looking stupid in the oversized parka. Her hair was still stringy. But she was wary now. Different. He faced west, listening over the falls, afraid of seeing the Cessna rise above trees, full of fuel to get to north Texas before having to stop. *We'll be out of this area*—that's what Rohmer had said. *No chance of being spotted or stopped. Then it's dead south, over the Gulf.*

"I'll tell you what I think."

"That's what's you do, Marion." He threw the empty bottle out into the pool. "And that's *all* you do."

Don't, he thought. Stay on message. In some way, being in a hurry and wasting Ross would mean he'd lost to her. But he couldn't help looking above the trees. The thing was to just leave, and everything would be cool. He saw himself driving away and tipping his cap to her, leaving her on the dock with her buddy. It would be better, because that way he could send her postcards.

"He won't use it."

"What's that, Marion? What won't he use?"

Real good, send her postcards. *Hey, Marion, what's the haps? How's the family? Check out this beach.* Perfect. Or a snapshot of him fishing. Duke Wayne hauling in some humongous billfish, a marlin or sail, standing next to Captain Haysoos, whatever. With his shirt off, with the hair and a good tan, Ernest Fucking Hemingway—

"The plane."

"Uh huh. Sure, Marion, he just leaves it here."

He looked back down at the woman in the boat, then bent at the knees and held out his hand to her. Or a shot taken of him in a casino, captioned *Your hard-earned dollars at work!* He smiled, liking that one even better, motioning for the woman to take his hand. Shit, he could send Ross a card every week, that was reason enough not to throw her sorry ass off the dock.

"You think he owns it?" Ross said behind him. "You think it's his very own Cessna?"

"Take my hand." He didn't turn but wanted to, to see Ross's face. Of course he owned it, people rented cars and houses, not planes. He wanted Ross to stop running her mouth.

Below where he stood, the shy one was still looking up, wary. Something was wrong with her.

"We're right on the border of a foreign country," Ross said.

Hearing her move on the bench, he straightened. It was just to get to him. To piss him off. "That's nice. So what?"

"So, he doesn't need a plane. He isn't carrying anything illegal. He can just drive over the bridge at International Falls, into Canada. When he's good and ready, he'll leave for wherever he wants. The money's in Costa Rica, but he doesn't have to be there. He can go anywhere."

Just leave a Cessna? Pick up and just fucking *leave*? It had never occurred to him.

"But I may be wrong," she said. "You'll know when you get there."

He looked at his watch, listening. "Get out." He motioned to the shy one and she stood. "Come on, get up here." He waited as she clumsily held to the dock, then jumped. The planks were slick and she fell.

He jumped down into the Stratos, Marion still talking as he reached for the ignition and saw the keys were gone. He looked on the floor, felt his pockets, looked to the dock. Ross was trying to get the woman up.

He grabbed her ankle.

"Let go—" She kicked and he clawed her leg, knowing from the force in her she had the keys, all of them on one ring, the boat, the truck. Pulling her toward him, he saw Marion had her by the parka.

"You can't do this!" The woman kicked him. "You're evil!"

"Give me the keys, now—"

"Let her go, Jerry—"

"*Give me the keys!*"

Half on the dock, legs over the side, the woman kicked again but he had a good hold on her, felt her arms windmilling. His cap came loose. Marion lost her grip, and he pulled hard—

Searing pain—he heard himself scream. Across his forehead, all the ties, the delicate knots of the hairweave broke in her fist, torn, with each knot a pop like a button snap.

Blood already in his eyes, he wrestled her back down into the boat. The torn-away part of the hairpiece hung and flopped—he felt it off on one side. With a final yank he pulled the woman fully into the boat.

Only now could he touch himself. It was torn half off. His hand was bloody, the broken knots like pig bristles under his shaking fingers. He leaned over the gunwale and cupped water—cold, freezing. Something fell from his shirt pocket, the phone. He slapped water to his torn scalp, tasting blood.

In peripheral vision he sensed Ross looking at him, seeing the hair.

He tried now to put it in place, seeing the cell phone sinking in brown water before he looked to the floor for his cap. He bent and snatched it, straightened. In great pain, he pulled the cap hard, front and back, down over his ruined scalp before stepping over the woman and putting out his hand.

"Give them to him," Ross said. "Please, Heather. Now. God, Heather, do it."

Sprawled on the floor, the woman reached in her parka pocket and handed them up. He put them in his pants pocket.

"Get up."

"Don't hurt her."

"Get up, Heather."

He stood away so she could stand. When she did, he turned to check Ross, and saw himself in the Stratos's windshield. Blood was coming from under the cap. He took it off, seeing now the full damage. It looked to him like popped rivets. This one was just like Doreen, the quiet ones you couldn't trust. He touched himself. Any facial movement pulled the wounds. Cool air fell sharp on raw flesh. Wiping blood, he patted his pants for the keys to be sure, then stiff-armed Heather.

She fell back, sitting down hard on the gunwale.

He shoved again.

"Don't! No!"

She landed on her back, and began thrashing the water. When she got to it and snatched for the boat, Lomak slapped her hand away. He scooped more water and patted his head. It helped, it was soothing, the woman chattering and yelling at him, pointing now at his head, laughing.

"Yeah, Heather, I'm funny but you're fucking hysterical, Heather, that's what you are, fucking Loony Tunes, that's funny—"

He kept talking that way, keeping it going so he couldn't hear what she said—talking, talking, crazy fucking woman laughing—"Yeah, honey, okay honey, that's good, you send a postcard where you're going—"

The puffy down coat was buoying her up, keeping her high in the water. But she was moving fast now, caught by the current.

He felt the bow sink behind him, Ross still yelling. He stumbled to the stern and balanced with his hand.

On the still-hot motor housing.

He took it away, touching his head delicately. A float cushion sailed out, tied to yellow rope. When he looked to the water, the woman was thrashing to the cushion, grabbing it, but then she lost it, drawn by the current.

He was laughing now, it was funny. "Really good, Heather, you can take the cushion with you over fucking Kettle Falls, in a barrel, man—" That's right, the cushion could be like a souvenir for her, in Canada, where she was going with rocks and shit—

He heard and felt it at the same time. A blow, an audible thud that humped him over the hot motor from behind, sharp and hard, an axe handle. But not. The head pain confused him, but the new thing that had happened quickly overwhelmed what still pulsed on his scalp. His legs tingled, he tried to reach around, hot through his jacket from the motor housing. He tried to push off but couldn't. Something was stuck to him, in his back. He reached and cried out from the movement. Something was *in him*. He felt his legs going, something to do with his spine. It was Ross, behind him, in the boat.

One second, take your eyes off them one second, they would fuck you over every time—

Lomak reached again, awful pain spreading in all directions. He pushed off the motor, hands burning. The Stratos bobbed under him, sinking his knees. Ross was yelling somewhere different, this time from the dock—Jesus Christ, screaming, loud fucking back-stabbing woman, and he was going down now, dropping, hearing himself suck air. As she shouted, Lomak saw more yellow rope tangled under him, felt it still in him, how she had done it as he was touching the hair weave.

The drag anchor, fucking aluminum. Stuck in him.

And for some reason, dropping down now with a grunt on his knees and forearms, facing the gray indoor-outdoor carpet of Schmidt's boat, what he was thinking—the complete bullshit that came into your mind—was of this guy, some guy that looked like a snake—actually like a real snake, his eyes wrapping round the side of his head. On the news with Jim Lehrer, some expert, this snake guy running his mouth on how you couldn't blink, you had to stay on message.

Not a good deal.

Ross was crying now. The back was bad, but better if he kept the way he was. On his forearms. The sound of the falls muffled her. That was good, a steady drumming. He remembered the one in the water, but it was not cool being like this, down for the count, on the floor.

"Ross—" He listened for her, hearing himself breathe, the thud of water. "Ross!"

"You bastard!"

"Hey counselor—"

He coughed, in great pain but he wanted her to get it. To start thinking on it right now. "See you in court."

No answer. Good, maybe she understood. "How'd she do, Ross? Half gainer with a tuck?"

He coughed again, but it was all he had to use. "In court you can tell it. Show slides. Marion? Hey, Marion. Lots of good shit for the jury. How you did me twice. Goes on the resume, Marion. Lots on your plate, busy Monday."

Too hard. He was out of breath and saw more blood, brownish red. It was coming off his nose, sopping into the indoor/outdoor. Charlie kept a tidy boat, Mr. Clean. Lomak thought of him in the barn, taped on the jet skis. This was not good, but that was fucking humiliating. Or the Ross house. He remembered it, forgotten all day, her house with the field-stone, the library and antiques, flowerbeds waiting for dozens of flats of annuals. And detonators in the basement.

Unable to feel his feet or lower legs, but remembering the house and knowing it would blow up today—that was some-thing. You had to think positive. He remembered the plane and listened for it, but knew better. Rohmer was gone. Police and shit, whatever would happen…

No matter. Ross's house, that was something.

Very tired now, he listened to the falls. He reached up painfully and lay the weave in place before resting his head on the carpet.

CHAPTER

40

He was cold and wished he had taken a jacket before leaving.

Braking hard on the gravel drive, Schmidt got out and ran up the Nielsons' front walk. The door was unlocked. He entered and trotted through to the kitchen. On the back landing, coats hung from pegs. He pulled on a plaid wool jacket, stepped out and moved quickly down the grassy slope, toward the covered boat shed.

He got out the keys. A Lund and a Seabreeze hung suspended. Reaching the dock, he decided on the Lund, moved to the winch, released the pawls, and spun the flywheel. The boat lowered as he turned, cradled in canvas cinches—slowly, slowly. It touched water, floated free. Schmidt pushed the boat out from under the shed, moved along the dock and hopped down. Seconds later he had it started. He spun the wheel and swung out into the lake.

The motor whined, the hull rose.

He had no plan. Nothing. He touched his face, cool air finding places where duct tape had taken skin. The missing eyebrow. If John Nielson had called the landing, someone would soon exit the channel. Gustofson, or Pierson from the Dew Drop. Whatever happened, he'd soon have help.

Jerry. He saw him seated, tapping his lips for silence, the deer rifle balanced. Of the two, he was the killer. Schmidt looked to shore and back to the channel before sitting. It was a thing people like that had. Playing cowboy. It made him think of Lillie, an adult-ed course she'd taken in Milwaukee, after the kids were gone. Something she said the instructor had quoted—how did it go? Something like, the reason for most of the trouble in the world had to do with people who couldn't be still in a room by themselves.

True. Alone in a room. He couldn't do it for long himself, it didn't work. Always he was up after a few minutes, feeling antsy. Scratching around, looking for Lillie or one of the kids. Bugging them to go bowling with him, to the movies.

He was glad for the Lund's windscreen. Eyes watering and the bare places tingling on his face, he wondered whether Brenda Contay was like that too. Always ready to pick up and go, to do. It was in her face and movements.

Jesus, he thought. The stuff that came to you at the wrong time.

Even so, steering but hardly seeing, knowing the channel by heart, Schmidt saw himself getting ready for bed, the room smelling of camphor and wood, seeing her red hair and feeling guilty in front of his wife's shoes lined up in the closet. But trying to start again, in the old way, with people he knew—it was starting over from the same place. That's what was wrong with it. To start again, you couldn't just start over. You had to actually let go. Take a chance.

He saw an aluminum skiff ahead in the lake. It was empty but running, not drifting. As it came about in a lazy turn, he recognized the dented transom as his own. He looked to the American shore, to his house. The plane still rested at the dock. He aimed for the utility, and now saw the upper body folded forward, then Rohmer's pink head.

He throttled back, saw the tiller angled away, the boat circling. He looked again to his house. No movement. At low speed, then in neutral, Schmidt waited for the utility to complete the circle. He floated nearer and grabbed the transom. He managed to kill the ten-horse, and held on until motion stopped. From the entry wound, he knew Rohmer was dead.

Rizzo. No, Lomak. He had been gone an hour, maybe more. Schmidt pushed the smaller boat forward and away, brought it back, working to reach the rifles. He glanced again at Rohmer, and for a moment wondered what should be done with the plane.

Someone had put the scope sight back on the Remington. He grabbed the rifle, and shoved the utility clear. He sat again and put the Lund in gear.

◆◆◆◆◆

"I believe him, that's all," Tina said. "If he sees us trying to signal, he'll hurt them."

"He won't see." Arms loaded with more bedding, Brenda stepped to the catwalk. Sonny was looking up at her, sitting on the heap of blankets and life preservers she had thrown into Brian Reese's Lund.

"*Move.*"

He barked at her, ready for play.

"Call him, Tina."

"Sonny! Here!"

The dog jumped to the houseboat and crossed to his mistress.

"It's the way he gave orders," Tina said, wrapped now in her own parka. "'Do what I say, I'm in charge, I'm the boss.'"

"I met him, I know."

Brenda tossed the bedding. She would use gas from the tank in Brian's boat to soak the blankets, then get down in the water and tow the boat out into the cove. Then set it on fire. Maybe someone would see.

"Acting like a theater director," Tina said. "'This is my play, don't change the script.' I think setting a fire is dangerous, Brenda. He had it all planned out, rehearsed."

"He won't see it. At night, yes, not now."

"What if you're wrong?"

"Tina, we can't just sit here. He throws someone overboard, forces two women to go with him—"

Determined, she went inside for matches. Brightness filled the lounge, the harsh glare at odds with the cold, gray morning. She stepped to the pantry and opened drawers, looking. She checked the shelf before the houseboat's controls, the sideboard—then remembered Brian Reese's matches in her windbreaker.

She went back out and swung up the ladder. Crossing the deck, Brenda looked out to the channel. Nothing and no one. Just grays and browns, small pine-covered islands. It made her angry. A criminal, a hater of women had taken her friends, but somewhere nearby, locals were making breakfast, fishing, reading bird and geology guidebooks.

She turned to the land spit. Scanning now, searching the slope for the stand of birches and campsite, she found it. Right there. Their observation point, the empty beer bottles. She imagined Schmidt beaching the Stratos, jumping out and heading up the slope, just as she had done an hour before. To spy. And now the sleek boat was coming toward them to help with Heather's fish, the man with spooky hair. Then killing the pike, and blaming the fish for his own clumsiness.

She thought of horses hanging in a barn, saw the rancher—*It's a teaching moment, missy, killing horses this way helps teach my boys it's a tough world*—

She ran inside to her cabin. Digging in her windbreaker, she remembered Charlie Schmidt and Louis Rohmer looking up as they arrived for dinner. It now seemed staged to her, an act. She got the matches, dropped the jacket, and heard the distant, muffled sound of an outboard.

Brenda ran out and crossed to the railing. Louder now, it was not the Stratos. She saw nothing and felt defeated. There would not be enough time. Whoever it was would pass within sight of the inlet before she could tow the boat and light the blankets. The sound of the motor would blot out her shouting.

"Hear it?" Tina called.

She waited, watching. The motor's pitch had altered and now seemed aimed for her. The change convinced Brenda it was him. In the next moment the boat appeared, and in seconds it entered the cove. She wasn't sure, and then she was—his hair and features, driving someone else's boat. He was alone, and Brenda felt enormously relieved. But quickly she took it back, scolding herself, denying any certainties or loyalties. He corrected several degrees and aimed for the houseboat. He was watching her, keeping track of the boat, looking up.

She went down quickly. Tina shoved up from her chair, the dog at her side. She believed in him, and she was no fool. But behind the wheelchair, in the narrow span of water between houseboat and land spit, the captain's chair still floated, tacky underside face up.

She looked at him, this time in a different boat. He put the engine in neutral and drifted the last few feet. When he again looked at her, there was something different about him. His pant leg was ripped. Propped in the bow was a rifle. He looked now to Tina.

"You all right?"

"Yes, someone—"

"He took Heather and Marion," Brenda said.

Charlie looked at her. "Rohmer's dead." She said nothing. "I'm just telling you." He said it defensively, in reply to whatever must be in her face. "I came to check on you. Someone will be here soon, I have to go."

"I'm going, too."

"There's no point. I'm looking at random. I don't know where they are."

"He mentioned something about a plane," Tina said. "Just that, a plane."

"Wouldn't they need a dock?" Brenda asked.

He looked at her again. "If he was picking someone up, yes. But he wasn't, that wasn't the plan. Rohmer never planned to fly out."

She looked at Tina. "What did he say?"

"He said they were going to Kettle Falls. He told Heather to hurry up, he had a plane to catch. He told Marion she should get her gloves, he said she was in the steno pool. Meaning she would be typing something."

"Kettle Falls. Okay," Schmidt said. "That's it. Lomak went there because they have wireless from the hotel. He thinks Rohmer's waiting for him at my place."

"Somewhere with a dock," Tina said.

Charlie nodded. "It makes sense. Louis mentioned going there yesterday afternoon."

"They're my friends," Brenda told him. "I'm going."

"This guy is bad news."

"We know."

She jumped to the transom. He stared at her, standing in a strange boat, strange himself, holding to the houseboat. His face looked both blanched and red. His left eyebrow was gone. "Don't argue," she said. "He's got Marion and Heather. I can steer if you have to do something."

She looked at the rifle, then at Tina. "Is that all right?"

"I'm fine, you go."

Charlie shook his head, but held out his hand. She took it, jumped, and stepped quickly to the passenger seat. He shoved them clear, put the boat in gear and backed away.

♦♦♦♦♦

The smaller Mercury motor sent the Nielsons' Lund slapping over the lake in heavy lunges. Schmidt was glad the noise made speech impossible. He stood at the console and kept the bow aimed for two islands that concealed Kettle Falls. Brenda sat next to him, right hand gripping the windshield. Her eyes were slits, yellow rain parka flattened to her chest.

He saw she was looking at the deer rifle in the bow. Maybe she thought he was the one who'd killed Louis. He wanted to tell her no, but concentrated on the islands. What was the point? If she thought it, she thought it.

Hours before, they had made this same crossing. The light had been fading, Johnson Bay behind them, the falls ahead. That had been long ago. He felt her disappointment next to him, like some kind of laser. It's not my fault, he thought.

But whose, then? Who had brought them here? Whose fault?

♦♦♦♦♦

Spray slapped the windshield. Again, and again. Water drizzled off the glass like thread.

Nothing looked familiar to Brenda. Coming back last night, suddenly the islands had been there, static and ghostly in the dark. Something was flapping on her right. She looked and saw his left pant leg split up the seam. His leg was exposed, white above the knee. She saw his calf was hairless, thin blue veins disappearing into his shoe. The shoe itself was clumsy-looking, splattered with paint. On his way to sixty, that was easy to forget with him. Until you saw a hairless calf with veins.

Holding to the windshield, she looked up at his remaining eyebrow. Below his jacket, a strip of duct tape flapped from his shirt. He had been bound, held somewhere. There was no plan he was part of. Not then, not now.

"It has to do with money!" she yelled.

Charlie nodded, but didn't look at her.

"The one who took Marion and Heather…There was a trial!" He shook his head and leaned. "A Trial! It's someone Marion sent to jail!"

He nodded and straightened, looking out. "I see now why…brought him. He's…gofer."

"Can't hear!"

"The Gofer! The flunky! Louis set this up!"

The boat hit a swell and slammed her down. Gripping the windshield, she saw Louis Rohmer's pink face at dinner. Lively, intelligent eyes, bald head, the beard. His college sweetheart was going fishing where Charlie Schmidt had a house, in Northern Minnesota.

She felt him touch her shoulder. Brenda looked up, and he leaned. "They were playing around with a laptop computer. At my house. That's part of it. Marion said her husband's in England."

"All week."

"The husband's doing some deal?"

"Setting it up. His son's with him."

Charlie nodded. "Husband out of the country. The son. Daughter with a friend. He knew all about it."

"Then he calls you."

Charlie said nothing and straightened. Seeing he felt blame, she looked away. *Hey Louis, how's by you? Fishing? Why not?* That's how it had been, easy-touch Charlie Schmidt, the good-guy widower with an empty house and no plans. For the first time it registered with her—*Rohmer's dead.* Again she focused on the rifle in the bow. He had not said how it happened.

Brenda glanced down again at his leg. She watched the hard, solid calf muscle flexing against the boat's motion. The idea threatened her, that he had killed someone. Not because she feared him, but because of what it would mean for them.

It changed something. It put him on the other side of a line she mustn't cross.

He slowed as they neared the islands. As she had last night, Brenda crept forward to look for rocks. She looked down. Under a gray morning sky, the water gave back nothing. Twice the hull tapped something. As they passed slowly between the islands, limp trees jutted from granite walls.

"There!"

His voice came loud, it startled her. She turned, seeing him looking up, and raised her head in time to see broad wings. They sailed overhead, silent, motionless. That was the word for it, sailing. Floating. She had never seen an eagle, but knew that was what now disappeared behind trees.

When Brenda looked at him he was already back to business. He had wanted her to see it. It was important to him, even now.

She faced forward with selfish regret. On a normal day, he'd be telling her all about it. They'd be tying up and walking to see the nest. Carefully, from a distance. He'd be telling her things about eagles, how they raised their young, helping her love this place. Wanting her to. Focused once more on the black-brown water, she felt a rush of resentment for all men, how they made things interesting, how they got your attention, got you thinking with them, then ruined it with games and toys, ambition, all their damned *technique*.

The sound of the motor rose as they again passed out into open water. Brenda crept back to her seat and held on. Very soon, she could see the flat line of the spillway, the broad, smooth broken O that formed the pool before Kettle Falls. Just above the waterline, the dock ran out into the bay. Again the motor slowed. The boat rose on the backwash and settled. She looked at him, at the hairless eyebrow, wanting now to ask about it.

"Get me the rifle."

"Why stop? What for?"

"To see what we have. Just hand it to me."

She glanced at it and saw the scope sight. One minute she liked him for eagles, in the next she thought he wanted to shoot someone. Brenda again crouched forward and came back with the rifle. He raised it and sighted at something. After several seconds, he said, "I see Marion, that's all. The boat's tied up."

"Is she all right?"

He waited for Brenda to stand, then handed her the rifle. She raised it, bracing elbow against chest as he had done. The eyepiece held a bright, jittery disk. She trained it on the shore, found the dock, and followed it out slowly. Marion sat alone, small in her Hudson's Bay coat. She was seated in profile, facing away on a bench, hands between her knees.

"He took Heather somewhere."

"No, he wouldn't leave one of them."

She studied her friend's sloped shoulders, the outline of someone broken. Marion was staring at the falls.

"Let me see something," he said.

She handed back the rifle. He sighted again, following the shore.

"Come on," Brenda said. "Let's get her. Shoot the thing, let her know we're here."

"He might want that."

Slowly, maddeningly, he sighted a full minute. Marion did not seem to move. Lomak didn't appear, neither did Heather. At last Charlie lowered the rifle. He shook his head and motioned for Brenda to sit. He shoved the throttle and she sat back heavily. As they gained speed, she watched Marion, wanting her to hear them and stand.

They neared the dock, and she saw familiar things—the shuttered bait shop, a whitewashed gas shed, the gravel road. Charlie throttled back. At last Marion turned on the bench.

She did not stand. After a moment, she glanced down at Charlie's Stratos.

"Are you all right?" he yelled.

The Lund came about, and in those seconds, on her feet now, Brenda saw the figure on the floor of Charlie's boat. He was on all fours behind the seats, like a Muslim at prayer. The boat's anchor was jammed in his back. Yellow rope trailed away, tied to a bow cleat. Stains formed a loose circle on his dark brown jacket.

His foot moved.

Their boat nudged a piling. Charlie grabbed hold and she scrambled onto the dock. There was blood on the planks. She moved to Marion, sat next to her and put an arm around her shoulder. She clasped Marion's folded hands with her free hand. Marion's were icy.

"She's in shock."

Still in the boat, Charlie looked above the dock, tying up. "Get her up and walking, take her onshore."

"I'm not in shock." Marion sat straight and turned to Brenda. "Heather's dead. He killed her and I hit him with the anchor. We've been talking."

"Go on, help her off the dock," Charlie said.

"I don't need help." She stood, Brenda with her. They moved several steps, but Marion stopped, looking down at the dock. "That's his blood. Do you have my phone?"

Brenda shook her head. Again she took Marion's icy hand and led her forward. Now she heard the falls, felt them underfoot. Their shoes scuffed gray planks. "That's it," she said. "Almost there."

"Don't treat me this way," Marion said. "I know where I am. I have to call Drew and Carrie."

"We will."

"I'm not in shock. I have to call them."

"Okay."

They stepped from the dock onto the gravel road and started up. Now the sun felt warm on her head. She remembered benches along the path leading to the lookout.

"Tina?"

"She's all right," Brenda said. "We left her, she's warm, she was amazing, she managed somehow to get into the Lund, she was looking—"

"You can tell her I'm responsible."

"Don't, Marion."

The gravel rose more sharply. Soon, the hotel's roof line came into view. Branching right was the path to the falls. They needed to sit a minute. Brenda led Marion into shade, smelling pine. A red squirrel ran across the trail. Pursued by a second squirrel, it tore up a jack pine. Both animals circled the tree and stopped, tails lashing.

"Why else do you think he came here?" Marion said. "Why do you think he killed Heather?"

"If you need to blame somebody, blame Rohmer. He put it all together. He brought Lomak here."

"Where is—"

"He's dead." She said it sharp, with finality. To ward off the next question.

"He's crazy." Stiff and aimless in her movements, Marion stumbled. "Jerry Lomak."

"Watch your step."

"We talked some. He may be dead now. He was with Doreen Taylor. They worked for Damon Plumbing, she was a bookkeeper—"

Again Marion stumbled, but this time she caught herself, hand to the ground. She straightened and they continued. She brushed off her palm. "I told you."

"I don't remember." Brenda again took her hand.

"In the car. Minnie and Mickey."

"Oh, yes."

"A perfect fit. Perfect couple. He formulated policy, she implemented."

Good. Marion was sounding like herself again, her voice and words. "We're almost there. Minnie and Mickey, go on."

"That's right, Brenda, keep me talking. You know what to do, you really do." A wan smile. She squeezed Brenda's hand. "With Heather, too, you were a quick study. Got her in one. The house and drinking, the mister in his shop, turning out those kitsch bird feeders—"

She was crying now, squeezing Brenda's hand as they moved. They reached the benches. Wedged into terraced space between trees, the seats faced the water. The bay below was half hidden by tiers of limbs that stepped down the slope. The women sat. Marion wiped her face with her sleeve.

"That cute kid in his hockey jersey." She shook her head, smiling, patting Brenda's knee. "Heather took the keys. It's what set him off. She was that angry, Brenda. Little Heather took his keys. One good thing, though. One thing."

They needed a good thing. Brenda searched her pockets for Kleenex.

"Know what it is?" Marion asked.

Finding none, Brenda turned and took Marion's hands. "You tell me."

"That fish she caught. That was your doing. Taking her out, taking Heather Reese fishing. What that must have meant to her, catching that damned fish—"

Marion pulled away and wiped with the coat sleeve. She brought her fists down and pounded her knees. "That's it—" She straightened on the bench. "Listen to me trying to salvage this with a damned fish."

She stood and Brenda started to follow. "No, Brenda. I just need to move."

She sat back, watching Marion trudge up the incline. Heather had stopped Lomak by taking the boat keys. It was out of character. Dangerous, risky. Perhaps it was you, Brenda thought. Maybe it wasn't Rohmer who got her killed, or Marion. Maybe it was you.

At the next bench, Marion stopped and looked up into the canopy of trees. The squirrels were barking somewhere.

"I want to say something," she said. "I knew Heather all my adult life. You knew her two days. That's enough to have a sense of someone. Not to know her, just to have a sense. Minnie and Mickey, Doreen and Jerry. You think you know dependency, the terms—"

"You told me."

"No, I didn't. Not what's important. I told you boiler-plate—master-slave, what everyone loves to hate."

Marion made fists and walked back, searching for the thing that needed saying. Again she stopped and looked up. The sun must be fully out now. It was streaming through in places, slanting down in static channels, like something in a cathedral. Like all the angled light in moody forests that had been drained of meaning in hundreds of ads and films and greeting cards. There was no significance to the light. None.

Still staring up, Marion hugged herself. It hurt to see. It was Heather's gesture.

"Everyone should be a person, right, Brenda? Be independent? Make decisions, make their own choices? That's you and me and all the capable people in my office. That's Tanya Walker, times ten. But what about people who can't? What about the Doreen Taylors who can't figure out what to do next? That's not so bad, is it?"

"No."

"That's not crazy or strange. It's all a matter of degree." Still hugging herself, Marion looked into the woods. "Tell her what to do and how to do it, Doreen Taylor could take it from there. Lomak was telling her for years, but in court, I did the telling. What to wear, how to sit. Someone gets her pregnant just out of high school—if you knew her you'd see how that had to happen. The teen father leaves before the baby's even born. Doreen lives with her parents, her father dies. Then the mother. So, there's Doreen and her son for the next seven years, in the little house they left her. In the job her father got for her, keeping books. Along comes Jerry Lomak, snaking out people's sewers—"

This was not good. Brenda stood. "Come on, we should go up to the hotel."

"You listen!" Marion glared at her. "That guy down there killed Heather. I want someone to know why."

"What about Carrie and Drew? Let's find a phone."

Marion blinked. She ran a hand through her hair. "God, my mind." She came forward. Side by side they started back down the slope. At the intersection they started up. With each step, more of the hotel came into view.

"What can I tell him?"

"To come back. Tell him to call the embassy, see if they can get him and Jay on the next flight."

"You don't know the rest. Drew's buyout, all his plans. How can I talk about this with Heather dead? God, he has to know—maybe he does. Leonard would try to reach him. Our broker. Tell him what his crazy wife did, a good broker would do that, wouldn't he? And Carrie. Laura Remnick will make sure she's all right. You don't—"

Brenda stopped. "No, Marion—" She took her elbow. "He's back there. He can't hurt her. Come on."

"What about others? Someone in Detroit? This took planning. Oh God—"

"There's just the two, him and Rohmer. Carrie's fine, she's at the Remnicks'. Come on."

"No, it's not over, it's not!" Marion dropped to her knees. "Not over, oh God—"

She knelt, grabbed her friend and pulled her close. Marion kept repeating "not over!" and Brenda was seeing her father's hand, palm up, her father dying on a beach, and she was kneeling beside him, tapping with her fingers, terrified of losing him.

She looked to the water, to Charlie on the dock, with the rifle. He was watching them. He glanced down at Lomak and then he was running, pant leg flapping. Marion was weeping hard now, out of control, pounding her knees.

In seconds Charlie reached them. He knelt, laid the rifle aside and quickly, roughly grabbed Marion under the arms and pulled her up.

"Not now." He said it loud and steady, turning her by the shoulders. "Not now."

She heard and looked at him.

"We're going up this road," he told her. "You and me. There's a hotel with a phone, come with me now." He looked at Brenda. "The safety's off—" he nodded to the rifle. "Take it and wait on the dock. People will come in the next half hour. I'll come back when I can."

He turned Marion firmly, held her under her right arm and began marching with her up the incline.

CHAPTER

41

Lomak moaned.

Brenda stood on the dock, looking down at the anchor. It was new and still bright. The prongs were not yet dulled from use. The bronze product label was still in place, where the foils joined the hinge. Seeing it made her feel stupid holding the Remington. Useless and helpless. The thing was solidly lodged in the middle of his back.

Lomak coughed, and spat. He was facing away, face hidden between his forearms. Brenda moved to the wooden bench and set down the rifle. She stepped back, then sat with her legs over the edge of the dock. She eased into the bow of the Stratos. Once it steadied, she stepped between the seats, around Lomak. He didn't move. She looked out over the water, heard no sound. After a moment, she squatted down before Lomak's head.

The sun had burned off the morning haze. It glinted on gold strands of the hairpiece. The thing hung from knots still tied to the side of Lomak's head, matted with clots of blood. There were small open wounds. Wedged between the seats, Lomak looked like someone searching for a contact lens. Brenda glanced again at the anchor. Both prongs had sliced neatly through the twill jacket. One might have reached the right lung, the other would be close to or touching Lomak's spine.

"Can you hear me?"

"Yeah."

"Try moving your feet." She craned to see. Lomak was wearing cowboy boots. She remembered the broken shoelace.

"Fuck."

"Can you feel your legs?"

"Huh-uh."

"People are coming," she said. "They'll need to know how bad it is."

Lomak spat weakly. A trail of spittle and blood was coming from under his face. His forehead rested on the gray carpeting, next to his cap. Brenda glanced to the controls. The keys were missing. Heather.

"This is bogue—" The man spat. "This is shit."

She heard nothing. It had taken extra time to cross in the slower boat, maybe twenty minutes. If the hotel had phone service, in a few minutes Charlie would be calling Northern Lights. Half an hour to negotiate the Ash River, add another fifteen or twenty minutes to get here. In under an hour others would arrive with radios and questions. After that, it would be lawyers and autopsies. Interrogations. Depositions.

Only now she remembered. Heather Reese was dead. Brenda stood now and looked to the spillway. Held against the current by yellow nylon rope, a seat cushion flapped twenty feet from the dock. The rope was stretched around the outermost piling, tied clumsily. That's how it was, she thought. Marion tried to save her.

"Tell me what happened."

She stared at the cushion, the pressure on it. Charlie had said that by month's end, the spillway's safety line would be in place. They left it off in spring, allowing everything that got this far to go over. People were warned, took precautions. She remembered the base of the falls as the two of them had looked down the night before—the broken, violent journey's end for branches and limbs. Whole trees collapsed under their own weight and fell into the lake, lazing then in Kabetogama or Namakan, root stumps high above the water until they grew sodden and sank, aimless and seemingly without direction, heading here.

She looked down at the humped figure on the floor. The boat felt defiled to her now, an instrument, covered with blood and sin. Without the Stratos, they couldn't have done it. It made her feel sick, a stupid thing. A kid's thing, bought for Charlie's son, for skiing, no kind of grown man's boat.

"You bastard," she said. "Why'd you do it?"

"Fuck you, Red." Lomak spat. "Look at my fuckin' head, ask me why."

There was something still left in him. Even on his hands and knees, knowing he might never walk again, might not live, he was still the tough guy. A man who kills women, then blames them for it. She edged her way to Lomak's feet. Above the left boot, the pants had hiked up. She reached down and touched Lomak's calf.

"Feel that?"

"Fuck you."

She took satisfaction in it, with no shame attached. "Where are the keys?"

"Pants. Broke my fucking back. Stabbed my fucking back, fucking—"

"You feel nothing." Disgusted to touch him, she reached down, shoved her hand into his pants, and pulled out the keys.

"I feel like shit."

Brenda straightened, remembering Charlie's face as he neared the houseboat. It had been full of guilt and shame, her own full of suspicion. He had known how it must seem to her. No Charlie Schmidt meant no Louis Rohmer.

"Who else is in this besides Rohmer?" Looking now at the anchor, she fought off an urge to grab it, twist it, just to hear him scream. "Look, help is on the way. You're going to make it, and you can do yourself some good. Right now. If someone else is in this, tell me now, it can help you."

Quickly, she shoved past Lomak and crouched again at his head. "What else did you do? Help yourself, Jerry, you can do yourself some good—"

"F'geddaboudit. You know this movie?"

"Who else is in this!"

"Fucking Indians everywhere." Lomak coughed and spat. "Duke Wayne, these settlers. No, maybe *Green Berets*. Surrounded, VC everywhere. Someone says 'Now we got 'em right where we want 'em.'"

Lomak coughed a laugh. "Right there, in court. Right where I want 'em, no shit. In court. Tell my story, blow up her fucking house, fucking space station—" He coughed again, trying to laugh.

"Marion's house? You did something to it?"

"Write a book, Red. In prison, no shit. Write a book, get me an agent…"

Brenda stood and looked again to the lake. She wanted others, right now, to free her from choice. To stop her from choosing. The distant islands floated in bright sun. Against the sky, the pines looked to her like a ragged, two-dimensional graph. Like vital signs on a monitor in some patient's room.

"Tell me what you did to the house!"

"Seventy-two hours, Red. 'To the moon, Alice—'" He coughed again. "Gimme my cap."

She looked down. Lomak's head was still bleeding. The cap lay next to the fuel tank.

"Put it on. Fix the hair, put it on."

Another ragged cough. Disgusted, Brenda reached down. She lifted the hairpiece with two fingers and settled it

in place. She got the cap and set it on Lomak's head. "Push
it down tight." Bent at the knees, Brenda shoved down with
both hands, wanting to hurt. Lomak moaned.

She wiped her palms on her knees. "Do you want some
water?"

"I like it."

"I said, do you want water?"

"Just like a movie." Lomak's hand moved. "Send her postcards from the slammer. Why not, Red? Every week, once
a week. 'How they hangin', Marion? Wheelies in the yard,
Born on the Fourth of July. Just like Tom Cruise. Boogie up my
wheelchair, pimp my ride. Three squares a day. Lift weights
with the brothers in the yard. Get me a wife. Fuck… Give me
any kind of lawyer, I'm out in seven."

Brenda shoved up and looked a last time out to the lake.
He was right. It would be his word against Marion's. Second
degree murder, not first. No premeditation. No intention. A
trial, lots of publicity. Book and movie people would soon
know who was involved—prominent lawyer Marion Ross,
Pulitzer winner Brenda Contay. They would come running,
she knew all about it, from her own book. Knew exactly how
sensational experience got turned into money. The difference
was, she had no daughter. No son, or husband.

Two skinned horses swung lazily in dusty sunlight.

"What did you do at the house!"

No answer. Seeing nothing, hearing no outboard, she
stepped around Lomak, to the controls. She had watched
Charlie. A rocker switch raised and lowered the boat's heavy
motor. She inserted the key, and depressed the switch. An
electric whine. Finger still on the switch, she turned to watch
the glossy engine slowly lever up. Brenda held the switch until
the housing was fully raised. Charlie had done it last night on
their way back, saying this way, the Stratos drew less than a
foot of water.

She used the seat to step up onto the dock, then moved to the stern tie-up rope. She worked the knot open, and not looking down she stepped quickly forward to the piling tied with the bow line. The second knot, pulled tight by pressure, was harder to work open, but she got it untied and stepped back.

It made sense to her. Given more time and the hard current, both ropes might have come loose on their own. But the Statos wasn't moving, still huddled and lodged against the dock.

You don't get off that easy, she thought. You just don't.

Looking away, feeling the cowardice of *not* looking, she sat quickly on the dock and pushed the Stratos with both feet.

She stood now, and watched as the bow was caught by the current. It swung sharply, the stern scraping the dock. No longer snagged, the boat moved fast and cleared the last piling. To bear witness, she stepped to the end and watched the Stratos now whip left. Lomak's hunched form was visible a few seconds, then not as the boat neared the spillway. Once there, it slammed the cement. Now it ricocheted along, *tat-tat-tat*, edging its way along the cement wall.

Did he know?

She heard nothing but the rush of water, the hull's grating, gradual progress, until the boat's bow extended into the spillway. It swung up sharply. Without delay or snag the glossy black hull slid quickly down, the motor last.

CHAPTER

42

Nearing the hill's crest, Schmidt stopped. The gravel footing on the far side would be even worse going down. He balanced on one foot, pulled off a shoe and emptied out stones. He slipped it back on, hopping, and did the other.

He started up again. The shoes dated from another era, Johnston & Murphy wingtips he kept for painting. They had no laces, and for no reason this made him think of Lars Nielson. When the old man didn't wear his dentures, it was like wearing floppy shoes. Maybe Lars was alive, but Schmidt didn't think so. People here lived by routine, like toy trains on a track. It was why the son had come this morning, looking for his father.

He heard birds and looked up. There were streaks of cirrus cloud high up. The sun felt warm despite the cool air. You could have a blizzard, or this, or both at this time of year. Even on the same day. Cold fronts, warm fronts. The idea led him to speed up, the changeable weather making him question leaving Brenda alone. He had not worried about Lomak, but now wasn't sure.

She would be glad to know Marion was back in control. They had found a crew opening the hotel, a phone that worked. Marion was using it now, calling London.

◆◆◆◆◆

The bay's smooth pool had a mesmerizing effect. It was glossy and almost circular, embraced on three sides.

Brenda glanced from it, out again to the lake, the islands. Any time now, people in uniforms with radios would be tying up and stepping onto the dock. They would introduce themselves before helping her down into their boat, or up the hill to take her statement. She had seen the drill often enough and felt ready.

However long it went on, whatever the questions, it was on her. No one else. It was good knowing this. A relief.

She heard a sound and turned to see Charlie skating, sliding down the gravel road, arms out for balance. He knows already, Brenda thought. He comes over the hill and sees you on the empty dock, hands in your pockets as though just figuring out what to do with the day. It was his turf and boat, his house. Some nice woman killed by his houseguest. He would feel responsible, and need something from her. Nothing was his fault. He'd been used, exploited. It must be awful for him, and Brenda watched Charlie running now, down the steep incline, heedless of falling.

The distant whine of an outboard came from her left. She looked out over the bay, but saw nothing. When she turned back, Charlie was standing at the end of the dock, all slit pants and ill-fitting, too-small coat. He was staring at the place where his boat had been, the sleek, black phantom with a praying figure on the floor, replaced by a watery hole in the world.

He looked at her, more reluctant than confused. Brenda stared straight back at him, sure he saw how it had been. She was sure he did, how she'd untied the Stratos, how she sat on the dock and shoved with both feet, the thing rocking out, catching the current, the figure still at prayer as the hull snapped straight and slipped toward the spillway.

He came now, glancing down and back, crossing the hollow dock. His face looked seared.

"Tell me about Marion," she said.

He looked to the lake. "Someone's coming. Maybe Lester Gertz, the Orr sheriff. She's okay, on the phone."

"That's good, but there's more. Lomak did something at her house. Something happens there in seventy-two hours."

He faced her. "We have to get this straight real fast."

"It is straight, Charlie. Just say what you know."

He frowned and shook his head. It made her want to wrap him in her arms. The sweet dunce wanted to make a plan, a story.

He looked back out. "I went up with Marion. I came back and you went up alone. To tell her what Lomak said about her house. I was here, I decided and untied my boat."

"Bullshit, Charlie. This is mine, not yours. Lomak had a plan. Even from prison, he planned to keep it all going."

"Lester's no country bumpkin. We need to keep it simple."

"Charlie—"

"That's it, Brenda. It was my party and my boat. In your place, I might've done the same thing. So that's what I'm saying, that's what happened. Don't say anything else."

"No."

"Yes, and if you say different, I'll tell him you're lying. Hysterical."

"No." Not knowing why, she grabbed his hand and pulled. "Come on—"

He resisted, jaw locked, determined.

"Come on, hurry—"

He let himself be taken, the top of his hand sticky. She understood he was indulging her, not yet understanding.

Yanking his sticky hand, she made him jog with her, off the dock, up the slope. To be out of sight of the arriving help.

"Marion's all right," he said. You don't need to worry."

She didn't answer, desperate now, the approaching boat louder. As they moved she looked back. Still there was nothing, the lake empty, islands static. When they reached the path leading to the lookout, she grabbed his coat and pulled him with her.

"What are you doing? The hotel's straight...Brenda, stop."

He resisted, but she kept pulling, starting to see what might be done, concealment just ten yards away. Five. Breathing hard, she dragged him into the cover of tiered pines and let go of his hand. She dropped on the nearest bench and breathed through her mouth. Again, from this point she could see only slices of water. They were hidden.

"If you're thinking about Heather, I'm sorry but there's nothing—"

"Just shut up." He thought she wanted to see if Heather had lived. She took deep breaths and studied him. She felt challenged, blocked, but at least they were now hidden.

"If there were any chance, I'd be down there." He looked up the slope.

"Down where?"

"At the falls."

"You can get there? From where we are now?"

"On this path. It goes down on the Canadian side, to Rainy Lake."

"You're saying you can get there on foot."

"It takes about ten minutes. It's no good, Brenda. Lester will contact the Park Service, they'll have boats. We can't do anything."

"But we can actually do it. Get there from here on foot."

She stood. Still he didn't follow. He wouldn't, he was a good man and for that reason a bit unimaginative. She knew better and had seen things. Written about them. The motor was louder, and whoever was coming would soon be in the bay, nearing the dock. Finding no one there, they would walk up to the hotel.

"Are there people in Rainy Lake? Fishermen?"

"Could be. If they saw the boat go over, maybe a crowd."

"Is there a clear view? From where we'd come out down there?"

"I don't know. It's usually misty. Why?"

"He was dying."

Finally, the light dawned. "No, Brenda. I don't think so."

"He killed Heather Reese. She has daughters and a son. He plays hockey—"

"That's not— it doesn't matter, it's done."

"It matters. No one saw him. Just you, me and Marion. He managed to get up, I was in the bow, somehow he jumped—"

"Oh, is that right?"

"Stop fighting me and *think*, Charlie. You have daughters, a son."

He turned and started down the slope. Brenda ran in front of him. She turned and pushed his upper body with both hands, backpedaling. He kept coming.

"*No*—" She kept at it until he grabbed her arms. "Really selfish, Charlie, self-centered—"

She kept shoving him with her palms, angry. "I *did* this thing, I *made* this decision. Now you want to hang *tough*, stand tall, all this Eagle Scout *crap*…. I did the easy part, but this is *not* easy, this is something else…Charlie Schmidt, big-time local hero. *Bull*shit!"

He had been trying to pass her, but now stopped.

"That's right," she said and dropped her arms, amazed at herself and breathing hard, knowing from his face how crazy she must look to him. "That's right, it was easy. Making a decision, doing the right thing. I believe that, Charlie. The man killed Heather Reese, we know that. Just like we know what comes next if I didn't do what I did. So, Charlie, *this*, right here, this is the hard part. Right here. Going against your Mr. Nice Guy take-the-blame pledge of allegiance. Let's see it, Charlie, that pledge, show it to me. Does it say anything about your daughters? Your son who gets to sell dad's place and never come here again? What's the pledge say about *them*, Charlie Schmidt? What about *me*!"

He half smiled. "Believe me, you don't know the place."

"I know enough—"

She shoved him again, feeling angry, all in now, having chosen and now driven. "I know if we go right now, down to Rainy Lake, it will end with Lomak. No one else gets hurt. I know this. You did not do this, I did not do this. You took Marion to the hotel, you came back, we took this path to Rainy Lake, hope against hope, looking for Heather. We heard something—"

Maybe it was working. He was no longer moving toward her, pushing back.

"You think Marion won't come to Minnesota?" she said. "Oh, yes, she most certainly will. You think you're the only Eagle Scout? She'd be back here on visitor's day and Christmas and Groundhog Day—every fucking time her conscience rings the bell— 'Hello, Marion, time to go chat up Charlie Schmidt in some jerkoff prison, the guy your client screwed for keeps.'"

Maybe it was working. "And Tina, Charlie—"

"You really—" Still loosely holding her upper arms, he was studying her now, his own face a mix of fascination and disgust.

"Really what, Charlie? Really *what*? Tell you what you don't want to hear? What you didn't think of? Too bad. That's right. Tina, Charlie. Whose only close friend is no more— Tina back in Milwaukee—"

"Don't leave out the dog—"

"—reflecting on recent events. Oh yes, of course, it will be a whole lot better knowing Charlie Schmidt's in prison. Getting corrected for *what?* Oh yes, that'll be good, a real comfort."

She watched his good face stuck with adhesive and thread, looking for signs that her blackmail and sabotage were working. *And what about me?* But in the moment she sensed as Charlie now sighed, getting where she wanted him to go, that whatever might have been waiting for them, to be found or created, would not be. Not now.

She took his hands in both of hers and squeezed hard. He let her. The motor below had slowed, and in the following seconds fell silent. Someone would be tying up, looking around. If there were two, one would go up to the hotel, the other stay on the dock. Marion would tell them what had happened, and they would have radios. Call and ask whoever was on the dock about Charlie and a second woman. No sign of them here would be the answer.

That's right. She yanked Charlie by the hand. No sign. He was still making her pull him, and she was breathing hard again, conscious of being out of shape. But now he seemed to decide, came alongside and began trudging next to her, holding her hand.

It revived her. They moved higher. The falls grew loud. It was as she remembered it and this, too, gave her something. Petting-the-dog, the good guy—Brenda held him close, marching. Give me this, she thought. Don't change your mind.

She let go and put her arm through his as they neared the lookout. "I knew there was something wrong with him," she said. "Yesterday. When he came over to help Heather and me. He had to impress us. Show us what he knew, but he couldn't. He was clumsy, he fell getting into our boat, it made him angry. He comes over to these two women, he falls on his ass—"

"Don't talk," he said. "This is wrong."

"The hell it is."

He mustn't quit on her. Brenda kept him close, measuring her steps to his. "I mean, it *is*. Of course, all of it. But, Charlie, that's why the rules aren't for this. The rules are for something else."

"No, they're for everything." He shook his head, rejecting what she had said. But still he was matching his steps to hers.

"Not for this. And don't you back out on me, because I *will* say you weren't there, Charlie. I mean it. I'll tell them what happened and then this Lester, this sheriff will be stuck. And so will Marion. I mean it, I'll do it."

"I see you mean it," he said.

"You and Marion went to the hotel. When you came back, we did this, what we're doing right now. We went up and over, down to Rainy Lake. For Heather. You knew it was hopeless, but you humored me. We heard something and when we got there, we saw whatever it is. Say yes."

"All right."

"We don't know what happened. When we got to the Canadian side, that's when we knew." When they passed the gravel path to the lookout site, she made him stop. "We should look, Charlie. We wouldn't make this walk and not look down."

He was letting her decide now, walking passively. Every time their eyes met, Charlie's had a look about them. Discovery, suspicion. But he had decided, and he now followed her through the narrow funnel in the foliage, bright at the end. She remembered how it had been, a railed deck twenty feet square, braced above the falls. But you could see to the dock from the north side. As they approached, Brenda turned and blocked the way.

"Don't do anything, Charlie. Stay off the north side. We have to be careful. All we want is to see what's in Rainy Lake. We're looking for Heather."

He nodded. They passed out onto the bright platform, quickly stepped to the railing and looked down. It fumed below—massive boulders and tree trunks in a brothy haze. She felt again the power of movement under her feet, a hypnotic tumble of brown water falling, drifting down. Bearing no resemblance to anything else, the hull of the Stratos, bottom up, glistened below. It appeared to be intact. She did not see bodies.

"One thing, Charlie—"

Hands on the railing, looking down, after several seconds he turned to her. She saw he was going to make her do all of it, seeing again the mix of interest and disgust about his eyes and mouth. Some of the thousand-plus muscles in the human face were eloquently letting her know what he was thinking, as he waited for the one thing.

"Did we see your boat from here or not? Had it already gone over, or later?"

"Later. Otherwise, he didn't have enough time after we left."

"To do what?"

"You tell me."

"He was paralyzed. I got the keys from him to raise the motor."

"It could have already been raised."

"An autopsy would show his wounds made it impossible for him to get up and untie the boat." She looked at Charlie's hand on the rail. "He was a klutz. A fuckup. He tied the ropes wrong, they came loose. I didn't do it, you didn't, he tied a granny knot and it came loose."

She wanted them to be together, united. Nothing changed in his face.

"Don't make this harder, Charlie. You don't know what he planned." Brenda remembered. "God, the house, something about blowing her house, and seventy-two hours. This is not everything. But I made a decision, Charlie, no one should have to go through what was coming. This is a bad thing that needs to be done. You have to help."

He looked back out. For the first time, following his gaze she saw fishermen, three boats clustered at one end of a small island. It was a painting, Hudson River school. Everything below was bathed in fresh light, a watery maze of islands and shore, perfectly blue water.

Holding her hair back, Brenda now looked straight down. She felt shock and disgust. She had killed someone, and now she was seeing a painting. But there was no sign of others below, no curiosity seekers near the falls.

Looking back out, she saw the three boats were at anchor, two people in each. One man made a cast, then a second man. The two graceful, whip-like gestures came close together—men lost in thought or talk, watching their lures, reeling in. It filled her with hope, a sense of victory. Half a mile from the violence of the falls, sportsmen were enjoying themselves, oblivious.

It would work. She felt ashamed, but it would work. She had killed someone, Jerry Lomak had not been dead until she untied the ropes and sent him over the falls. And it didn't matter that he had seemed to say he wanted her to do it. Wanted his hair on right and his cap, for his last big scene.

Charlie straightened and moved quickly toward the tunnel of foliage. Brenda followed. She thought he saw it now. Right or wrong, he understood and agreed with her.

"We came here," she said. "We looked down and didn't see anything—"

Moving behind him, she glanced down again at his shoes. They had no laces, and she saw Jerry Lomak jumping, his shoe catching. She would see it forever. Charlie kept moving and didn't answer. But his own idea was now part of the plan—they had not seen his boat from the lookout.

CHAPTER

43

"**Brittany, this** is Mrs. Ross. Yes, hi, please put Carrie on..."

By the time Brenda and Charlie reached the hotel, Marion had regained her take-charge self. She had been questioned by Sheriff Gertz, and as Gertz questioned the two of them, Marion had reached her husband in London. He and Jay would leave on an afternoon flight. Now, Marion was calling Carrie.

"Brittany, I can't talk about the trip now, please get Carrie.... She *what?* Walked home when? Clean clothes? She had plenty of clothes..."

Seated in the hotel's dining room, Brenda now stood.

"Dammit, never mind, put your mother on, I... Shopping, of course, that's perfect, that's all she's ever done in her whole life, what's her cell number..." Brenda crossed quickly to the lobby. "Brittany, how the *hell* can you not know your own mother's cell number!"

She took the phone. "Hi, Brittany, this is Brenda Contay, Mrs. Ross's friend."

"Stupid girl!" Marion glared at her, looking trapped.

"Did I do something wrong?" the girl asked. "I mean she just walked home, I don't—"

"No, Brittany, she's not mad at you, she's just worried—"
Marion was staring at something, seeing something. Her
face now seemed to lose shape and collapse. Her shoulders
dropped, and she began heaving for breath.

"Just a second." Brenda put down the handset and wrapped
her arms around her friend. Marion was now hyperventilating,
and it was scary.

"I see it! I see everything!"

"Please, Mar, Carrie's fine, she just walked home, it's
nothing."

"I know exactly how he thinks, I see it! That's what
Lomak meant—"

Marion was now struggling to get free. "I have to go, I
have to get there! *Let go of me!*" Brenda held on, hearing and
feeling the most capable person she knew going to pieces.
Seated at another table, Sheriff Gertz and Charlie got up and
now came from the dining room.

"Damn you, let go, you don't see it, you don't understand—"

"See what?" Marion was twisting, pushing.

"You said seventy-two hours—let me go! You said seventy-two hours, you said there's someone else."

"He was crazy, he's dead, Marion, he can't hurt anyone now."

She let go and Marion spun away, blocked now by the
two men. She began shaking her head. "There's no one else,"
she said. "It's all him, no one else, it's all Lomak. I know what
he did, I see it, I know him." Wild-eyed, head still shaking,
Marion was again seeing something in her mind's eye.

"*Space station.*"

"I don't understand."

"You told us he said something about a space station."

"He was babbling, he was fantasizing about writing a book."

Marion's chest rose and fell. She looked at all three of
them, but now glared at Gertz. "It's part of his plan, it's
how a loser wins, you can't see it. Lomak worked for the

gas company, before he snaked out sewers he worked for MichCon. God!"

Between them, the two men began helping her to the door leading to the hotel porch. "You have to find my daughter, she went to the house, he planned everything!"

The door opened and closed, but Brenda could still hear Marion's voice—shouting, pleading. She remembered Lomak humped in front of the outboard motor. *Get an agent, seventy-two hours, fucking space station...* The last thing had made no sense to her, but everything else did—the talk of a book, sending postcards from prison. Brenda watched her friend through the lobby window being led down the stairs—remembered the phone, and picked it up.

"Brittany, it's me again. Mrs. Ross isn't sick," she said. "There may be a problem at the Rosses' house, that's why she's concerned about Carrie."

"She left like maybe a half hour ago."

"I see. Okay, Brittany, tell your mom to call when she comes in, will you do that?"

"Sure, but—"

"And Brittany, this is important. Do *not* go near the Ross house, stay where you are."

"Don't you want—"

"No, please, Brittany, don't do anything and stay where you are. The police will handle it. So whatever you do, stay where you are, and have your mom call the number I'm going to give you, got a pencil?"

She waited. At the base of the porch stairs, sobbing and broken, a different Marion was being supported on the front drive. Gertz was using his cell phone. It was awful, a strong person needing others to help her and tell her what to do. Like Doreen Taylor.

She gave the hotel number, handwritten on a piece of tape someone had stuck to the cradle of the old-style phone. She looked again to the window, and as she repeated the number, a pickup truck appeared.

She said goodbye as the truck came to a stop. The men guided Marion to the open door.

Watching her get in, Brenda thought of the Ross house. It was spacious and refined, a thing of beauty. She saw Carrie Ross going up the graceful staircase to her room. You've seen it, Brenda thought. A teenager's room full of rock posters and stuffed animals. Last year, a gas explosion had caused six houses to blow up on a street in a Detroit suburb. All but one of the houses had been empty. But a young mother, and two children she was home-schooling had been killed. An ugly story, the street cordoned off, littered with toys and bricks, pieces of furniture. They didn't put such images on local news broadcasts—not yet—but someone had posted to YouTube a photo of a child's severed foot in a shoe. It was the kind of story she had covered before leaving tabloid TV.

Gertz slammed the pickup's door, and the truck moved off toward the road to the dock. Brenda crossed the lobby and stepped out. The sheriff and Charlie were talking now. Gertz nodded, and Charlie started jogging across the lawn. A good sign. He had asked permission to do something, and Gertz had said yes. The sheriff watched him a moment, then turned and crossed to the stairs.

"He's going down and help with the second recovery." Gertz came up.

"Someone's taking Marion to the landing?"

"Right now, there's a boat waiting. They got an EMS back there, they'll give her something."

Brenda raised her pack of Marlboros. He nodded—more permission—then went inside. She lit up and watched through the window as he sat again at a table in the dining room. He raised his phone, and resumed writing on a legal pad.

Maybe it's nothing, Brenda thought, watching him. Maybe it's only this up here. All this insanity, and Marion's just lost it. Except Marion knew Lomak. So did she, in a way. Just for ten or fifteen minutes, but she'd seen him in action, heard him—an actor, a poseur playing cowboy, impressing the ladies…

She turned away and moved to the handrail. Two men were scrubbing awnings on the sunny lawn. One said something, and his partner looked to the hotel. On hands and knees, he dropped his head and mumbled an answer. Both men were using wooden brushes, dipping them in buckets of frothy water. No, she thought. Boys in their teens, not men. Working on a weekday in early May probably meant they were dropouts. But what did she know about it? Or anything else here? School in northern Minnesota might have a different calendar.

Please let Carrie Ross live—

She realized what she was doing. Praying. *Please let Carrie Ross live.* She never prayed. Ever. It was hypocritical and empty of her to pray, but that's what she was doing, *please keep Carrie safe—*

She lit a cigarette, feeling chilly in the shade of the battleship-gray porch. Something would happen in seventy-two hours. But seventy-two hours beginning when? If the time started on Friday, that meant whatever Lomak had planned was meant to take place today. While he was on his way out of the country.

Again Brenda turned. Framed in the lounge window, Sheriff Gertz was still talking on his phone. Nodding. Waiting.

Everyone called him Sheriff, or Lester. He had sat opposite in a rocker with his legal pad, a booted foot on his knee, asking questions as they repeated their story. The two men clearly knew each other, but that had not made Brenda confident. Seated next to Charlie on a worn leather couch in the lounge, she had fought hard to not look at him. If she did, Gertz would glance up from his legal pad, see she was seeking support, and immediately know she was lying.

Now, what she had done seemed unimportant. Trivial. As the sheriff talked inside, Brenda studied his profile. Gertz no longer looked like a local yokel to her. He looked deceptive. Intelligent. With a fleshy face you sometimes saw on thin men. Maybe Charlie would tell him his own made-up version later, when she was gone. She imagined the two alone at the table inside, Charlie leaning on his elbows, starting in on his fake confession. Local to local.

Again Brenda turned and faced the lawn. She had a strong impulse to step down and talk to the two boys, anything for distraction. No, she mustn't, that would lead to questions. Everyone knew everyone here, the parks and rec people, the deputy with Gertz. All of them were potential sources of information about the redhead with Charlie Schmidt.

Smoking, and perhaps for that reason, Brenda now thought of the husband in his garage, Brian Senior back in Milwaukee. He raised his safety goggles and turned off the table saw as someone began telling him the news. He too was smoking, and very deliberately stubbed out his cigarette in the smokeless ashtray.

The door opened behind her. Gertz stepped out, put on his broad hat and closed the door. "Your friend's on her way to the landing," he said. "We got a second boat coming in now, to take you. Gustofson put someone on that houseboat, it's underway, too."

"Our friend is on it," she said. "Tina Bostwick. If it's all right, I'd like to go back with her."

"That'll work, and it'll be better if what else we need to do gets done back there." Gertz shouldered into his brown Eisenhower jacket. He came forward, and waited for her to take the steps before following. "By then we may have the second recovery. Stevie?"

One of the awning scrubbers looked up. "Wyan't you get that other pickup and drive this lady down to the dock. Can you do that, please?"

The boy stood and waved. He ran forward shaking soapy water from his hands. During the interview, one of the Canadians had come up and talked to Lester about grappling hooks. They had found Lomak's body, but not Heather's, and the idea was gruesome to her—dragging Rainy Lake with hooks. What seemed the most respectful, the most humane thing would be to leave Heather Reese to return to the elements. It was how Tina Bostwick had imagined her own death, before changing her mind.

"I would think you want to make some calls yourself," Gertz said. "That'll be easier from the landing." He walked with her along the path, head down. "Now, Mrs. Ross will fly home, and you'll follow with your vehicle tomorrow."

"If that's allowed," Brenda said.

"Gus will help you on that, getting to Milwaukee."

"If that's all right."

"Can't be sure just yet, but where we are now, I don't see a problem. But you and Mrs. Ross will need to come back, say in a week or ten days."

"I understand."

"There'll be the paperwork, and the state troopers will have something to say, but they'll mostly rely on me."

They waited in silence on the sunny drive. Add nothing, Brenda thought. Volunteer nothing.

"The Birmingham police say a Doreen Taylor died Friday night," Gertz said. "She was Lomak's girlfriend. He burned her house, she died from the smoke. Your Oakland County people faxed Lomak's sheet. He was up for sentencing this week."

"Marion said it was this Thursday."

"It could happen a lot more than it does," Gertz said. "Going after the lawyer. Why wasn't he in the county lockup?"

"I think it was his first offense."

"Too bad. If they'd of looked at his Navy discharge, maybe this wouldn't of happened. Well—"

A second pickup came from behind the hotel. "You just go on now with Stevie. I'll see you sometime this afternoon." He touched his hat, and began walking back toward the hotel. The truck was crossing the lawn, tire tracks a darker green marking its progress.

"Miss Contay? Just one more thing."

He was waiting at the base of the stairs. Heart pounding, Brenda walked back toward Gertz, studying his face. He had delayed until she was alone, to throw her off and build false confidence. Now, Gertz would tell her he knew she was lying. She stopped in front of him.

"I talked to the chief in Birmingham, I told him what Mrs. Ross thinks Lomak might've done. It sort of fits with the house he torched. Birmingham police and fire are coordinating, they're getting a bomb detail ready."

"What about Carrie? The daughter?"

"Well," Gertz said, "she's in the house or she isn't. By the time Mrs. Ross gets to the landing, someone should have more." He touched his hat again, and went up the stairs.

Did you untie the rope? He had not asked her. Flushed with relief, Brenda walked quickly to the pickup. As she got in and slammed the door, she felt it was going to work. For no reason, Charlie being allowed to help search for Heather convinced her.

Then she remembered Carrie.

The truck reached the gravel road and started down. "Charlie's boat," the driver said. "You saw it go over?"

"Heard it first," she said. "We were on the trail to the Canadian side. I insisted we go, just in case. Charlie said there was no hope but I insisted. Then we heard this hollow boom. You couldn't see from the trail, but it was there when we reached the Canadian side."

Shut up, she thought. Too much detail, too much talk. But that was their story. Where the path to Rainy Lake ended at the water's edge, side by side they had stood on matted bark, mounded with froth from the falls. In a shower of sun and vapor they had been able to make out Charlie's boat. The hull had stood upended in boulders, the motor gone.

"Never happened since sometime like in the forties."

Brenda looked at him. The boy was hunched forward, the truck now creeping down at a steep angle. For the first time, she saw he had a large purple birthmark on his neck.

"It's posted all over," he said. "You have to want to go over, almost. People come to Voyageur's, they got a lot of maps and brochures. It's not like parks where you have RVs and day-trippers. You have to want to be here. People know about the falls."

He was defending the place against outsiders. Brenda sat back, and they rode in silence. At the base of the hill the driver eased to a stop. She got out and thanked him, slammed the door, then walked toward the dock. Seated on one of the benches, a man in uniform now stood and raised a radio.

As she neared, he lowered it. "Sheriff Gertz says to put you on the houseboat."

◆◆◆◆◆

In three minutes, she could see it, cream-colored and top-heavy. It looked like a huge mobile home, lifted in a tornado and dropped where it least belonged. As they neared, Brenda saw Brian Reese's boat trailing behind, still mounded with bedding. The canoe was where she had left it. She would have to tell Gus Gustofson.

The driver was again using his radio. Seated on the padded engine cover, Brenda now stood. She worked her way to the cabin, grabbed a handgrip. "Are you talking to the houseboat?" He nodded. "Ask if the woman onboard knows anything."

He brought up the mike. "Yeah, Dean, the lady there? Anyone talk to her about this?"

"She knows what happened at Charlie Schmidt's, not the falls."

"Okay, good." He looked at Brenda. "You still want on?" She nodded, and he again raised the mike. "Yeah, Dean, hold up a minute."

She worked her way back to the motor cover. It had an official seal, eagles rampant with talons gripping gold spears. She sat, seeing for the first time the boat's equipment, tools and instruments she couldn't name. All the ropes were arranged in perfect circles on the spotless deck. It was serious to her. Military and threatening.

◆◆◆◆◆

Two minutes later, they reached the houseboat. As the launch slowed, Brenda saw boats with fishermen, off the south shore. Men in one of the boats waved, and without thinking, she returned the wave. It was crazy, she dropped her hand. She had killed someone, and was waving. But it was just the ordinary world reasserting itself, where people woke to rain. Then conditions changed, and they went fishing.

Someone Gustofson had sent now stepped out onto the stern of the houseboat. The launch nudged forward. As it touched the houseboat's bumper, Brenda stood and gripped the driver's arm. She stepped across, and was helped down from the transom. She turned, shielding her eyes as the launch drifted back.

"Is she up front?" The launch now rose and swung away.

"Pretty cold there, from the broken window. She's in one of the back cabins."

BARRY KNISTER

Still looking out, she waited for him to enter. What to say? What *not* to say? That she had taken a life? Taken it for herself? *What about me!*

Seconds later, vibration came underfoot as the big outboards began to rev. A sluggish wake formed off the stern. Tied there, Brian Reese's runabout now swung sharply. The current had taken Charlie's Stratos in just that way, to the lip of the spillway. The rope rose from the surface, and the small boat drew in behind.

Ties that bind. Someone had said the two halves of Karma were the cards you were dealt, and how you played them. Brenda sensed herself using whatever was at hand. Words, images, catch phrases.

She turned away, entered and closed the door. Gently she knocked on Tina's cabin. The dog barked. "No, Sonny. Come in, Brenda."

She was propped in her bunk, Sonny at her side. The wheelchair stood crowded against the washstand. The engines grew louder, impossible with the door open. Brenda got the wheelchair and scissored it closed. She rolled it out into the passage, went back in and closed the door.

She moved to the end of the cabin and leaned against the closet. "Heather's dead."

Tina nodded. "I thought she must be. The boats and police. No Heather."

"She. Drowned."

Tina looked out her window. Dappled water was now sliding past. "Do you think she suffered?"

"Yes, but not long."

Brenda fixed on the force of moving water outside. To think about what might already have happened to Carrie Ross, or what she herself had done—it would do to her what had happened to Marion. Then she would be useless. To herself and others.

"Not long," Tina said. "That's something. I didn't think he would hurt them. For some reason, I just didn't. He was loud. He wanted to frighten us, wanted attention. For some reason I just didn't think he would really do anything like that. I wanted him to take me, but he wouldn't. He knew I didn't care. He needed people with families."

She looked from the window. "Charlie Schmidt?"

"He's helping the Canadian police."

"A decent man. You thought he was part of it."

"I was wrong."

"I wish I were closer to her husband and son." Tina reached down and scratched Sonny behind the ears. He raised his head, eyes closed. "Maybe it's better I'm not. I know them, but Heather's the connection. Have they been told?"

"I don't know. You and I will drive back tomorrow."

"I'm very glad you'll be there. I'm a real baby at such times."

"So am I."

"Two cowards," she said. "Strength in numbers."

Watching Tina with the dog, her lined face full of consciousness, Brenda felt bold. There was no need to pity her. "I am not decent," she said. "But I am resourceful. Some would say opportunistic."

"Decent and resourceful aren't mutually exclusive."

"What happened is bad and ugly. There's more and I'll tell you, but not now."

"No, not now."

They were silent. Brenda watched Sonny being scratched and felt jealous of the dog's pleasure. Its simplicity. "Tina dying," she said finally. "I feel cheated. But this is what I want to say and then I'm going to clean up. What I got in meeting her is meeting you, I—"

"You said Tina, you know."

Brenda looked up from the dog.

"You used my name instead of Heather's."

"The point—"

"You're worried about me and made a slip," Tina said. "I find that very moving, Brenda. It reveals what I think you want to say."

"Tina…"

"No, go ahead."

"Not coming here would have meant not meeting you. But now—"

Tina smiled the slightest of smiles. "You're afraid, because of what happened, I'll see your interest in me as some do-gooder act."

"Yes. That's exactly right. And it's important to me that you know I made up my mind yesterday, before all this. You and I got to a point so fast, it meant something. Heather, too, that's my regret. We had one or two talks. I almost wish we hadn't."

Tina took a deep breath, and let it out. "I can tell you this. She admired you. Before the man came this morning, I was up, we were having coffee. She told me what you said before taking the canoe. About us all being types. It's true, Brenda. Until you know someone, that person is just a handful of details. And I'm full of regret you only knew Heather that way."

Tina looked down at the sleeping dog, still stroking him. "If you want to come see me, come see me," she said. "I never would consider you a do-gooder."

CHAPTER

44

Another way to Rainy Lake led down from the service area in back of the hotel. It was a staircase made from railroad ties, and as Schmidt reached the top step he saw a tractor with reel mowers was now parked on the gravel. Next to it, the kitchen's big smoker grills had been scrubbed and opened to dry.

He moved down the drive toward the main building, then along the hotel's north end to the front greensward. The red and white striped awnings were gone from the lawn. He looked up and saw they were now in place, over the upstairs windows.

Preparations for the summer season, and the sameness from year to year gave him something like confidence. Schmidt moved along the front walk. A flagpole rose on his left, surrounded by flowerbeds. There was too much sun here for impatiens, so they planted petunias or dahlias.

What the hell was wrong with him? People had died, people might still die, and he was thinking about flowers. He looked up, walking, and saw the flag was still missing. The ordinariness of his thoughts seemed…disrespectful. Out of touch. She killed someone, he thought. Never mind why, that's what she did.

He reached the porch stairs and went up, seeing Lester inside. He was talking with Chuck Anders' boy, Stevie. Crossing the porch, Schmidt knew what had to be done. He would get it over with, right now. They had been his guests, his party and his boat, and he had sent it over the falls. But as Schmidt reached the door, the boy with Lester glanced to the window. He had his cap on backwards, like Schmidt's son Andy, before he got serious. Charlie let himself in.

"Those times," Gertz said, pointing at a card in his hand. He gave it to Stevie and looked over. "I hear they made recovery." Schmidt closed the door as the sheriff turned back to the boy. "Got that now? You give the card to Carl, so he knows which calls and who to bill."

"Okay." The boy started for the back entrance.

"Cold?" Gertz said. "You look like a man could make use of some whisky." He folded a sheet of paper and tucked it in his inside jacket pocket. "Come on, I'll buy. We'll bill the county."

A door opened and closed at the far end of the dining room. Gertz followed where Stevie had gone, Schmidt behind him.

"We reached the deceased's husband," he said. "Her friend in the wheelchair knew where he works, we got him there. He's an underwriter for Northwestern insurance. You use them?"

"Travelers."

"Yeah, they merged with someone, I think. The husband had some family between here and Duluth, they're coming for the boat. This Lomak mention anything about family?"

"A girl."

"Doreen Taylor. No, that doesn't work. He torched her house on Friday night, before he left Michigan. You say him and this Rohmer flew in the next day."

"About three, they said. I got there after dark."

The passage ended at stairs leading down to the bar. Gertz took them and moved along the part of the floor that was level. Charlie followed as Gertz raised the hinged bar top and creaked over duckboards. "They got their priorities straight here. No water yet, and still on the generator for electric, but they got the bar set up."

He lifted a lowball glass from a pyramid of clean glasses under the mirror, and held it up to the light. He blew in it and set it down. "Ever tend bar?"

"Short-order cook," Charlie said. "After the service."

"What you want?"

"Well bourbon is good."

Gertz looked down. "Nope, nothing in the well yet. You get to go premium." He turned back and reached for the Wild Turkey. "Was Lomak on the sauce?"

"He drank. Mostly beer. How's John Nielson?"

"Didn't talk to him. We divvied it up with the troopers, them to your place and us out here. They towed your utility to the landing for the coroner. Last I heard, they sent John home. What do you bet he's out in the barn, working on lawn mowers? I'm glad we divvied it that way."

Gertz poured and put down the bottle. "That way they get to sort out what's what with the plane."

Schmidt sipped his whisky. "I forgot about that."

"Yeah, well, not at the top of your list today." Gertz braced both hands on his hips and stretched. "I bet that woman *never* leaves home again."

"Not the daughter—"

Gertz shook his head and dropped his shoulders. "Still waiting on that," he said. "First they want to evacuate the neighbor houses. My guys put the mother on a plane, the troopers said she could go. If Mrs. Ross isn't just crazy worried, it would fit with the house he torched in Hazel Park.

Taking care of business, tying up loose ends. He did work for the gas company."

Schmidt sipped his whisky. It was like some new weapon to go with smart bombs and video war. A device with different times and places, going off whether you were alive or not.

"I don't suppose we're going to find out why they killed Lars Nielson," Gertz said. "Gustofson says this Rohmer sent a check to the landing. For a rental car he wanted to drive to Canada. From what Mrs. Ross told me, Rohmer planned to cut his buddy loose, soon as they made the wire transfer to Costa Rica."

Gertz disappeared below the counter and opened a cabinet. He snapped it closed and came up holding a can of Coke.

"The medical examiner called, I passed on what Mrs. Ross said about the anchor wounds." He popped the top. "Yeah, money or no money, to see that—" He shook his head.

"See your friend go over. I guess, though, she didn't actually see it. She was throwing float cushions, then she put him down with your anchor."

Schmidt couldn't think about it. He saw John Nielson kneeling in front of him, pulling at duct tape, his father dead. But Lester was right about him. By now, John would be fixing mowers out in his father's barn. He would still wave to Charlie Schmidt up here. Help put in the dock in the spring. But it would be different. Full of things both of them were thinking, and couldn't say.

"Yeah, plenty angry," Lester said. "And your lady friend. If it was someone I knew, I think I just might untie that rope and sing Nearer My God to Thee all the way home."

"But she didn't."

"I'm talking about myself," Gertz said. "Show up and hear all this shit? What Lomak already did and still had planned? Alone with him? Sheriff or no, yeah, that's maybe what I'd do. Which would explain the keys still in the ignition. They told me, when they found the motor it was angled up, that's how your Stratos cleared the spillway. But that's all just speculation, Charlie, and you don't need to say anything at all here. And you shouldn't, because you and Miss Contay had your say clear enough, don't you think? How's Andy doing?"

Gertz drank from his Coke in a long swallow, expecting no answer. He lowered the can and sighed. "She wouldn't say, being a lawyer, but five'll get you ten Mrs. Ross would agree with me. Especially if her house goes up."

CHAPTER

45

It was almost three when she finished her shower in the upper-deck bath.

Toweling off, Brenda looked out at the Canadian shoreline. She remembered Sunday morning, how she had showered as the big boat slowly worked its way through the Ash River. With the skylight hatch open, she had felt a sense of welcome. Even intimacy. Now, toweling her hair and looking out at the lake's shoreline, she felt all nature holding her at arm's length. Sunny and alert, it was now a thing apart.

She swung at the waist to inspect the baby-pink scar against white skin, where they had removed her left kidney five years ago. Her butt still looked decent. The boys washing awnings had checked her out. Men still turned on the street when she passed, interested enough to see whether the promise of her face and hair carried over to the flip side. Facing forward, she decided it pretty much did, and would a while longer.

It had to do with people dying, looking at herself this way. She rubbed her hair hard with the towel. If she bothered to keep track, it would probably turn out that such body inspections occurred after funerals, or visits to hospitals. After reading certain news stories.

Enough. She hung up the towel, pulled on fresh panties and a tee shirt, then stepped out and moved to her cabin. It was less chilly up here, all the windows closed, the sun heating up the roof. She got clean jeans from her bag and pulled them on, then reached for the black cashmere turtleneck.

No, not black. Black would somehow help the worst thing to be true. Brenda stuffed the sweater back in, pulled out and slipped on her green chamois-cloth shirt. Her feet were still slightly orange from the soggy boat shoes. After buttoning the shirt, she found her Nikes under the tin sink and shoved into them. She knelt to tie the laces.

Lomak jumped and fell.

Finished, she stepped across to Marion's cabin and began collecting things from hangers and drawers. She laid the clothes on the bed and started refolding shirts, sweaters. Shrinks called it displacement. Channeling disturbing thoughts into action. Most of the clothes were familiar to her from fall dinners on the Rosses' patio, or at her own A-frame cottage in Port Sheldon. Sometimes, Carrie was there.

If she lived, if she was not maimed or killed, those times were not over. She crossed the arms of Marion's red crewneck. If Carrie was all right, Brenda Contay and Marion Ross would remain friends. For a time, when she saw Marion in the fisherman's knit sweater, or in the bathing suit—it was still damp from yesterday—if Marion was in this same one-piece Speedo and pulling herself up out of her backyard pool, just as Brenda stopped her car on the driveway and got out, there would be a moment of confusion. If Brenda was quick to smile and wave, her friend wouldn't notice. Such moments would weaken. Each new time would be more easily remedied with a quick switch to different topics, waiting distractions.

But otherwise, looking at each other would be impossible. Every time, forever, they would remind each other of Carrie. Of something too awful. Too dark.

Balled socks lay in the bunk's open drawer. Brenda got them and tossed them on the bed. She set her friend's leather duffle on the bed, spread it, and placed the folded clothes side by side in two stacks. A plastic shoe bag with drawstring had been stuffed into one of the pouches. She tugged it out and shoved in the wet bathing suit. She wedged the bag in the corner, the socks, Marion's running shoes, her robe. She zipped it closed, then looked around for more to do.

Heather's things, she thought. That's why you're taking so long up here.

Brenda moved the duffle bag, and sat on the bed. She braced with her hands, feeling the bunk's rigid wooden frame behind her knees. Beside her, Heather Reese sat clumsily. Her pants were down around her ankles. Her eyes were pinched shut, and she was laughing.

◆◆◆◆◆

"**So many.** Where'd they come from?"

The stern door slapped shut as Tina angled her chair and locked the wheels. On the right, men and children were standing on docks, women with arms crossed outside cottage door walls. All were watching the houseboat slip past, a crowded *tableau vivant* of figures frozen in the moment.

Brenda stepped to the starboard catwalk, and looked ahead to the landing. Patrol-car lights flashed in the parking lot. Now she saw Janey Gustofson. She was standing alone on the dock's broad loading area, smoking. If anything, she looked even less believably the mother of three. She was wearing an oversized sweatshirt and a cap, and kept flicking her cigarette.

"Where's Marion?" Tina asked.

"Probably on a plane."

A police car pulled away as a man in coveralls came around the lodge. Then another. As the giant houseboat slowed, the two men reached Janey. She said something, and they moved to ready lines at either end of the platform.

Brenda looked again to Gustofson's wife. She kept dragging on the cigarette, raising and lowering it. There was something else. She wasn't waiting on the dock out of courtesy, it was something else.

The big outboards growled and the boat's forward motion slowed to a stop. One of the men secured his line. He backed away and lifted the loading ramp as his partner slipped the second rope over a piling. The first man dragged the ramp to the stern and dropped it in place with a loud thud. He walked on board and swung open the gate. Sonny trotted across.

"Ready?"

Tina nodded and unlocked her wheels. He moved behind her and shoved her ashore.

Janey had grabbed Sonny's collar. "Are you all right?" Holding the dog, she knelt beside the wheelchair, her child's face shadowed by the cap, thick blond hair tucked behind her ears.

"I am, thank you."

She stood and the man pushed the chair up the incline. Sonny strained, but Janey held him close. She looked to the boat. "Your friend had to go back."

"I know." Brenda came down the ramp.

"It's not her, it's back home. Her daughter. I didn't get it all, but she went to her family's house, and there's something wrong there."

Fucking space station—

Brenda looked to Tina as someone inside swung open the shop's door. She was wheeled in, the door fell shut.

"Your friend—"

She faced Janey. "Marion Ross."

"Marion, that's it. The troopers drove her to I Falls—International Falls. To catch the plane to Milwaukee." Still holding the dog, Janey dropped her cigarette and stepped on it. "I wish, you know, I could help. She was really, you know—" She spun a finger. "I would be the same, that's for sure. She doesn't know where her daughter is. Carrie? She called this…" Janey snapped her fingers, closed her eyes.

"Brittany Remnick."

"Called Brittany, and Brittany said Carrie still didn't come back. So Marion was really concerned on that. I think she wants you to keep calling the police in Birmingham." Janey stuffed her free hand in her hip pocket and waited.

All at once, Brenda felt disoriented and dizzy. Maybe it had to do with stepping on land. More than anything, she realized she was starving. "My friend hasn't eaten today," she said. "Neither have I."

"Pardon?" Janey took her hand from her pocket. "Oh, sure, no problem. We can order out or I can get you something like soup. There's leftover spaghetti."

"It must sound crazy to you, after what's happened. I'm sorry."

"No, I don't think that at all. Not after everything out there. You come with me." Back on solid ground, Janey Gustofson and Sonny led the way up the incline. "Or we can grill some brats, I could make a salad."

"You have customers," Brenda said. "Just show me where things are, we'll manage."

CHAPTER

46

As the family business grew, the Gustofsons had added on to the original lodge. Convenience store, tackle and gift shop, a dormitory for summer employees. Their own rooms were reached through a narrow passage leading from the store.

Brenda made her call to the Birmingham police from the all-purpose kitchen-family room. Tina was there in her chair, looking out, Sonny lying next to her. A big picture window framed the dock and river.

"Please hold."

Below the loading incline, the huge houseboat stood motionless. Brenda paced, phone clamped to her ear, watching as the two workers continued unloading, stacking everything on a handcart.

The desk officer came on. "Yes, I'm calling on behalf of Marion Ross, I'm Brenda Contay, a friend of the family. I need to know whether you've gone into the Ross house.'"

"Hold on... Okay, I see your name here. You're in Minnesota?"

"Yes."

"The bomb unit didn't go in yet," he said. "The mayor and chief decided to hold off—"

"God, *Why?*" No, Brenda thought, and pinched her eyes shut. Never challenge cops.

"If you give me a chance, I'll tell you," he said. "We're waiting on two MichCon technicians, coming from Flint. The mayor and chief decided the gas company techs can better assess the risk before we start making people leave their houses."

Local politics. Before making people leave their houses in upscale Birmingham, the mayor wanted to be sure it was necessary. Brenda hung up as Janey Gustofson pushed buttons to microwave leftover spaghetti. She opened a bread box and pulled out a plastic bag of rolls, then pointed to the overhead cabinets. Brenda nodded and Janey left.

The microwave shut down. Starving again, she found a potholder and got out the spaghetti. She opened an overhead cabinet, got down plates and plastic glasses. Tina turned from the window to watch. She looked very tired.

"Nothing new on Carrie?" she asked.

"Nothing. They haven't gone inside yet. No one knows where she is." Brenda opened the refrigerator, hoping to see wine.

"Brenda." She looked over the refrigerator door. "Carrie will be all right."

She nodded, wanting to believe it. But didn't. During the delay for the MichCon technicians, somewhere in the Ross house a clock or timer or cell phone hooked up to a bomb would tick from 71 to 72. Carrie would be up in her room, happy to be alone after three days with crazy Brittany.

She looked back in the refrigerator. "The choices are milk or orange juice." She spotted a canister of grated cheese and got it out.

"Milk, thanks."

She got out the carton and brought it with glasses to the table.

"Do you like to cook?" Tina asked, trying to distract her. "I used to be quite the baker."

"Baking's too hard," Brenda said, pouring milk. "Pastry chefs are supposed to be the most highly paid, and most bad-tempered. My college roommate taught me whatever I know. She's Italian."

"That's comfort food," Tina said. "Tuscan, Sicilian. I do a good tetrazzini."

Brenda returned to the counter, opened a drawer, then another. She found a large spoon. Unable to wait, she put it down and opened the bag of rolls. She got one out and began eating. It had to do with Carrie, starving this way, shoving bread into her mouth to stifle fear. Still chewing, she now used the spoon to scoop spaghetti onto the plates. She brought them to the table, and the cheese. Ravenous, she sat and forked in pasta. It was meaty and bland, just right for kids, and a hard-working husband who needed plenty of carbs.

"Lots of sausage," Tina said.

"I'm used to more seasoning and garlic, but it's good."

For more than a minute they ate without talking. Hearing the distant sounds of customers and A.M. radio, Brenda drank milk, seeing the men had finished unloading. Canvas bags, rod cases, coolers, and suitcases rested on the handcart. The house-boat now looked invulnerable, indifferent. Today or tomorrow, someone would install a new window, then it would be ready for the next contest winner or corporate bigwig.

"Bert loved his garlic."

Tina was using her napkin to wipe at something in her lap. That had happened several times last night at dinner. It would be related to the MS. "In all forms," she said, still wiping. "I sometimes want to write these experts pushing garlic as the heart-smart cure-all. If it was really good for the ticker, Bert would still be here."

Personal history, she thought. Little details. They were the meaning of life. What details figured for the man she had killed? When she learned what they were, that's when what she'd done would have its own full meaning.

"Your husband," she said.

"I never told you, did I?" Tina smoothed out her napkin and took up her fork. "Bertrand Glen Bostwick. He ate garlic cloves the way you eat olives. I never understood it, it was just his way. About now he'd be saying, 'Tina, what gives?'" She sprinkled on more cheese. "You wouldn't think someone dealing with the public could get away with it—he managed a savings-and-loan. There were Certs in every coat pocket when I went through his things for the Purple Heart."

Brenda was about to ask whether they'd had lots in common when Tina said, "Bert had many fine qualities."

That's all you needed to know. She took another roll. Because if you weren't bitter or angry about your marriage, that's what you might say. Not *we had little in common*, but *he had many fine qualities*. It's what Brenda thought her mother would say. Her parents had had little in common, but Reva Contay had never expected more than Many Fine Qualities. If you ate well, didn't fight much, could shop whenever you wanted, and rely on the summer rental on Cape Cod, good enough.

"Brenda?"

She glanced from her plate to see Tina looking out the window. There, just at that moment, slipping behind the big boat she saw Charlie standing up in a runabout with Lester Gertz.

She set down her fork. Eyes locked on the bow of the houseboat, Brenda waited. There he was finally, nosing past, the two of them still standing. Sheriff Gertz was again using his phone, Charlie at the controls. He spun the wheel and brought the boat at right angles to the wharf. Still talking, the sheriff stepped forward. When Charlie jumped on shore, Gertz threw him a line. He seemed himself to her. She had already grown used to the missing eyebrow. Gertz now came ashore. He pocketed the phone, turned and said something. Charlie nodded, they parted. Charlie began walking toward the office.

"Go talk to him," Tina said.

He looked to the house, but would not see them in the picture window. "Janey will send him back here," Brenda said.

"No, go outside to him. "It's better. Mary Oliver would agree."

Brenda used her napkin, pushed back the chair and crossed to the passage. It was dark, covered in wood-grain paneling, with a corny, light-at-the-end-of-tunnel effect. The store's radio grew louder with Frank Sinatra's "All The Way." That was perfect for Charlie Schmidt. Her hunger was gone, and with it her sense of fear. He had come back with Gertz, and driven the boat. She did not think he had changed the story.

She heard the door open. "Hi, Charlie, they're—"

When Brenda stepped out, he looked at her, and back to Janey. "You have their keys."

She turned to a pegboard and handed him a ring.

He held it out to Brenda. "I want to trailer the boat. Lester got a call. A relative is coming."

"Heather's?"

"A sister-in-law. If they have a trailer hitch, we might as well have it ready for them."

Practical in all things, she thought. It was just his way. Like someone popping garlic instead of olives or peanuts.

"If you back the Suburban up, I'll attach the trailer." He waited, holding the door, then followed her out. They walked toward the lot. The plaid jacket was gone, his shirt collar buttoned. He looked cold.

"I hope you didn't say anything." It was overcast now. She wished she had pulled on the rain parka.

"It's all right," he said.

"Tell me you didn't—"

A worker came from the side of the building. He nodded and passed, trailing the smell of solvent or glue.

"I didn't have to," Charlie said. "Lester's no fool, and he didn't ask. Leave it alone."

She understood. *Thank you.* And then, as they walked side by side, the knowledge shocked her. No, she thought. No. Others would see and understand. Even a county sheriff.

They reached the gravel parking lot. The Suburban was parked alongside the Gustofsons' pickup, and a pontoon boat. The patrol cars were gone.

"Lester got calls from police in Birmingham, and the EMS crew," Charlie said. "Marion's in the air. But I guess you know that." She nodded, walking, waiting for more, sure he and Gertz knew something else. Something that had happened while she was eating. "She was still…you know. Lester said the EMS guys gave her a shot."

They neared the Suburban. He had more information, but was not telling her. The Ross house was gone and he was not telling her, protecting them both, because Charlie Schmidt knew what it would mean for them. Practical in all things, including her.

"If you back it in over there, the third from your left—"

He pointed to a row of boat trailers at the end of the parking lot, then left her. She watched him. Ask, Brenda thought. Call to him, learn the truth. But she couldn't. Readying the keys, she stepped to Marion's Suburban, climbed up and used the key. The engine turned over. She buzzed down the window and looked back to the row of trailers. Charlie had already pulled one out and was wheeling it. A piece of duct tape still clung to his shoulder.

"Come on back—"

Knowing he was cold, she put the truck in gear and twisted around, seeing that the workers had already neatly packed the gear. She sat straight and guided the truck in reverse, using both outside mirrors.

She slowed, foot on the brake. "A little more—" She eased up, the truck creeping. "There!" She stopped and set the hand brake.

The hitch dropped in place with a solid *chunk*. "Cut the motor." She did this, then swung down and walked to the back. He was kneeling just as he had to fix the flat tire, using a wrench. He looked up at her. "If you ever have to do this, it's a little tricky backing down the ramp. I'll do it this time. After I float the boat, it will help if you pull back up."

I'll do it this time.

"You show me, I'll do it."

She was sure again that he was protecting her—but also schooling her for life here. Life with boats. He was hopeful, but there was no hope, because Carrie Ross was gone and without her, nothing could be saved or recovered. Not after such darkness.

He refitted the wrench and turned. "I like that about you."

"What? That I do what I'm told?"

"No. That you like to learn."

Still working, he was waiting for something from her, something she liked about him, a signal. Again full of fear, Brenda said nothing.

He tightened the hitch bolt with a last turn and leaned down on an elbow. Maybe good news was all it would take. Carrie alive—maybe that alone would be enough. People made choices in the wildest ways. Who to love, what toothpaste to buy. She remembered the broken, praying figure on the floor of Charlie's boat.

He got up, knees cracking, and wiped his hands on his pants. "You never saw my house. Maybe in the morning."

Giving her no chance to answer, he stepped clear of the trailer and started toward the river. She thought to call after, to say no, it's not possible, not now. Do it, she told herself. Even if Carrie's alive, you killed someone. Make a clean break.

She couldn't, watching his back, touched by the sound his knees had made. Because she wanted to think she could face it here next year, and the year after. Wanted to think that was the answer, his house at the other end of the lake, miles from Kettle Falls. A different world, different everything.

"Brenda?"

Janey was crossing from the lodge, marching fast. "It's the daughter. She wanted her mom, I told her you were here—"

Charlie had heard. He waved to her—*go, I can manage.*

Carrie Ross was on the phone. Sixteen this past March, and on the phone. Flooded with gratitude, exultant, Brenda watched Charlie move toward the boat slips. He hadn't known—and all at once it troubled her, her own darkness, the way she had assumed the worst. It was something about her own nature to think that way. Even now, she thought. Because Charlie Schmidt had turned away without waiting for an answer. As though moments ago, with nothing from her, he was giving up, giving her back to those with better claim.

She jogged for the lodge, Janey next to her. "She only had the office number," Janey said. "She's in the house next door."

Next door would be the Heanys.

"I went back to check on your friend. She was tired. I put her in the kids' room for now."

"Thank you."

"Gus says the police are making you stay through to tomorrow. I can get you something if you want, but we've got room. The kids like the dorm better anyway. There's a hideabed in front."

"If you let me buy tonight's dinner, I'd prefer to stay here. I know Tina would, too."

"That's good, then, I'll feed the kids first." They went in. "Gus took the cordless, I think he went to Nielsons'."

An elderly customer was waiting at the counter with bread and tonic water. Her stylish aqua running suit and champagne-perfect hairdo suggested a city wife indulging a retired husband. She looked at Brenda as Janey stepped behind the counter.

"You were on the boat," the woman said. "I saw you come in." She shook her head.

Janey placed an old-style phone on the counter, like the one at Kettle Falls. She held out the handset. Brenda took it and faced away. "Carrie?"

"Tanya's dead." The girl sighed. "I came home. When I opened the door, there was this smell, like when the freezer downstairs got unplugged."

Voice shaky, Carrie sighed again, a sigh identical to her mother's. "I saw her check, I opened the basement door and turned on the light—"

Brenda had been through it herself. More than once, she had reported from crime scenes with bodies left for days or weeks in crack houses. Putrefaction started within two or three days. It was horrible, the sense of smell the most primitive, the most basic. The stench of death was nothing you could ever grow up to manage, or prepare for.

"I'm very sorry," Brenda said.

"She was at the bottom of the stairs, she fell bringing up towels—"

Lomak, she thought. A man who killed women. Carrie was crying now, lost and weeping, a young girl who did not need to know about Lomak. Better by far for her to think Tanya Bates had died a sad, ordinary death, a bad-luck death that was nobody's fault.

"Your mom's on the way," Brenda said. "Just stay with the Heanys."

"That's when the firemen came in," Carrie said. "I was on the basement stairs, I was so scared, I heard people and noise."

Someone was speaking to Carrie.

"They said it was dangerous and I should go back where I was staying. But I ran next door, and Mr. Heany was on the ground." Carrie sighed again, her mother's sigh, the very same. "He broke his wrist. Do you know where my mom is?"

"On her way. I promise, Carrie, she'll be there soon."

Brenda took the phone from the counter and walked with it, trailing the cord into the passage. "But you're all right," she said, speaking she hoped with authority.

"Yes, but it's so awful."

"What about Mr. Heany? You say he fell?"

"He was on a ladder. He was changing the light over the front porch."

"So you helped him."

"He was on the ground, I went over. Mrs. Heany called Beaumont."

"And you helped him."

"I just saw him on the ground—"

"And you helped him get inside." A good girl, Brenda thought. Nice girl. "Lucky for Mr. Heany you were there."

"But Tanya's dead, it's so awful—"

"You couldn't do anything, Carrie. Is that Mrs. Heany with you?"

"She stayed here with me when the police took Mr. Heany to Beaumont Hospital."

"Let me talk to her." Brenda knew the Heanys. They were in their eighties, long retired and devoted to meticulous land-scaping. Frail but clear of mind.

"Brenda, hello," Mrs. Heany said. "This girl, I don't know what we would have done. I was making lunch when she brought him in. I called Beaumont, I was filling the ice pack and looked out, I saw all these patrol cars, a fire engine—"

With the inflections and words of her generation, Mrs. Heany made clear her gratitude. Brenda remembered her from last summer. Small and birdlike, in denim wrap skirt and lime-green polo, she had stretched out on a chaise next to the Rosses' pool, keeping watch on her great grandchildren. I would be her granddaughter, Brenda thought. The children's mother.

"But it's just awful about Tanya Walker," Mrs. Heany said. "Such a good person. One of the officers said she fell bringing up laundry."

"Marion would be very glad to know you're there," Brenda said.

"Well, you *bet* I'm here for this great girl, I can tell you that for sure. And you tell Marion not to worry. Carrie's going to be fine here, aren't you?"

Mrs. Heany went back to the police and Tanya. How many disasters occurred in a life of eight decades? How many moments of delight? So many of both, waiting to happen. To oneself and one's children and their children, attachments and things that gathered meaning—sighs and duct tape, cards fanned out on a table, retrievers in fog, broken shoe laces. That, really, was the whole of it, and you had to accept it all, otherwise you lived a remembered lie. That, really, was everyone's story—the *chunk* of a trailer hitch, a sound full of people and places. The feel of folded paper in a breast pocket.

"So they didn't evacuate the street," Brenda said.

"They didn't have to," Mrs. Heany said. "But one of the firemen told me it would have been very bad. The men who got Carrie found some kind of detonators with timers or switches. On the gas line."

Carrie was speaking. "That's right," Mrs. Heany said. "When the police took my husband, they told us this thing was set to go off in seven-point-two days. They said it would've blown up the whole house, and us too. On Thursday. Think of that."

"They told you Thursday?"

"That's what they told me. Whoever did it wanted the house to blow up on Thursday."

Brenda shook her head, half hearing as Mrs. Heany went on. No, she thought. Seventy-two hours, not seven-point-two days. It fit with everything else, another mistake. Lomak had meant for the house to blow up today, not Thursday. For a big finish, an exclamation point. Like coming to the aid of help-less women with a tangled fish. But he had confused the time of his getaway with the day he was due to be sentenced.

A minute later they said goodbye. Brenda hung up, still in the passage. The store's radio had been turned down, so she could hear. Looking ahead to the family room, she saw the hideabed she would sleep on tonight. It was grouped with worn chairs around a pine coffee table. The Gustofsons would make adjustments tonight, change their routine.

Knowing she would see Charlie Schmidt in the morn-ing, Brenda turned and started back with the phone. She remembered them side by side at dinner, listening to him tell about his house. It's red, he told her. Like a barn, at the end of the lake.

ABOUT THE AUTHOR

Barry Knister was a university professor before turning to full-time writing. His first novel, *The Dating Service* was published by Berkley. His second, *Just Bill* is a novel for adults about dogs and owners, and was published by Gold Mountain Press. Knister has published two others novels in the Brenda Contay suspense series. The first (*The Anything Goes Girl*) draws on his years as a Peace Corps Volunteer. The third (*Godsend*) is set in Naples, Florida. Knister is the past secretary of Detroit Working Writers, and served as the director of the Cranbrook Summer Writers Conference. He lives outside Detroit with his wife, Barbara, and their Aussie shepherd, Skylar.

Visit the author at his website: www.bwknister.com
or at his publisher: www.bhcpress.com

www.ingramcontent.com/pod-product-compliance
Lightning Source LLC
LaVergne TN
LVHW090844050425
807822LV00032B/473